P9-CFV-763

STRANDIA

STRANDIA

SUSAN LYNN REYNOLDS

FARRAR / STRAUS / GIROUX
New York

Acknowledgments

I would like to gratefully thank the Ontario Arts Council for their support through a Works-in-Progress grant.

I would also like to thank others whose support has been less concrete but no less important. Thank you to Mary Jo, who introduced me to Jung, among many other things. To Guy, who celebrated the "thunk" of a finished manuscript. To Michael, for his encouragement as I wrote it, and to Greg, for his encouragement as I searched for a publisher. To Geraldine, for an old, old favor returned in kind. To Luisa, who enables me to "get out of its way." To Janis, who celebrates life with the joy of a dolphin. To Linda McKnight, for her friendly patience. To my mother, who swore when she was growing up that she'd never tell *her* children to "get their noses out of that book!" and managed to keep her vow under stressful circumstances. Thanks to my editor Lee Anne Martin for her invaluable perspective and her tact. And thank you to Larry, who teaches me daily about joy and courage and reverence for life and love.

*This book is dedicated to my sister
Sandy, the original*

Part One

The Island

Prologue

In the beginning there was only the sun and the sea. The sun was Raza, Father to all the life that swam in the belly of the Mother. For uncounted ages they existed alone together. But then the spark of a new being appeared beyond the sky, growing closer and larger and more beautiful, until he eclipsed even the beauty of the sun. The newcomer's name was Kryphon and the Mother's being surged toward him. Their meeting was portentous. And then he left her, retreating into the black night once again.

But from their meeting grew new life: a girl and a boy. From deep beneath her, the Mother raised a place where the sea and the sky met for these children to be born, for she knew they would belong both to water and to sky.

In time Calleby and Bedjar were born in this place. They were covered with iridescent scales and breathed both air and water with equal ease. But unlike any creature ever seen in the world before or since, they also had legs and arms which streamed away from their bodies as their father's legs had streamed behind him. When their ears and eyes opened, the Sea Mother spoke to them in crashing words: "Look to me and honor me, and as long as there is beach to stand on, I will care for you."

But Bedjar looked up to the sky, breathed deeply, and turned his back on the sea. He looked beyond the beach, found a lactus tree, and climbed its ribbed trunk. He brought the fruit of the lactus to Calleby and said, "We need her weaning no more. We walk upon legs that can climb. We can find our own food and do not need her gifts."

Calleby, seeing his blue eyes sparkle with the light of Kryphon, tasted the fruit of the lactus tree.

The Sea Mother shuddered with rage. She slapped them down with a thundering wall of water and drew them back into her womb. She stripped them of their iridescence, the shimmering scales falling from their bodies like schools of minnows. She smoothed the gills at their throats and the gills disappeared, leaving no mark. Finally, she threw them up onto the beach, leaving their soft new skin to bake on the sand.

The Sea Mother called out to all the creatures that coursed through her, "From this day forth, ignore the hunger calls of Bedjar and Calleby." The mollusks and conchs and bonitas and krill all turned as one in the sway of her voice and closed their ears forever.

All but doraado, who spoke out, "Oh, Mother-of-all, home-to-all, smoother-of-stones, your punishment is too severe. Calleby is blameless, yet you curse this helpless child because she yielded to Bedjar's eyes, just as you did to Kryphon's light."

The Mother's fury boiled at this reminder of her foolishness. She threw doraado onto the coral and raked the gills from his cheeks and the scales from his back. She flattened his tail and poked a hole in his head so he would be forced

4

always, like Calleby and Bedjar, to take his life from the air.

This is how doraado got his name: dor-a-a-do, "not a fish, not a man," for he could not walk upon the beach or live long in the deepest reaches of the Sea Mother's being.

And this, too, is how doraado became the friend of Calleby of Strandia and all the daughters that came after her.

Chapter One

Sand bowed her head while Coral and Shell braided the traditional bridal blossoms of jinnange and monarri in her hair. Coral was reciting part of the dressing ritual in a monotonous singsong.

Sea-blue jinnange for the Mother when she's calm,
Star-white monarri for the wave crests during storm . . .

Sand bit her lip and glared at her hands lying still in her lap, palms upward, fingers curled. She was concentrating, imagining vines growing, tying her wrists to her legs, anchoring her feet to the ground, reaching up and folding their leaves like hands over her mouth. She made this image real in her mind, so real that it became physically impossible to leap up and shake her sister to make her shut up.

Shell's wistful voice finally distracted her. "There. Your hair is done. Look up, Sand."

Sand glared at her friend. After one puzzled glance in

return, Shell continued, "It's almost perfect. Too bad we can't bind some fern into your hair to go with your eyes. But it's not traditional."

"Traditional!" Sand spat out the word.

Coral and Shell both fell silent and looked at each other over Sand's head. Their hands fell to their sides.

In a subdued tone Coral said, "You can stand up now. It's time to put on the shannal."

Sand put her concentration to work once more as she stood to have the sixteen yards of material draped around her in the ritual folds. She was a tree, a bael-nut tree festooned with parasitic vines. She must stand tall and straight to maintain her dignity. With this exercise she sought to forget that she had only a few minutes more before her fantasies would be replaced by an act that would change her life forever.

Anemone darted into the room like a hummingbird. Sand deliberately looked away from her. Her mother's hands fluttered like moth's wings and then stilled. "You look lovely, darling," she ventured.

Sand continued to stare out the window.

Covering the awkward silence as best she could, her mother twittered, "Well, Coral, since you've finished dressing her, perhaps you could help me? And we can leave Sand and Shell to their last few moments together as maiden friends."

Sand stiffened.

Coral hugged the bride. Even in her cold fury, Sand was careful of the gently swelling stomach of her older sister.

"May the Mother bless your union as she has blessed mine," Coral whispered, before she followed their mother out of the room. "What's wrong with her?" she asked once they were beyond earshot.

"I don't know, I'm sure. The silly child insists she doesn't

7

want to marry. You'd think she'd be flattered. Tamin has offered the biggest bride-price I've ever heard of." Anemone dropped her voice to a whisper. "Since you'll know soon anyway, I can tell you now. I've been longing to tell someone. Three taells of beach!" She savored the delicious pause while Coral registered shock, and then continued, "But even that has no effect on her. She just keeps saying she doesn't want to marry."

"What does she want, then?"

"Kryphon knows!" Anemone was punctilious about lady-like behavior, and this oath indicated the extremes of frustration she'd weathered over the past few months.

Coral's eyes rested on the small knot of guests already gathered on the beach. "I can't believe I've been so blind to this. But then Sand hasn't been around much lately."

"That's the truth. She's gone before breakfast and half the time doesn't come home till dark. Sometimes I know she's been home at all only because her sleeping pallet's still warm under the covers when I go to wake her."

Coral's voice dropped to a whisper. "Do you think she has a lover?"

Anemone shook her head impatiently. "If that was the case, she'd no doubt be whining that she wanted to marry someone other than Tamin. But she just keeps saying she doesn't want to marry anyone—ever."

"I wish I'd realized," Coral mused. "Maybe I could have talked to her. After all, I didn't really want to marry Kran either. I didn't think I was ready for a man to share my room and the bed I'd slept in since I was a baby. But "—a smile curved her lips—"marriage has been a series of delightful surprises."

Anemone shook her head. "I didn't want to bother you. I hoped that she would learn from your example. After all, it has unfolded right before her eyes. But she won't look. And then, too, her situation is so different from that of most brides. I keep telling her how lucky she is. After all, instead of staying here with us, she will practically be mistress of her own household. Tamin's mother, Iola, has never been either a strong talent or a forceful personality. And she's fairly elderly—she didn't have Tamin till she was almost past the age of bearing children. Sand will be able to organize things as she chooses. I've emphasized how challenging that will be. I've tried to make her understand how satisfying it is to provide nourishment for your own household through the power of your talent. I told her how rewarding children can be. I might as well try to smooth the waves. Sand has no ears for my words. She wants to live a life that doesn't exist. I believe she would be a man if she could. She says life is more than using your talent to get food. More than babies and creating new ways of wearing your clothing and your hair. More than visiting other women to talk about babies and clothing and hair. But when I ask her what else this grand life she envisions consists of, she falls silent. She can't or won't tell me. And then, because she has no answer, she changes the subject and accuses me of betraying her. Of selling her to get more beach. You see how she won't even meet my eyes anymore."

The two women walked slowly toward the water, smiling and greeting their guests as they went, complimenting them on their finery. Most of the guests were nearby raeth, or the groom's neighbors and relatives. The number of them gathered today in fancy dress created a vision of bright, swirling excess, from the yards and yards of intricately draped whisprain cloth, to the elaborate hairstyles that had taken hours to prepare.

A little distance apart, a small knot of people huddled together, dressed much more plainly. The fishermen talked quietly, the women and children stayed silent for the most part. But their eyes were wide open, absorbing the strange sounds and sights for discussion when they returned home. Now and then a couple of the Midisle wives actually pointed and whispered at a particularly outlandish coiffure.

In turn, Coral stared at the cropped hair of the Midisle women. Her hands absently stroked her own unbound hair.

As they reached this drab group, Anemone cleared her throat for the little speech she had prepared. "Thank you for coming to my daughter's wedding. Thank you especially for taking the day away from your fishing and your other duties. Your loss of a day's income is an extra tribute to the bonds between our families."

In the flat silence that followed, a woman's voice interjected, "It's not as if we had much choice." The comment had not been intended for everyone to hear, but in a sudden lull in the conversation it carried.

Anemone paled, then flushed. She turned away and Coral pattered after her.

Behind them, a little girl piped a lilting sentence ending with "long hair?"

Someone shushed her, but another woman said loudly, "You can tell they don't do anything productive with hair like that, can't you?"

Enraged, Coral tossed her head, making the tips of her hair swing across the top of her thighs as she walked. She commented, "Kran has told me of several incidents in the market lately, but I didn't realize that the discontent touched even the fishermen who rent our beach and their families."

Anemone sighed. "Nothing is as simple as it used to be. And Marris just lets them get away with anything. I've told him fifty times that if he'd make an example of one of them, the others would soon settle down."

Coral smiled indulgently. "You and Father should trade

duties for a few weeks. He would love that—choosing the menus, visiting with neighbors, spoiling the babies. Then you could deal with the fishermen and the contracts and smarten everyone up. You know Father will never do anything so drastic as 'making an example' of one of them. He's always believed in treating the Midislanders as equals."

"He's always been a fool," her mother snapped.

They didn't break the new silence between them until after they'd checked that all was set up on the tables. Coral reverted to their earlier topic. "Sand will settle down, Mother. We all do."

"I know." Her mother sighed. "I hope it's soon, that's all. This has been very trying. What makes it worse is the great value of Tamin's gift. I wouldn't want him to demand his marriage gift back because he hadn't received due value for it." She bit her lip and glanced at Coral. "I know sometimes it sounds as if I *have* sold her, but it's not that way. Not at all. Though I can't deny that I have plans for those three taells of land."

They caught sight of Tamin and his parents coming through the lactus grove. Anemone's hands darted to her hair and then down to twitch her robe into place. Finally she fixed a smile on her lips and moved forward to welcome them.

"Greetings, Mother-by-choice," Tamin said, kissing her cheek.

Anemone moved her hand quickly in a warding gesture. "Not for another hour!" she reproved him.

He shook his head in exasperation. "All these bride-day superstitions! In an hour that name will be yours by right. What's an hour of mortal time to the Mother?"

"Bad luck!" she insisted.

The smile faded from his lips. After a moment's silence he asked formally, "How fares my bride this day?"

Anemone wove her fingers tightly together so her hands would not betray her. "A little nervous, perhaps. Otherwise fine."

Tamin's father, Calut, looked out to sea. "I haven't seen a single doraado."

"Don't worry about that. Sand has never had any problems contacting or controlling the providers. Even when my own talent has failed me—a bad storm or distance—Sand could always make the catch. Her talent is so strong that she apprenticed to the temple for a while, you know."

Calut's gaze pierced her. "Of course we know. But I've never known why she left."

Anemone shrugged, wishing she'd never raised the topic. "A girl's whim, I'm afraid. She didn't feel suited to that life of service. But she had no problem fulfilling her duties."

Calut continued to study her. "I guess we'll soon see."

Anemone's features twitched with irritation, quickly hidden. "Excuse us. We have a few more duties to see to."

Coral fumed as they strode away. "I can't believe how rude he was to you!"

Her mother laid a soothing hand on her arm. "I understand Tamin's parents are a little disappointed with his choice. This is their last chance to register a protest, and it was pretty mild."

"Disappointed! What's wrong with Sand?" Coral's voice rose.

Her mother's fingers closed on her wrist and squeezed. "Hush!"

They reached the cooking fires, damped down for the moment by mats of seaweed. A salty, pungent smoke wove thin gray strands in the air. The two women began to lift the mats, checking each fire to be sure it was burning neither too fast nor too slow.

"Nothing is wrong with Sand. But they had really hoped

that Tamin would prefer Shell. Do you remember how inseparable the three of them used to be as children?"

"Shell? That colorless wisp!"

"Her family is very wealthy and their land adjoins Calut's. And, though it's never mentioned, Shell worships Tamin. I've seen her watching him."

Coral snorted. "So why aren't we guests at Shell's wedding instead of tending the cookfires for this one?"

"Tamin decided he would have only Sand. The Mother alone knows why; Sand has never encouraged him at all. The opposite, in fact."

"He likes a challenge?" Coral speculated.

"Evidently. He's grown into a rather arrogant young man. When his family began pushing him to marry, he said fine, but only to Sand. In the end they gave in."

"Was there never a daughter at all?"

"No daughter, no nieces, no sisters . . . nothing. His mother is the last of her line; Calut is an only child. It is critical for Tamin to marry as quickly as possible, and preferably to a strong talent, if their beach is to thrive. And Sand is very lucky to be the chosen one. If she stayed here, she'd be the younger sister to a strong talent." She laid a fond hand on Coral's shoulder. "I'm going to be around myself for a long time, and I have no intention of turning over those duties of honor and power one second before I have to. No ambitious young man is going to want to marry a raeth daughter with those prospects.

"Of course, it will be a little difficult for her at first—it's not easy moving in with another family. And it's so rare; it's not as if it's something she has always lived in knowledge of. But Sand has never fit in well here. She can hardly be worse off with another family."

Coral stayed tactfully silent. She might have answered that Sand had really only ever had problems "fitting in" with

Anemone's strict ideas about what was and was not proper behavior for a raeth daughter. Sand adored and got along very well with her father, and until Coral's marriage, the sisters had been very close, too.

As they turned from the fires, they saw how thick the crowd of guests on the beach had become. A hush spread through the assembly. There was some stirring when Sand appeared in the doorway of the house and the guests shuffled around to try to get a better view of the bride.

As Sand walked down the steps and across the tufted beach grass, Coral saw her set white face. Her chin was thrust forward. She moved unfalteringly, gliding like a sleepwalker, toward the water. Marris, her father, walked a couple of paces behind her. As she reached the beach, the guests parted. Sand deliberately kept her gaze on the horizon, refusing to meet anyone's eyes. She stopped only when she reached the water. The incoming wavelets washed over her pearl-embroidered slippers.

Anemone started forward, intending to drag Sand backward, but Marris's hand on her arm stopped her. "She's on her own now, wife."

"Look at her feet," she moaned. "Those slippers belonged to my great-grandmother—she wore them at her wedding. They're ruined!"

Marris shrugged. "If they're ruined already, there's no point in making a fuss."

Tamin thrust through the crowd to join Sand at the water's edge. For the first time since Sand had left the house, she turned her eyes from the sea. As their eyes met, he fell back a step. Conscious of the guests watching them, he deliberately moved nearer again. "Your glance stings like sea salt in a cut."

She turned her face away.

"Remember the night I told you I'd marry you, that I'd have you and no other? Here we are. Just a few more minutes and we'll be married, Sand." He was annoyed with himself; he was babbling. Why wouldn't she look at him? All his friends had teased him, telling him that the more reserved a woman acted before the wedding, the more passionate she'd be on the wedding night. He fervently hoped they were right.

He glanced away down the beach. "Look. Here comes the priest."

Unwillingly she turned her head to see the priest in his turquoise robes weaving along the water's edge. Two novices trailed behind him, tossing handfuls of meltara into the water. Wherever the fishmeal struck, the water boiled as myriads of rainbow-colored trawna fought for the pieces. It was an impressive display of fecundity, calculated to encourage the gods to bless this marriage with children. Preferably daughters with powerful talent.

Sand slowly turned her head to the left and saw the priestess, with two attendants, coming toward them from that direction. The waters stirred violently behind her as well.

The bride looked down at the waves washing over her feet and said her soundless goodbyes to her family and this life she had known.

The two dignitaries met and stood together in knee-deep water in front of Sand and Tamin. The novices handed each of the clergy a robe, which they immediately donned. As the hems of the garments hit the water, the rainbow iridescence of thousands of tiny fish foamed around them again.

During her service at the temple, Sand had learned that the renewed activity of the trawna was caused by cakes of meltara sewn to the hem of each robe. But as the crowd gasped in delight, even Sand had to admit that it was effective.

The priest raised his arms. "On this beach today, we will

bind together Sand and Tamin, before the island and in the eyes of the gods."

The novices stepped forward and stood on either side of the bridal couple.

The priestess turned to Anemone and Marris. "Is this your daughter?"

They answered together, "She is the daughter of our flesh, joy of our days, wealth of our raethdom."

"Shall she be joined in marriage to this man?"

"She shall join with him and bear him children to keep the beach prospering in the family name."

"Will the providers serve her?"

"Yes. They serve her willingly. She and the providers are as one."

"Can she feed her family?"

"They will never go hungry."

"Summer or winter, sunshine or storm?"

"Yes. For all time."

The priestess turned to Sand and said, "You have heard. Now you must prove yourself."

On the priestess's signal, Shell and several other raeth daughters who were Sand's attendants today broke from the little knot of Midislanders and waded waist-deep into the water, spreading the net between them.

This was the moment. All Sand's will should be directed at finding the minds of the great silver doraado and binding them to her wishes. However, Sand concentrated instead on everything that followed.

The priest asked Tamin, "What do you offer this family for the loss of this talent?"

Tamin opened the bag his father handed to him and took out three stone plaques with his family's symbol on them. "Three taells of beach." They had been taken from the cairns, set one every taell, marking raeth holdings around the entire island, except of course for Midisle. To change ownership, one family's marker would be replaced by the mark of the new owner. But beach didn't often change hands.

A gasp swept through the guests like a sea breeze. There had been rumors of a fabulous marriage gift, but this was unprecedented.

"Do you accept this consolation?"

"Yes, we do."

Sand ground her teeth to shut out the quick pleasure in her mother's voice.

Tamin handed the plaques to a waiting mason—a man called Obron with a flair for the dramatic. He set them on a stone block, raised his hammer, and brought it down suddenly, shattering all three at once.

Sand winced at the sharp report. That was a little premature, she thought. They should have waited until after the fiertha was provided. Her mother was not going to be pleased.

There were more ritual questions and responses, and then quiet fell on the assembly as they waited for the providers to appear, herding the fish in for the fiertha.

Almost involuntarily, Sand sent out the thinnest tendril of a search and found a school of doraado playing about a taell out to sea. She had done this so often; it would take so little effort on her part to project to them the images of racking hunger that would cause the sea mammals to round up clouds of fish and send them scurrying to shore.

Instead, Sand concentrated on fear, consciously making her heart beat faster, sending waves of adrenaline through her body. "Danger! Get away!" she sent to them.

With one will the pod broke the surface of the water, flinging themselves into the air. When their sleek gray bodies clove the water again, they were heading farther out to sea.

Calut grumbled in his wife's ear: "All she has to do is provide dinner. I dislike these showy acrobatics." She glanced at him wordlessly and looked out to sea again.

Everyone waited. And waited. The girls holding the edges of the nets began to shift from foot to foot in the cool water, passing nervous glances among themselves. The guests stirred uneasily.

Anemone cursed under her breath. Wondering what her difficult girl child was up to, she decided to feel out the situation for herself. She had only begun the search, however, when her husband pinched her. She opened her eyes and glanced at him guiltily.

He scowled and whispered, "Woman, what are you thinking of? Will you have people say that the girl has no talent and her mother provided the fiertha in secret? Will we repeat the legend of Aleta and Kenan?"

She shook her head, but her face was as white as Sand's had been but a little while before. "No, of course not. But I wish I knew what she was doing."

A moment later Anemone's wish was granted. Lifting her chin, Sand turned away from the priest and priestess to face the guests. In a high, clear voice she said simply, "I can't." Turning to Tamin, she added, "I'm sorry." But her eyes sparkled.

Her poise broke then and she charged up the beach, pushing through the guests. When the way was clear, she dashed for the house.

A hundred conversations erupted in her wake; a rumbling hiss of outrage and amazement. She covered her ears as she ran.

In the momentary sanctuary of her room Sand sat down with her back to the door. Her fingers shaking, she began to frantically unplait her hair and scratch the flowers out of it. She kept her face still and smooth, but inside regret, guilt, and triumph battled for dominance.

She began sifting through images from the water's edge, images that had impressed themselves on her mind at the time but that had stayed unexamined until now. The rage on her mother's face, the shock shown by both her father and Coral, and an odd expression on Shell's face. Sand's hands paused for a moment, tangled in her hair while she pondered this. She identified it. Shell's eyes had held hope.

Sand shook her head and then continued with her task. I have made one person happy today at least, she thought. How long had Shell been in love with Tamin? She thought back to years before, when she had called the providers that first time. The three children swam out to play with them. Tamin had teased one of the gentle mammals and Sand had bristled with indignation. When she turned to Shell for support, however, she saw nothing but admiration shining from her eyes. Poor Shell. Sand shrugged and gave a wry twist to her lips. Perhaps now Tamin would solace himself with Shell's adoration.

Sand heard the door open behind her and tensed the muscles in her shoulders.

"You little idiot." Her mother's voice slid into her heart like a thin, icy blade. "You have shamed us beyond speech. This will never be forgotten. Our raethdom is shamed; our name is tainted." Her mother's voice was climbing the scale inexorably toward hysteria. "Do you know what people are saying down there? Do you? They're torn. Half of them insist you are a no-talent, that we've tried to cheat Tamin's family into accepting you for the sake of the bride-price. The other half merely say you've always been spoiled and this outrageous behavior is no more than we deserve for our indulgence toward you. They're right, of course."

Sand fought to keep all emotion out of her voice. "Please,

Mother. Let's not exaggerate. All the raeth know I can call the providers—"

"Do they? And how would they know that? You're never around when the raeth wives come to call. Always sneaking off, the Goddess knows where. Neglecting your duties. *I* hardly know anything about you . . . it would be a miracle if my friends did."

Sand couldn't reply to this in any way that her mother would be willing to hear.

"So all they know of you is what I've told them. If I was trying to marry off a no-talent secretly, I wouldn't be spreading the secret all over the island."

Sand was beginning to understand some of her mother's rage and she didn't want that. She tried to end the discussion quickly. "Well, there's no point in talking about it. It's done. I'm sorry."

"*Sorry?* That's not good enough, Sand. It's too easy. You think you can blithely say 'I'm sorry' and everything will be all right again?"

"Mother, what's the point in talking about it? I tried to talk to you before and you wouldn't listen. I had to act."

"That so-called discussion you tried to have with me consisted of you saying 'I don't want to marry Tamin.' No explanation. No reason. That's not good enough either. What's wrong with the boy? He's offered the greatest bride-price ever seen on Strandia for you. You show your gratitude in this way? You might as well have spit on him and his family."

"Bride-price? What do I care what he offered to pay? I should be *grateful*? But that's what *you're* really upset about, isn't it? You've lost those three lovely taells of land. And I've embarrassed you in front of your friends. You will never understand me, Mother, and neither would Tamin. You and he are the same species—all you understand is possessions.

Well, I'm not interested in possessions. I don't care about having them, and even more than that, I don't want to be one!"

"Well, what *do* you want? I hear a lot of 'I don't want this' and 'I won't do that,' but I don't hear any positive suggestions."

Sand clenched her jaw.

"I know what you must do—go back to the temple and re-enter service there. It's the only way to clear your name and atone for what you did today."

"I won't do that."

"Well, by the Goddess, what will you do? You can't stay here now, a living stain on our name. You don't do anything, you don't contribute anything. If you don't go back to the temple, if you won't be a raeth wife and you're not behaving like a raeth daughter, what will you do? There's no place in raeth life for a burden."

"Then I won't be raeth." Sand's mouth said the words as they formed in her brain—uncensored. She stood up and reached for a sharp knife. "I've tried to tell you a hundred times that this is not a life I'm happy with. There's never really been a place for me here. You don't need my talent— you and Coral have more than enough between you to provide. The temple is a life of slavery; every second there is something scheduled to be done. There's not a moment's freedom. I will die before I marry Tamin. He just wants me because I don't want him. He wants to win. He wants to be able to say I'm his wife. If those are my choices as raeth, I *won't be raeth.*" She sawed off one long honey-colored lock and felt for another.

Her mother gasped. "What are you doing?" And, when Sand grimly continued to cut, asked again, "What will you do?"

"Find my own way."

"Don't be ridiculous! There's no such thing as your own

21

way. You're either a raeth daughter or a Midislander. Just cutting off your hair doesn't mean you can live in Midisle, you know! You have no skills besides your talent. And without a raeth husband or your father's beach to compel from, you have no place to use that talent."

The knife continued its work.

Her mother's voice climbed even higher; it was the sound of gulls fighting over a fish. "If you leave here like this you can't come back. Raeth women do not roam the island unattended like Midisle *girls*." She emphasized the last word, implying that only her breeding and good taste kept her from calling them something much more accurate and insulting. "You will no longer be our daughter. You have done enough damage to our name."

"Fine. You were my mother-by-chance and by the Mother's will. By my own will and by yours, you will be my mother no more." The last strand fell to the floor. Sand twisted her head back and forth experimentally. None of the ragged hair on her head brushed her shoulders. The loss of the weight she had borne all her life, without realizing it, made her feel as though her head might simply float away.

She set the knife down and faced her mother. "Goodbye, Anemone."

She pushed past her mother and marched from the house. On the porch she bumped into her father.

The sight of her hair turned Marris's face pinched and bloodless. "You are leaving?"

She nodded silently.

For a long, long moment he said nothing, and Sand looked away from the wetness that filled his eyes. "Well, perhaps it is best for right now. But, Sand"—he reached for her hand and clasped it tightly—"when you have a longing to see your family, you are welcome in my home." He pulled her to him and hugged her fiercely.

"You'd better talk to your wife about that," Sand whispered in his ear as she hugged him back. Then she pulled away from him and began walking quickly toward the raethdom that adjoined theirs.

"Goodbye, Sand," Marris called softly.

She didn't cry for at least five steps.

Down on the beach, Tamin and some of the guests followed her with their eyes until she disappeared into the trees.

Chapter Two

When her anger and frustration finally ceased to pre-occupy her, Sand found she was already several taells away from home. She'd stormed along heedless of the number of cairns she'd passed, the number of beaches she'd violated. Trespassing was strictly forbidden and now she threw a guilty glance over her shoulder.

She began to ponder how she would survive. Much as she hated to admit it, her mother was right. She had no skills beyond the talent she'd been born with. Without a raeth's beach to compel from, she had no way to use her talent, and a raeth woman used only her father's or her husband's beach. She'd have to develop a new way to support herself. Sand shrugged. Surely for a day or two she could just exist without worrying about what was to come.

Rounding a small point, she caught sight of a group of fishermen gathered on the beach before her. She hesitated. From their clothing she realized that none of them were raeth.

Sand lifted her chin. She was raeth—no Midislander would dare challenge her on a raeth beach. For all they knew, she was there by invitation. As she approached, she first surveyed them imperiously, and then acknowledged their existence with a gracious inclination of her head. They muttered greetings in various tones of respect, but no one met her eyes. The name for a Midislander who courted raeth women was perentha—a deadly insult. Since she'd become eligible for marriage, she'd not spoken to any man save in her own family, and servants.

One of the men did not have his eyes deferentially dropped. He stood calf-deep in the sea, handsome as a statue of Kryphon himself. He stared at her pointedly as she walked by.

How dare he look at her like that! Then she remembered her hair, that ragged remnant of her previous pride. By the Mother, no wonder he had stared. Involuntarily she ran her fingers through it. She must look like an eldrin—one of those mad people who wandered the sands alone, eating seaweed and talking to themselves. She quickened her pace until long after she'd passed from their sight.

She cursed the impulsive fury that had prompted her to cut off her hair. She hadn't realized that, until she got some Midislander clothes to match her cropped top, her hair would make her more conspicuous, not less. And the combination of ragged hair and the voluminous folds of her shannal would mark her as even more queer. Where was she going to get some other clothing? She didn't know a single Midislander.

She continued to march until her legs began to tire and her arms ached from carrying the weight of her wet wedding dress. She began to keep her eyes open for a likely hiding spot to spend the night.

She rounded a rocky point and froze. Sitting at the

water's edge before her was a girl of maybe twelve years. Sand considered hiding until the other went away. But the girl's shoulders slouched dejectedly. Sand decided that this young one was no threat to her.

The child turned her head at the sound of Sand splashing at the water's edge. She scrambled to her feet and backed a few steps into the sea. Her eyes were red and puffy from recent crying. The length of her brown hair proclaimed she was raeth, but it looked as if it had never seen the civilizing influence of a comb. Her only garment was a man's shirt belted at the waist. Far too big for her skinny frame, it hung almost to her knees. The hem washed back and forth with the waves.

"What are you doing here?" She tried for authority, but her voice came out in a squeak. "This is raeth beach. You don't belong here."

"Honored raeth daughter," Sand began in a low voice. "I'm sorry to trespass. I was going to turn back but I saw you here. You looked as if you were in trouble."

The girl's fingers tightened on the net she held. Her eyes filled again and Sand saw her jaw clench in an effort to keep the tears from spilling down her dirt-streaked cheeks. "Who are you, anyway? Are you eldrin?"

"No. I am raeth, as you are."

"You look eldrin," the child said frankly. She took a step forward and Sand blinked at her intense scrutiny. "Your hair's all ragged and it's got stuff sticking out. What are you wearing?"

"My shannal. I was to be married today."

Turning away, the girl lifted her net high and then slapped it down on the surface, spraying water everywhere.

"Grandfather says I'll never marry. He says I'm a skinny, ugly no-talent and no raeth son will ever want me."

She turned back to Sand, her eyes full of tears again.

Sand reached a hand toward her, but the girl flinched away.

"Is that why you're crying?"

"No, of course not." Scorn laced the child's voice. "He says it all the time. I'm used to that."

"Then why? Is there something I could do to help?"

The girl paused a long while and then held up the net in her hand. "Can't reach the providers," she muttered. Then louder and plaintively she continued, "They hate this beach. They always play far, far away. Usually I can hardly hear them. Tonight I can't hear them at all. I haven't been able to bring them in with fish for four nights now. Grandfather gets so angry when I come home with an empty net."

"Why don't you just demand some deepwater fish from the fishermen who rent your beach?"

The child stared at Sand. "You *must* be eldrin. Look out there." Her arm swept the lagoon. Farther out were dozens of reefs, marked by where the water broke over them. "What fishermen could use this bay to anchor in?"

"You don't rent out your beach to fishermen? How do you make a living?"

A shrug. "We eat the fish I can get. If there's any extra, I walk to Midisle to trade them for what we need."

"What happens when you don't catch any?"

The girl looked up across the beach to where the undergrowth began. "There are always bael nuts. And, in season, lactus fruit."

Sand thought of the floury consistency of the bael nut and imagined a steady diet of them, night after night. She made a wry face at the young girl. "Let's see if we can get you something better for tonight. Take my hand."

The girl hesitated, but hunger made up her mind for her. She slowly extended her hand until her fingers touched Sand's.

27

"Now we'll both reach together," Sand told her with quiet assurance. "They must come."

The girl raised her eyebrows skeptically. Then she obediently closed her eyes. Sand began a search, weaving a net of awareness out across the waters. In a couple of minutes a pod of doraado broke the water far from shore. Sand kept track of them while she searched for others, closer. The child was right. The doraado stayed far from here.

Bending the focus of her whole will on the group she had found, she waited until she had acknowledgment of her presence from several individuals. They waited, lazing about on the surface of the sea.

Sand began to concentrate on her hunger. She projected gut-wrenching emptiness, a painful void. It helped that she hadn't eaten for two days; the prospect of imminent marriage had killed her appetite.

She felt the providers respond to her call. Each of them ranged back and forth below the surface, startling schools of fish, herding them in toward shore.

They threaded their way through the honeycombed reefs in the bay, anxious to assuage the pain they felt.

"They're coming!" the child whispered breathlessly. "A lot of them!"

"Shhh." Sand divided her attention between the doraado and the girl. "Be quick; let's spread your net out."

The girl handed her two corners and they waded out waist-deep in water. Bending over, they held the net below the surface. They waited.

The red globe of the sun was almost resting on the edge of the world. The light lay in an unbroken beam across the quiet sea. Then its symmetry split as a dolphin broke through. The first was followed by another, and another, and then several more—sweetly curved black silhouettes leaping and disappearing, leaving only a faint ripple.

"So many!" the girl whispered, awed.

"Shh! Concentrate," Sand scolded through clenched teeth.

And suddenly they felt the first slithering rush against their legs. A quicksilver shape skimmed around them and broke the surface on the other side, turning back the school. Against the net, below the water, they saw darting, slim arrows.

The girl began to pull up her side of the net, but Sand frowned at her. "Not yet!"

A moment longer and then the sea around them boiled. Hundreds of fish raced back and forth across the net. In their panic, they tumbled and flailed, their light underbellies in contrast to the dark backs of their companions. The dolphins danced at the rim of this churning mass, continuously turning its edges inward.

"Now!" They strained to bring the edges of the net together. Staggering under its weight, they dragged it onto the beach and let the net fall open, spilling its dark, undulating cargo across the white sand.

The girl swayed. Sand saw her face in the dying light, a pale disk surrounded by a dark mat of hair. "By the Mother!" the child gasped, looking at the sea's bounty. Before she could elaborate she fainted, her slim body collapsing like a suit of unfilled clothing beside the mound of twitching fish.

Chapter Three

Sand stared at the child's slack form, swaying herself. Turning away, she pressed her wet hands against her eyes, drawing upon reserves of strength she had rarely touched. When she lifted her hands, she could feel the salt water evaporating on her eyelids, stretching the skin till it felt stiff and tight. She blinked, looking at the doraado. They floated lazily on their sides, each watching her with one eye. They were her first responsibility.

Returning to the net, Sand picked out a score of the trawna, placing them in a fold of her shannal. She waded out to the closest dolphin. As he accepted the trawna she offered, she sent him a projection of gratitude, of warmth and relief, along with the words "Thank you, doraado. You are our truest friend always."

The dolphin rolled over and disappeared below the surface. With each one she performed this ceremony, until the last rose on its tail in salute and then flipped over and was gone.

She dragged herself back onto the beach and stared at the unconscious girl. Exhaustion was sucking at Sand now, too, fraying the edges of her thought. She longed to flop on the sand beside the child and succumb to it. Sand didn't know if it was a trick of the dusk or not, but the child's lips and fingernails looked blue. She knelt and chafed the girl's limbs. After a moment, the girl's skin seemed warmer and Sand left her to search the edge of the beach for dried seaweed and grasses. Before she covered her up, she borrowed the child's bone-handled fish knife from its sheath. Then, layering the insulating fluff over the girl, she unwrapped her sodden shannal and laid it over the seaweed, trapping the heat.

Finally she returned to the catch, which was still wriggling on the sand. She picked out plump perch and snappers. After a moment's consideration, she also chose some rarer delicacies: clown fish, groupers, parrot fish, and two triggerfish. All these she killed quickly and cleanly. As she was bundling the rest into the net, she recognized to her delight the iridescent blue-black scales of a bottle fish. Keeping him out, she dragged the rest to the sea and released them. As she watched, they revived and swam away, some bemusedly and some with a lightning flick of their tails.

She murmured, "Thank you, Mother, for the largess of your blessing. I return these little ones to your care that your body will always hold enough to fill my net and my need."

She used the net to tie up the fish she was keeping and anchored it in shallow water to keep cool.

At last she crept the short distance to where the girl now lay cocooned in warmth. After checking her breathing, she lifted an edge of the shannal and insinuated her own body underneath the seaweed. Sand's teeth chattered uncontrollably and the girl moaned and tried to push away the cold flesh next to her own. Sand slid easily below wakefulness and concentrated on relaxing each muscle. She stopped shivering, except for the occasional spasm. Next she imagined she was cold stone, lying in the embers of a beach fire, absorbing and storing the heat. She was so tired; focusing on this image and holding it was very difficult, but each time the thought wavered she hung on tenaciously. Gradually her skin temperature returned to normal; the child cuddled closer to her.

Sand let go then and her consciousness drifted away from her, gliding down across the beach and out onto the gently rocking surface of the waves like a shadow.

❋   ❋   ❋

Several hours later the girl beside her finally stirred once, then again, then sat up. Sand's consciousness winged swiftly back to her.

The girl's eyes in the starlight were empty, blank pools, but as Sand lay watching her, they filled with memory like bowls with water.

"How do you feel?" she asked the child.

"Weak. Empty."

Sand nodded. "I too." They were silent for a time, and then the girl finally looked around.

"Where's my net?"

"Keeping your catch fresh."

"Mmm."

Eventually Sand crawled out from under the coverings and stretched in the starlight. "It must be after midnight."

The girl straightened. "By the Mother! Really? I must get home!"

"Of course," Sand sympathized. "Your grandfather must be worried."

She snorted. "Worried? I don't think so. Just hungry and cross."

"I'm sure you'll be forgiven when he sees what you've caught."

The child walked down to the water's edge. The bright starlight on the breeze-roughened surface glistened back at her, making the water visually impenetrable.

She turned back to Sand. "Where is it?"

Sand waded out and, by looking at the landmarks she'd used on the shore and feeling the sandy bottom with her toes, she soon found the net.

The girl helped her haul it in. Feeling the weight of the catch, she suddenly realized the value of the gift Sand had given her. Abashed, she looked down at her hands.

"You've done me a great service, raeth daughter."

"My name is Sand."

"And mine"—she reached up and twitched the husk of a white star-flower out of Sand's hair—"is Monarri." She held it out to Sand with a shy smile.

They turned their attention back to the net.

"I was pleased to be of help to you. In a way, this is my fiertha. I have proven myself to the Mother in someone else's service." Reminded of her shannal, Sand picked it up and slung it over Monarri's shoulder.

"Here," she said. "This is for you. May it bring you luck in marriage."

"I can't take this," the girl protested. "What will you wear?"

"My undershift for now." Sand laughed. "Thank the Mother it's summer. As for later . . ." She shrugged. "I'm hoping that the Sea Mother will provide. Besides," she continued in a more practical vein, "the shannal is useless to me in the life I'll be leading. There's too much of it. It will tangle in everything."

Before they could argue further, Sand caught sight of a point of light moving in the vegetation beyond the beach. Twinkling orange-red, it wavered among the trees, creeping nearer and nearer. Sand spun Monarri around. "Look!"

The girl sighed. "It's my grandfather."

An old man stumbled onto the beach. He caught sight of them and raised his torch. "Mona!"

Sand heard relief in his tone. Whatever the girl might think, her grandfather cared about her.

"Mona," he repeated when he reached them. "Where have you been? It's so late! I dozed off and when I woke up and you weren't home I was sure something dreadful had happened. Are you all right, little Monarri flower?"

He tried to lay a shaky hand on the girl's shoulder, but she side-stepped him.

"Yes, Grandfather, I'm fine. I had trouble calling dinner tonight, until she came along." She pointed in Sand's direction. "Then we caught too much dinner and the talent-weakness took us."

For the second time, the old man raised the torch, and this time he used it to study Sand's face. In the dancing light his eyes glittered at her. The starlight breeze carried the sweetish smell of lactus brandy to her. Neither of them said a word. The seconds stretched out and finally he backed away from her.

"She helped me catch all this." Monarri tried to make his limp hand take the weight of her laden net.

"Thank you, mer-daughter," he finally said.

The child gasped in embarrassment. "Grandfather! She's raeth, not mer-kin. Her name is Sand."

His eyes sparkled in the light of the torch as he looked at Sand again, measuring her. Then he announced simply, "This one is no raeth. She is one of the Mother's own children."

Monarri's eyes were huge and pleading as she faced Sand again. "Please forgive him, Sand. He is eldrin sometimes. I guess it's from growing old and living alone so

34

much." The old man didn't appear to hear this treason from his granddaughter.

"It's all right, Monarri," Sand stressed. "Perhaps you're right, sir," she addressed him directly. "After today I'm not really raeth any longer. I can only hope the Mother will look after me as she would one of her own."

Mer-kin was a name sometimes given to the priests and priestesses of the Mother. More often, however, it referred to a mythological race of people who lived underwater. They were reputed to be mischievous and immoral. Though they could be helpful, they were more likely to trick an islander. The old tales said they were descendants of the half brothers and half sisters of Calleby and Bedjar. But they were the children of the Mother only, and had no sky-born father.

"Have you gifted her in return for her service?" the old man reminded Monarri.

"You've given me so much." The child's forehead creased in the torchlight. "What could I give you that you don't already have?"

"I don't have anything," Sand said in exasperation. "I'm starving; I need one of the perch we caught for my dinner. And I would like some fire from your torch."

The old man cackled. "Kryphon still calls to those with the blood of the Mother, eh?" He looked at her sideways and whispered, "He will return, you know."

Embarrassed, Sand forced a polite smile. "Oh, yes?"

He caught the disbelief in her tone. "Yes! Can't you feel it, mer-daughter? Don't you feel the Mother stirring, awakening? Reaching to the heavens to embrace him? You will soon!"

Grabbing her forearm in a bony claw, he forced her arm toward the heavens. "There! Can't you see him? He is returning to the Mother."

He was pointing to a bright star in the constellation of

the Conch that seemed unfamiliar. But Sand couldn't be sure it was new; there were so many stars in the heavens.

Monarri squirmed with the acute embarrassment of a twelve-year-old whose grandfather is behaving strangely in front of her friend.

"Grandfather, just give Sand your torch. I will find the path by starlight." She snatched it from his hand and pressed it on Sand. "Take it," she commanded as Sand opened her mouth to protest. "You'll need it to stay warm." Opening the net, her hand dove in and emerged with a plump fish which she pressed into Sand's other hand. "Come on, Grandfather. It's time to go home and sleep. In the morning you can have your very own fat grouper for breakfast. A whole one." She took him firmly by the hand.

He mumbled something in agreement and Sand saw that his eyes had dulled. He looked vague and lost now. Monarri began tugging him into the shadows of the trees, struggling with the weight of the net in one hand, and her grandfather's uncertain resistance in the other. "You're welcome to use our beach. I'll come here tomorrow evening," she called back, a question in her voice.

"I'll be here," Sand promised in return.

Sand was left alone. Her shadow danced beside her in the torch's light. She shivered as the damp sea breeze trickled over her bare shoulders. After a moment's thought, she turned back toward the rocky point she had clambered across late that afternoon.

Carefully picking her way over the big slabs of rock out toward the sea, she was almost at the end of the rocky spit when she found what she was looking for: a large, flat slab of rock sunk several feet below those around it, forming a natural shelter open to the sea on one side. Even now it felt warm under her bare toes; the heat it had absorbed during the day was radiating softly from its surface.

36

She propped the torch between two boulders and laid the fish beside it. Quickly she gathered dried seaweed, driftwood, and sea grasses. Piling them together, she touched the torch to the edges and soon a crackling fire cheered the corners of her shelter.

She clambered back to the beach and gathered up all the fluff she'd used to keep Monarri and herself warm. Hunting in the trees, she found two bael nuts and, with her arms full, picked her way back to the fireside.

The bael nuts she pushed into the heart of the fire. The fish she laid on a thin, flat stone and this, too, she placed on the fire. While they cooked, she set about smoothing the grasses into a bed. Finally she sat down with her back against the warm rock and retrieved her dinner.

She was shaking and weak, and it took her twice as long as it should have to smash open the bael nuts. She picked chunks of the nut away from the burnt shell and chewed them reflectively. With her fingers, she peeled back the charred skin of the perch and pulled off its fragrant, moist meat.

Savoring every mouthful, she gave thanks to the Mother for her feast. Tonight she was especially grateful. She'd been stupid. She could almost hear Teacki scolding her as she had done years ago when the talent-weakness had taken her. The old priestess was tutoring her then, and when Anemone flew into hysterics at the sight of her pallid, senseless daughter, Teacki had calmly taken over.

Later Sand heard how she'd dribbled lactus brandy and broth into her mouth, stroking her throat until she swallowed. All Sand remembered was waking to find relief on Teacki's usually unreadable countenance. The moment Sand was well enough to get out of bed again, Teacki sat down with her.

"Listen, young talent," she had advised. "And listen carefully. I will teach you many things; some of them are important, some of them not so much. But this you must remember all your life, or you will not have a life for long.

"You have talent—enormous talent. But the Mother does not gift one with such power without protecting her ocean children. Her gift demands some sacrifice and has limitations."

Sand looked at her, eager to comprehend but not yet understanding.

Teacki pointed. "Do you see that cookfire there, child?"

Sand nodded.

"The flame you see there, that bright dancing light, is your body. The fuel that feeds it and keeps it alight is the sleep you get and the food you eat. When you use your talent, it acts like a great wind blowing on the fire. The fuel must be replenished steadily and quickly or the fire will burn hotter and hotter and fall away to ash."

Sand shuddered at the bleakness in Teacki's eyes. With adolescent ghoulishness, she longed to ask if Teacki had ever known someone to actually use their talent to death, but she didn't dare.

With a wry glance at Sand's wiry frame, Teacki added, "You're not likely to need this knowledge for a while, but the opposite is also true. If you pile on too much fuel, the fire is banked. The air—your talent—can't get at the flame and can't be used. You will never find a fat or sluggish raeth woman if she is successfully using her talent. You must maintain the balance, Sand—maintain that delicate balance."

Today for the only time since that first mistake, Sand had pushed herself too far.

Finally she was full. She damped the embers of the fire with mats of wet seaweed, so it would last till she woke. She lay on her stomach, hanging her head and arms over the edge of the rock, and washed her face and hands in the waves. At last she lay down on the soft pallet she'd made and looked at the stars. It was so late that in the east the sky was graying. A gull flew overhead. Its stomach turned a luminous peach color as it wheeled and caught the rays of the coming sun. High above her the stars of the Conch began to fade as well, but the star the old man had pointed out to her could be seen long after all the others were lost in the blue welkin.

The waves kept whispering to her to sleep and so, obediently, she did.

Chapter Four

When she awoke, her face was turned away from the sun but the fierce heat bounced back at her from the rock walls of her shelter, beading her face and chest with sweat.

She rose, and after checking her fire to make sure the coals were still hot, she eased into the sea. The cool waves refreshed her and she paddled contentedly till the sleep was washed from her mind.

For breakfast she dug clams out of the sand in the shallow waters of the lagoon and roasted them, eating the meat and drinking their broth when they cooled enough to be held.

Picking the sturdiest-looking shell, she began grinding it on a rock, and soon she had honed a sharp edge. The idea of picking her way barefoot over the scorching rocks was unappealing, so holding the shell in her teeth, she swam to shore.

At the rim of the beach she found a young lactus plant. Bending one of its reeds toward the ground, she used her shell to saw through it, but the tough fibers quickly dulled the edge. "I need a knife," she muttered, scowling as she reground the edge of her shell. The reed finally came free and she held it to her lips and tipped her head back. Clear, sweet water flowed into her mouth. She drank till the tube was empty, and found she still wanted more. That meant she had to sharpen her shell again.

It was early afternoon by the time Sand had satisfied all her body's demands. She went swimming again, and floating on the surface of the waves, she reflected that without tools and servants, so much time is spent just existing.

She pulled her shift over her head and left it on the rock. Slipping naked through the sea, she swam cautiously out beyond the point, watching for hidden reefs. Turning over on her back, cradled in the waves, she closed her eyes and calmed her mind. She had just begun to reach outward with her thoughts when she was interrupted.

"Looking for me, little mudball?" The affectionate question formed inside her head, as she was lifted from the waves. She shrieked with laughter as she was dunked with a huge splash.

"M'ridan," she sputtered, "how did you find me?"

"I never lose you, mudball. If I bother myself to think about you, I always know where you are."

"Is that true?" Sand bit her tongue, but too late. Doraado didn't understand the concept of true and false. Things either were or were not. Sand had tried to tell him what a lie was once. "What if I told you the sun was green?" she asked, visualizing a blazing green ball in the sky.

"But that *is not*," he had replied.

"Suppose I insisted that it *is*."

He had circled her in the water, always watching her out of the same eye. Finally he said, "Then that would be a joke; but one that was not funny."

41

From then on, anything that was not true was referred to between them as an unfunny joke.

Doraado had an extremely well-developed sense of humor and they found the oddest things funny. Sand often could not understand M'ridan's more intellectual jokes. His practical jokes she understood all too well, as she was usually the butt of them.

So now she rephrased her question. "Is that an unfunny joke?"

He splashed her gently with his tail. "Gritty one, you should know better. All my jokes are funny."

Her name was a constant source of wordplay with him, and one of the original reasons for their friendship.

For a raeth woman to actually talk to a provider was so rare as to be legendary. Most people couldn't visualize clearly or quickly enough to keep the dolphin's interest. But one afternoon, when she had been Monarri's age, she'd been playing at the water's edge on her father's beach. A doraado had come up close to her. She'd greeted him and he had replied in visual mindspeech. Thrilled, she asked him where he had come from and he thought this was funny. "The sea, of course," he had answered her. He sent her flash after flash of images: coral reefs, sandy coves, forests of seaweed, deep blue water with the silver sky of the surface high above and the blackness of the ocean depths below.

"What do they call you?" she asked him laboriously.

He answered by sending an image of himself balancing on his tail, spraying water in delicate patterns over the surface of the sea. So she thought of him as M'ridan, which in her tongue meant "Wave-dancer." He seemed to think this was wildly funny, so she guessed she must have the meaning wrong. She apologized. She could feel his amusement even as he assured her that this name suited him very well.

"What are you called?" he asked her in return.

She projected him an image of grains of dry sand.

M'ridan seemed confused. "But what kind?" he asked her. He sent her image after image of different kinds of sand: flakes of mica stirred up from the bottom by a current; smooth white coral sand; muddy sand in the bottom of still pools; hard-packed clay sand; rich, loamy brown sand underneath fronds of seaweed; beige grit arranged in undulating lines by the waves; and many more images flashing by so quickly that her mind reeled.

"Which one?" he asked again.

"All of them," she answered in her confusion.

His merriment at this was unbounded. He stood on his tail and danced backward. Then, flinging himself in the air, he landed flat on the surface, spraying her.

"All of them," he kept repeating, laughing so hard that she eventually began to giggle, too.

"Come, let's swim together, little mudball," he had invited.

In time she discovered that the doraado have over twenty words for sand. Over the years he'd called her all of them with variations. Mudball seemed to be his favorite.

Also, in time they'd become more and more used to sharing mindspeech, until abstract thoughts became commonplace between them. Indeed, sometimes now he seemed to pick her thoughts up before she'd even organized them coherently. And since he was never offended by anything he found in her mind, truth-telling between them was easy.

"Shall we swim together?" he asked her now, as he had that first day.

Joyously she agreed. For a moment he disappeared and then she felt him surfacing underneath her. He rose out of the water and, with a click and a whistle, breathed in. She wrapped her arms and legs around him and felt the buttery softness of his skin.

43

"Ready?"

"Ready," she agreed, snatching a breath.

He surged and they dove. They were slicing through the water, her hair streaming behind her. She saw schools of colored fish scattering before them like petals thrown into the wind.

When she needed air, she loosened the pressure of her arms and legs and he took her back to the surface. A moment later he'd dive again. They swam over beds of seaweed and underwater gardens of coral sculpture. She wished she could see more clearly underwater.

Eventually she began to see little black fish swimming before her eyes. She knew they weren't really there. "Enough. I must stop for a time," she told him.

They returned to the surface and she lay on her back, rocking on the waves, reveling in the sun on her skin.

"Why are you so far from your home waters?" he asked her as they rested.

"My family wanted me to take a mate," she told him. "But I did not want to, so I left home."

"Why not want to? A mate is great fun."

"Not this mate. There would be no more fun for me with this mate. Or with any mate."

She had never told anyone about her relationship with M'ridan. This freedom, this uncomplicated joy she felt with him, was too precious for her to risk. If people knew, they would find a way to make her stop. If they knew how often she had shed her raeth duties and ridden so far out to sea on M'ridan that Strandia became the merest scar on the horizon—even her gentle, loving father would have responded harshly. Men were jealous of the raeth women's talent, but as long as it was used for gain they tolerated it. If they ever suspected it was a source of joy, however, Sand was sure they would stop her.

Her relationship with M'ridan had been hard enough to conceal while she lived at home. It would be impossible to hide as a sensible, duty-ridden raeth wife on another family's holding. There would be tedious social chores and curious eyes. And all too soon there would be pressure to have children; she thought of poor Coral—trapped forever, not even realizing it.

"Now I can't live with my family anymore," she told him.

"Why not?"

"I told everyone an unfunny joke and they're angry with me."

"What joke is so terrible it angers people?" he asked, genuinely puzzled.

"I told them I couldn't talk to the providers."

M'ridan began to chuckle. He laughed and laughed, rolling over on his back so that only his pale stomach and his silly fishy smile could be seen above the water. She finally swam over and punched him.

When he calmed down a little, he asked, "How could they get angry at that? It's the best joke I've heard in many days."

"What makes it so funny?" She wondered for the thousandth time how the doraado judged humor.

He thought a moment. "Because it's unexpected," he told her. "I can hear you better than any other one-who-compels. So it's shocking when you say you can't talk to me or my pod. That's what makes it such a good joke. It's ridiculous." She felt his merriment again as he considered it.

"But many people don't know that you can hear me at all."

"Oh." He considered this a moment. "Then they won't think it's very funny."

She smiled grimly. "They didn't," she agreed. "And now I can't live with my family. For a while I'm going to live here."

"With no pod? How sad."

"Don't you like to be alone sometimes?" she asked him.

M'ridan considered. "It's difficult to say. The sea pulses with life—true solitude is nearly impossible. But separate from the pod? Sometimes," he finally agreed. "But that is a matter of the moment and of choice. I would not like to be forced to stay away."

She shrugged. "When I get lonely, I'll find a new pod."

Soon they headed back toward her point of land. Surrendering both thought and mindspeech, Sand gave herself over to feeling and sensation. She hung on with just her arms, letting her legs stream out behind her, reveling in the caress of the cool water sifting through her hair and flowing along her skin. They dove and surfaced and dove and surfaced; she lost count of how many times.

Finally M'ridan brought her up into the sunlight and she recognized her niche in the rocks.

"I've got to find some supper," she told him. She grabbed his dorsal fin and he took her down to the floor of the bay. She pried a conch from the coral. It took more time and effort than she'd expected and she reached the surface gasping for air. She tossed the heavy shell onto her ledge, where it clattered against the rock.

M'ridan began to act silly. He flowed away from her, and before she realized what he was doing, she was surrounded by hundreds of trawna scurrying around her in the water. Giggling, she protested, "M'ridan, that tickles!"

She felt one brush her palm and closed her fingers on it.

When he slid up beside her with a whistle and a silly grin, she flung her arm across his back and offered him the tiny fish. He gulped it down.

"Thank you for an afternoon of pleasure, old friend."

"It was great fun," he agreed, and she knew he needed no more reason than that to have spent his day with her.

"I'll be living here for a time," she told him.

"I'll find you wherever you are, little mudball." He rose on his tail and danced for a moment in the afternoon sun. His dive sent a spray of water diamonds into the light, and before they fell back to the sea, he was gone.

She didn't try to follow him with her thoughts, though she could bespeak him at quite a distance. Lazily she turned and swam to her rock. She pulled herself onto its blistering surface just long enough to grab her shift and the conch. She slipped back into the water and wedged the conch in the rocks where it would be washed by the waves and stay cool.

After pulling her shift over her head, she swam into shore. She chose a low bael-nut tree with many branches, climbed into it, and slung her body between two of its limbs. With the breeze cool on her moist skin and the bael fronds rustling their lullaby, she set herself to catching up on the sleep she'd missed the night before.

❂   ❂   ❂

Sand awoke in the early evening. Climbing over the rocks to her shelter, she gathered dry driftwood on the way. At first she thought the embers of her fire had died, but she found two red coals still glowing under the gray ash. Silently she chastised herself for not tending it when she'd returned that afternoon. She snatched some of the dried grass from her sleeping pallet, laid it on top of the coals, and blew on them steadily. A bright flame seared the grass to black. With a sigh of relief she began building a blaze.

She retrieved her conch and set about trying to extract the meat: without a knife this proved impossible. She tried to crack it between two rocks, but it kept skidding back into the water. After she'd retrieved it for the fourth time, it had no noticeable marks on its shell, but she had tears of frustration in her eyes.

She was trying to talk herself into bael nut again when she heard, "Good evening, Sand."

Monarri stood atop one of the rocks behind her. "I could see the smoke from your fire. What are you cooking?"

"Nothing unless I can get this accursed conch out of its shell."

With a wordless grin Monarri pulled her knife from its sheath and set to work on the shellfish. In a few minutes she had the meat pried free. While Sand rinsed out the shell, Monarri went to cut some lactus reeds.

She returned carrying three. One they used to fill the now-clean shell. This they set in the fire again. When the water began to boil, they stuffed the shell with strips of conch meat. While this simmered, they sipped from the other reeds and talked of what they had done that day, though Sand made no mention of M'ridan.

"I must thank you again, Sand," Monarri finished. "I sold the bottle fish today for thirty-five flecks! And I got another twenty for the rest of the catch, not counting what Grandfather and I kept to eat ourselves. That's more money than we usually have in a whole year."

"You got a good price."

"I went first to one craftsman, then another, then another, and told each one what the last had offered me. It was a fine bottle fish. They all wanted it. Each time I got a price, I said I would think about it and went away and told someone else."

"Very shrewd. And what did you do with your wealth?"

"Most of it I brought back to the house and hid where Grandfather can't find it. Now when we're hungry, if I have to, I can buy our dinner—"

"Dinner!" Sand interrupted. With the help of a stick she wriggled the shell out of the fire. Using Monarri's knife again, she speared the strips of conch on the point and shared them with her friend.

"And what else?" she prompted with her mouth full.

"I went to the weavers' house and bought a new cloak for Grandfather. He gets so chilled sometimes. Especially when it's damp. And"—she reached into a fold in the ragged shirt she was wearing—"a comb." She exhibited it shyly.

"With your hair combed you'll look like a true raeth daughter," Sand told her. Monarri blushed and hid a smile. "I'll help you comb it after dinner if you like."

"I wanted to get you something special, too, Sand. I've never seen so many fish as you brought to shore yesterday." Her eyes went blank as the memory of it absorbed her. "I hardly helped at all . . ."

"That's not true! You worked so hard you fell to the seeftharl. Very foolish, by the way. Were you never taught to protect yourself?"

Monarri set her jaw. Ignoring Sand's interruption, she continued: "Anyway, I didn't know what to get you. You could just call in a batch of fish and sell them yourself."

"What would I catch them in?" Sand asked her gently.

"A net! I could get you a net!"

"And how would I have gotten my dinner out of its shell tonight if you hadn't come along?" Sand continued.

"You need a knife as well." Monarri set her chin on her fist. "I've been foolish. I should have thought of those things. But here—" She sat up and fumbled at her belt. "You must have *my* knife."

Sand protested, but Monarri was adamant.

"Here. Take it." She leaned over and fastened the belt, complete with sheath and knife, at Sand's waist. "I can borrow Grandfather's till I get another one. He never uses his, anyway."

Sand still looked dubious.

49

Monarri pulled the knife from its sheath and showed her its edge. "Look. It's a good knife, for all that it's second-hand."

"I can see that it's a good one. That's one reason I don't want to take it from you."

"You're not taking it." Monarri straightened. "It's a gift which I give you whether you will take it or not. You helped me in my need. To prevent me from repaying you in your need is ungenerous." She eyed Sand sternly.

Sand, hearing the earnest echo of adult wisdom in her shrill voice, began to laugh. "I pity the poor craftsmen you bargained with today. They didn't stand a chance."

Monarri, sure now of getting her way, grinned at her.

"Thank you for this gift," Sand continued more formally, taking the knife and hefting it. "And I will thank you in my heart each time I use it."

After washing their hands in the sea, they sat in the evening sun while Sand struggled with Monarri's matted hair. When she was finished, she could pull the comb through it from root to tip in one smooth sweep. Monarri looked like the raeth daughter she was. She kept drawing her fingers down the length of her hair disbelievingly.

"My mother used to make my hair feel like this." She sighed. "Then she died."

"You can comb it yourself, you know," Sand began, mis-understanding.

"Oh, I did for a while. Then I lost her comb, too, and it didn't seem to matter much." Monarri shrugged. She ran her fingers through the silkiness again. "But I love this feeling." She turned her gaze on Sand, inspecting her ragged locks.

"Enough!" Sand laughed self-consciously, putting up her hand and tousling her short hair. "I cut it like this because I told my mother I would no longer be either her daughter or raeth. Since my hair marked me as raeth I cut it off. It wasn't a well-considered action, but it's done now. And my hair looks like ragged seaweed."

"No, it doesn't," Monarri denied loyally. She sought for something to say that would be both complimentary and true. "It's a beautiful color."

They moved back to the fireside and sat close to it while they talked. When night had crept in completely, pushing the last of the sun's light beyond the west, they went swimming together, laughing as they raised their arms and phosphorescent streams blazed over their skin.

Afterward they pulled themselves back up on the rock and lay panting happily by the fire till they were warm and dry.

"I must get back to Grandfather," Monarri finally announced with a sigh. She hesitated a moment as though she were about to add something, but then she merely said, "Good night, Sand." She smiled in farewell, and her mouth seemed to fall into that curve more easily now.

Chapter Five

"Are you sure that you want to pursue it? After all, the more you make of this affair, the longer people will remember it." The older priest, Alesk, rubbed his palms outward across his forehead, and as he momentarily stretched the skin, the deep lines etched there disappeared.

Tamin leaned against the window. His face was turned away from the discussion in the room, looking out toward the sea, but his hands gave him away—the fingers drummed ceaselessly against his thighs. Tamin's father was going over the accounts, and the other three men felt invisible before him.

The younger priest, Rainis, cleared his throat. "May I point out, however, that it's not merely a matter of family pride. The Mother has been gravely offended. We mustn't let this go unjudged or unpunished."

An edge crept into Alesk's voice. "You feel the Mother needs you to catch her prey for her?"

Rainis clenched his jaw. "You always . . ." he began in a

strangled voice. Then he broke off and joined Tamin at the window, muttering something to him.

Alesk addressed Tamin's father directly: "Raeth Calut, would you be willing to let this matter drop?"

Calut grunted in irritation. ". . . eighty-six, ninety-two, ninety-five." He moved several flecks from one pile to another. Lifting his head, he glanced at Alesk and then stared at his son. Tamin dropped his eyes and fidgeted. Calut's face betrayed nothing. He looked back at the older priest. "My son disregarded my advice when he chose this raeth girl over another. Since he has no use for my words, why should I waste them? Let him deal with the consequences of his choice in whatever way he decides. I want no part of any more humiliation."

Tamin turned to the window again, but Alesk saw the tendons standing out rigid in the back of his neck and the hot flush under his dusky skin. "Find her. Punish her. It's my right. I want her punished."

Calut had gone back to his accounts and made no sound.

"We don't punish," Rainis reproved. "Only the Mother judges and metes out punishment."

With an audible snort, Alesk stood and bade them good night.

As they walked through the dark, Rainis said, "I think it's unwise to air our differences before others. There are too many Midislanders fragmenting from the old ways. We don't want the raeth following that lead. We must show a united priesthood."

He waited, but Alesk made no answer. He continued, "Furthermore, I don't think the Mother is well served by your pressure to drop this incident. You are allowing cracks to widen unchecked in the wall of faith."

Alesk just shook his head and continued to trudge through the dark.

Back in the home they'd just left, Tamin threw himself sideways into a chair and dangled his legs over one arm.

His mother, Iola, brought their nightly cups of mulled lactus brandy. She set the tray down and fiddled with the contents. Tamin tensed. He felt her unhappiness from a hundred minute signals, none of which he could have identified in words. "What's wrong?" he asked.

She compressed her lips. "That poor girl. Why do you have to persecute her? You wouldn't leave her alone when she wanted you to—and you got what you deserved. Why can't you leave her alone now?"

Tamin stared at her. "Whose side are you on?"

"It's not a matter of sides! It's a matter of right and wrong."

"Right. She's done wrong." He smirked in self-congratulation at his play on words.

"So have you! Why couldn't you stop pursuing her when she asked you to? Raeth men! They're arrogant and pushy, and when they don't get their own way they squawk like seagulls. Poor raeth girls never have a—"

"Enough!" Calut's word cauterized her voice.

She shot him a look, corrosive as acid, full of personal history and resentment. Tamin tensed, waiting for the fight to erupt, as it so often did.

But Calut merely rose and went to bed. When Tamin was certain his father was not returning to the room, he said, "I just want to teach her a lesson, Mother. She can't shame me like that and get away unscathed."

"So you'll kill her to ease your pride?"

"It won't kill her! Mother, you've never seen Sand compelling. She's got the strongest talent I've ever seen. Once we were playing on the beach and I dared her to see how far she could reach with it. She made a group of providers dance so far away they were on the rim of the ocean. I could barely see them."

54

"I've heard the story before, Tamin. Why not just leave her alone?"

"I don't want to be pointed at as the biggest fool on Strandia: offering the largest marriage gift ever for a no-talent. I want people to know that she's got talent. If she has to force the providers to bring her back to Strandia, I will be proven right."

Iola realized that by the word "people" Tamin really meant his exacting, discontented father. "But, Tamin," she pointed out, more gently now, "if they know she's got talent, they'll realize that she risked everything so she wouldn't have to marry you. Even with a hefty bride-price. How will that make you look?"

He fell silent. He rubbed his fingers back and forth over his upper lip, feeling the fledgling stubble there. At last he shook his head, avoiding her eyes. "I don't know. There doesn't seem to be a right answer." He sat up straighter. "But it's done now—it's in motion. I can't stop it. Mother," he pleaded, "don't you see, I couldn't let it go. I couldn't do nothing."

She glared at Calut's closed door. "No, I suppose not. You're too much like your father—you always have to be *doing* something."

◆   ◆   ◆

Sand's life on the point fell into a pattern. M'ridan played with her during the days and Monarri visited her in the evenings. The times of solitude in between the visits were a treasure and not a lonely burden as Sand had feared.

Sometimes the two girls would call in the providers to make a catch for Monarri. Sometimes they dug for clams. When she considered it at all, Sand felt that the Sea Mother truly was looking after her. Her existence here was

55

as perfect as anything she'd ever dared dream of. Until she was stung by a jellyfish one afternoon while swimming in the cove.

By the time Monarri arrived that evening, Sand was burning with fever and delirious. Monarri ran home to tell her grandfather that she wouldn't be home that night and returned with a blanket. All night she tended Sand, bringing her lactus reeds to drink from and keeping the fire blazing. In the darkest hours, Sand's fever reached such terrible heat that her skin felt hot enough to Monarri's touch to light tinder. The young girl insisted Sand slip into the sea to cool off. Despite the fact that her fever was so high, Sand was shaking with chills. She pleaded with Monarri not to force her into the water, but the girl insisted, inexorably gentle. By the time Monarri managed to get her out, Sand's fever had abated a little, but both girls were crying.

Sand fell into a deep sleep almost immediately after her dip. As dawn swathed the sky in pink clouds, Sand's fever broke.

She regarded Monarri with now-lucid eyes, and her friend brushed the sweaty hair from her forehead.

"Would you like some water?"

Sand nodded weakly. A few minutes later she found her voice and whispered, "How long?"

"One night."

Sand closed her eyes and sank back on the pallet of dried grasses. "I thought it had been weeks."

While Monarri went to get more lactus reeds, Sand lay awake watching the sun climb higher in the sky. Vulnerable for the first time in her new independence, she began to consider what could happen. Until yesterday she had been very lucky. The weather had stayed beautiful, and she'd been healthy.

She had put off thinking about winter. Now she admitted

to herself that the summer would end and her life must change. That was as far as she got before the healing sleep she needed pulled her under once more.

When she woke, she found Monarri curled up asleep beside her. Rolling over, she found M'ridan lazing in the water, under an overcast sky.

"You didn't call."

"I was very ill last night. A jellyfish stung me."

"Poor mudball."

Sand slid from her ledge, savoring the cool water washing the sweat from her skin. M'ridan watched her carefully.

Though she enjoyed the water, she had to climb out soon, because her arms and legs were so weak; she could hardly move them to stay afloat. Even getting out was a problem until M'ridan gave her a hefty boost.

"I'll swim with you tomorrow, M'ridan." As she spoke to him she could feel her strength leaving her like water trickling from a cup with a hole in the bottom.

Her eyes began to close of their own accord, when he answered gently, "Heal first, little grit."

It took two days to flush the poison from her system.

Though Sand quickly recovered her health, the jellyfish incident marked the end of her idyll on the point. The dawns that she greeted each morning were cloudy and at night a heavy, cold mist often obscured the stars, so that there was no light to see by.

Then the first of the winter storms hit. All day the winds blew and the waves got higher and wilder. By dusk they were crashing onto her rock. The coals, which had burned since she built her first fire from the torch, were doused by the combers that washed up on her rock.

Sand spent a chilly, sodden night huddled under the bael-nut trees. The rain stopped for a couple of hours the next morning. Just as she began to stamp and massage some life back into her limbs, Monarri arrived with a blanket and hot coals in a bowl.

"Poor Sand! I heard the rain trickling in the thatching all night. I kept waking up, worrying about you." Water streaked Monarri's cheeks, though whether it was tears or rain, Sand could not be sure.

"I'm fine, Monarri. I was wet and cold last night, but the sun is out now. And you, little dear"—she hugged the girl—"have brought me fire, which was the thing I was most wishing for."

Monarri chewed her lip. "Sand, you know that winter is coming?"

"Of course."

"The weather isn't going to get better, Sand. At least, not for very long. I asked Grandfather if you could come and live with us, but . . . but he . . ." Monarri burst into tears and couldn't continue for a moment. Sand put a hand on one of her shaking shoulders.

"I hate him," the girl sobbed. "He says that the Mother will look after her mer-daughter. I keep telling him you're raeth just like me. Stupid eldrin old man! And he doesn't want you to come for other reasons, too. He drinks too much lactus brandy. He's afraid someone else in the house . . ." Sobbing overcame her.

"Hush. Shh, little Monarri." Sand rubbed the girl's thin shoulder blades. "He's not so wrong, you know. I was raeth once, but I'm not really anymore. Not since I did this." She lifted some of her ragged hair and let it fall again.

"Cutting your hair doesn't change anything!" Monarri burst out in protest. "You're still raeth. You still have the talent. You can't just cut your hair and say everything's different!"

Sand silently acknowledged this, but tried to mollify her. "I don't really want to depend on raeth generosity for my shelter ever again. I'll find something."

"But I don't want you to go away!" Monarri flung her thin arms around Sand and hugged her tightly.

Sand patted her wordlessly. She wanted to assure the child that it wouldn't happen, but she knew it probably would.

They gathered wood for the fire. Everything they found was soaked and Sand had to split a fallen branch and hack out some dry shavings from the center before they could persuade the coals to flame. This time they built the fire on shore, under the protection of the trees. Out on the point Sand could see the waves still crashing onto the rocks. Overhead, the clouds were beginning to pile one on top of another again, creating a dense purple mass.

By the time the fire caught, with a lot of hissing and smoking, the rain had begun again. Gentle at first, the downfall soon accelerated into drenching sheets, which the girls watched sweep across the bay toward them.

Sand insisted that Monarri go home when she saw her begin to shiver.

"I wish you could come."

"I have my fire now, thanks to you. I'll be much warmer this night."

The girl leaned over and pressed her cold lips to Sand's wet cheek. "I'll come back as soon as the rain stops," she promised. "I'll bring you more coals, in case your fire gets put out again."

Sand's fire did not last for long after Monarri left. Though she tried to shelter it, sheet after sheet of driving rain doused it as effectively as someone throwing one bucket of water after another on it.

The rain continued. After the first hour, Sand was thoroughly soaked and cursing the small, insistent drops which continued to land on her. That night was agony. She was exhausted, chilled to the bone, and very hungry. By midnight she knew that if she didn't get up and keep moving, she might be dead by morning.

In utter darkness, with the rain lashing her skin, she crawled across the rocks that marked the edge of her cove. Standing upright on the other side, she stumbled along the shore like a blind person, back toward the beaches of her childhood.

Chapter Six

"Shipbuilder, you must come and look at it this afternoon. I can't fish again till it's fixed." Terent's voice hit a
piercing note.

"But, Terent, I promised to go to the boatyard as soon as
the rain stopped. Indeed, I was just going there now."

"You must come now. It's getting late. I've lost enough
days' fishing already."

"No." Berran started for the boatyard. But Terent wad-
dled after him, shrilling accusations about poor work-
manship and money-grubbing carpenters. Finally Berran
stopped in exasperation. He turned. "Terent, I don't dare
take you near the boatyard with those thoughts in your
heart, much less on your tongue. For your sake I will go to
see your Goddess-forsaken boat now. Though why I
shouldn't just let one of my men dent your head with a
hammer is beyond me." The easiest way to get rid of Terent
would be to look at his miserable tanth as he demanded and
show him the evidence. Berran knew it would be there.

As Berran walked the wet jungle path, he gritted his teeth to shut out Terent's continuous whining. The ground was muddy, the air was oppressive after the long rain. After being closed against the raindrops, huge pink sunblooms filled the air now with their perfume, heavy and heady as lactus brandy.

They emerged from the jungle, and Terent gestured impatiently toward the hull of the boat. "Look at that!" he yelled.

"Terent, this didn't happen just from the waves. Look at those scratches in the wood." Berran's calloused finger traced several deep gouges. "Something very hard hit this boat. Something like a reef. I am a boatbuilder, not a magician. I'm not responsible for your lack of seamanship. It's not my fault you can't steer a course any straighter than a drunken duck."

Other fishermen emerged onto the beach behind them just in time to hear this.

Terent's cheeks flushed. "Don't try to blame me, Berran. This happened because your work doesn't stand up to the sea. What kind of boatbuilder are you? This has happened to me three times now. Would that your father had not died before his son was fully trained."

Berran stood very still. He had turned away just before Terent delivered this last barb. He didn't turn back now.

Terent waited for the retort to his words. As the silence lengthened, he took a few steps backward. "Maybe that's saying it a bit too strongly, Berran. But I've lost two weeks' fishing already this year. If it was just scratched I wouldn't say a word, but the water pours into the boat. Here. Let me show you the break in the ribs on the inside." He bent and puffed and heaved, trying to flip it over, until a very tall fisherman stepped forward to help him.

"Thanks, Daulo." Gasps of surprise interrupted him. "By

the Mother!" he squealed, jumping back with uncommon nimbleness.

The boat had hidden a body. Sprawled on the sand lay a form, partly concealed by a muddy brown rag. The head was turned away from him, cheek pillowed on one thin arm. The other lay outstretched across the sand. The legs were thin, too, where they emerged from under the muddy rag, and lay parallel, feet pointing toward the sea.

The other men stood frozen in a circle—a widened circle, for they had all stepped back from this apparition. Berran moved closer, around to where he could see the face. The others began to mutter and Daulo whispered, "Careful, Berran."

The carpenter knelt beside the supine figure, examining the face. Patches of sand stuck to the hollow cheeks and forehead, but underneath, the skin glowed with blood.

"Is he mer-kin?" Terent asked in a loud whisper. The others silently craned to hear Berran's answer.

"No, I don't think so." Berran concealed a smile. He picked up the outflung hand and separated the fingers. "You see? No webs between his fingers."

They acknowledged the wisdom of his answer, murmuring among themselves.

Berran saw the eyeballs dart rapidly under the lids as he laid the hand back down. Still squatting, he carefully pulled the wet cloth back from the body. Underneath it was a ragged white shift. And then Berran glimpsed the small breasts beneath the damp material. "No webs between *her* fingers," he corrected himself.

He cupped the bones of her shoulder and rocked her. After a moment she moaned an incoherent protest and tried to push his hand away. He shook her harder. Her eyes flickered open and transfixed him. In the midst of the muck on her face, it was like finding two half-buried emeralds.

She gazed at him a moment, then opened her mouth and said something, but all he heard was a harsh croak. She wet her lips, making a face at the sand that came off on her tongue, and tried again. "Kryphon."

The more superstitious of the fishermen moaned in horror at this, and she turned her head to look at them. She sat up and pulled her tattered blanket around her.

Berran expected her to say something, introduce herself, ask a question, but she simply gazed around her: first at the fishermen, then out to sea and at the sun in the sky, and finally back to his own face.

The carpenter carefully examined her face. The memory of a summer afternoon returned to him—a distraught raeth daughter with ragged hair stumbling along a beach—this beach, in fact. He compared the face before him to the one in his memory. Satisfied he knew who she was, he glanced at the men hanging back. "It's all right," he told them. "This one's human."

Terent was the first to step forward. "Who are you and what are you doing under my boat?"

"My name is Sand," she answered with quiet dignity.

"Well, that's appropriate." Berran smiled.

"As for what I'm doing here . . ." She cleared her throat. A thin line appeared between her brows. "There was a storm. I couldn't find a dry place to sleep. I was wet and so cold. Finally, just to keep moving I walked along the beach. But the night was completely black and I bumped into this boat. I crawled underneath to keep dry. I guess I fell asleep."

"Why didn't you just go home?" Berran asked.

"I have no home."

This caused even more consternation among the men than discovering her had. Everyone on Strandia had a home, a place.

There was a long pause. Berran noted she didn't seem

self-conscious even with all these strangers staring at her curiously.

One of the fishermen asked, "What should we do with her?"

Before Berran could answer, one of the others suddenly burst out, "You're Sand-bel-Anemone!"

"Yes." She inflected the word with a question that asked, "So what?"

He turned to Berran. "She's the one that the—"

Berran flung up a hand to stop him. Turning to Sand, he suggested, "Why don't you go down to the water to clean up?" His tone of voice held more command than suggestion.

She hesitated a moment, curious about that unfinished sentence. Then wordlessly she stood and marched down to the water's edge.

She dropped her blanket above the high-water line, waded in thigh deep, and dove. The storm had blown in cold water from the depths of the sea, but Sand didn't acknowledge it by one second's pause. When she surfaced she rolled over on her back to watch the fishermen. The man with the blue eyes seemed to be trying to convince the others of something. The little fat man was gesturing wildly.

Sand turned over again and swam slowly out to sea. She toyed with the idea of calling M'ridan and escaping. She knew they could disappear by the time those sluggards on shore organized themselves to get the boats launched and start after her.

But her teeth began to chatter from the chilly water, and the thought of a couple of hours in it made them chatter even harder. Looking back at the men on shore, she thought of fire. Surely whatever they decided to do, she would be warm and fed. She didn't anticipate any real danger from them.

She swam back to shore, shook as much sand as she could off her blanket, and wrapped it around herself again.

The setting sun limned in gold the group on the beach above her. She overheard the man who seemed to be the leader as he raised his voice to reach the others. "So we're all agreed. No one is to report this incident."

Sand found this disturbing. Report to whom? Her mother?

"My name is Berran," he said quietly. "You will come with me."

He turned away, and after a second's hesitation, she followed. She consoled herself with the thought that she was never far from the ocean and could always escape with M'ridan's help.

As they reached the edge of the jungle, he gestured for her to precede him and they returned along the path Berran had taken before. Berran took note of the girl's composure. Completely uncertain about her fate, she nevertheless carried herself like a goddess—no hesitation; head up, shoulders back.

As they traversed the jungle, the twilight, hiding low in the vegetation, rose up and covered their path. Green trees, blue jinnange flowers, pink sunblooms: they glowed in the dying light and then faded to a uniform gray in the dusk. Ahead of them Sand saw orange light flickering in the darkness. While her mind whimpered, "More people?" in a feeble voice, her bones cried out in gladness, "Fire!"

"Wait here a moment." He disappeared into a hut and reappeared a few moments later with two steaming bowls. Handing one to her, he motioned for her to continue following the path. She cupped her hands around the heat of the bowl. The savory scent rising from it was almost too rich after days of fasting; it made her throat tighten.

They passed between several small dwellings and entered

a large clearing. A bonfire blazed and crackled in the center, surrounded by Midislanders. Close to the fire, on a raised mat, sat a smooth-skinned woman with luxuriant gray hair falling down her back. She stared at the fire unblinkingly. Then, as they entered the clearing, she raised her face to the heavens, where the red sparks in their upward flight mixed with the white stars already hanging there.

She spoke. "It is a good hour to share a tale."

A murmur of agreement rumbled around the circle. People began to call out suggestions. Finally the teller spoke again: "It is a good hour for the tale of Aleta and Kenan."

Sand stiffened and the hair prickled all over her skin. Why on earth would the teller pick that story just as she entered the circle?

Berran touched her shoulder and spoke low in her ear. "Let's find a seat."

People moved aside, making a space for them close to the fire. Sand looked about her then. So many strange faces after so long alone; she couldn't look away. But soon the teller's rich voice tugged at her concentration and the magic of the story absorbed her despite its implications for her own situation. As she listened, she lifted the broad, flat spoon out of the stew and blew on the contents to cool them. Her stomach began to growl.

"Long ago, when the bones of this island were much younger than they are now, a young raeth son known as Birck married a raeth daughter and joined her on her parents' beach. Her name was Pearl, and fittingly so, for her aspect was cool and lustrous, but inside was a core of adamant.

"They were a perfect couple. Each day Birck grew more helpful to Pearl's father, but he never failed in deference to the older man. And when her father returned to the Sea Mother at last, he went peacefully, knowing his son-by-choice would look after his holding and his daughter properly.

67

"Pearl had an unusually strong talent, and did all the compelling. Her talent never failed her; the providers never played so far away that Pearl couldn't reach them.

"The couple's only sorrow came upon them slowly but steadily. They had no children. At first they thought it merely hadn't happened yet. Then they felt it must come soon. But gradually they began to fear it would never happen.

"Until finally, when Pearl was almost past the age of bearing, they conceived a child. She delivered during the worst storm of the winter season. She almost died.

"For years the lives of Pearl and Birck were complete and full of joy. Their raeth daughter was a beautiful, grave child. They called her Aleta. They lived in happiness and asked no more from life than what they already possessed.

"It wasn't until Aleta had grown into a lovely girl of fifteen summers that her parents' joy was troubled. She showed no sign of the talent. Another year passed, and another. They realized that Aleta would never compel the providers, could never be a raeth wife. Their beach would pass from their hands and their name would be washed away like a sand sculpture at high tide.

"Aleta didn't mind. In some ways she was pleased by the idea that she would learn a skill and move to Midisle. But her parents wouldn't hear of it. After they had waited so long for her, seventeen years seemed far too short a time to have her under their roof.

"Pearl ordered her to say nothing about her lack of talent to anyone. And because she was a good-natured, obedient girl she complied, though sometimes it was difficult to hide.

"With her beauty, it wasn't long before the raeth men came courting. And when Aleta looked into the blue eyes of Kenan, she knew sorrow for the first time. She had no talent and could never marry him, a raeth son.

"She wept and withdrew to her room. The servants were

ordered to tell Kenan she was ill and could not see him. Day by day Pearl watched her grow thinner and more unhappy. Finally, calling Aleta to her, she asked, 'Why do you weep, my daughter?'

"Aleta would not answer. But at last she said sadly, 'Oh, my Mother, I have looked into the eyes of Kenan and they are as fair to me as Kryphon's were to the Sea Mother. And yet I may not wed him, for I am raeth in name only.'

"Pearl's heart was wrung within her. She promised Aleta, 'Kenan will be yours if you both wish it, for I have a plan.'

"When she explained her idea, Aleta was shocked and would not agree to it. But when she thought of Kenan and his eyes and his arms and his sweet words, she weakened. And finally she agreed to let her mother try.

"The next time Kenan came to see her, he found her pale and tired, sitting on the porch of her home. But by the time he left, she had more sparkle in her eyes and spring in her step. He began to visit her each night, and she encouraged this with smiles and words. Finally Kenan sought out Aleta's parents and spoke the formal words of proposal.

"Pearl gave him her agreement gladly, but when Kenan looked to Aleta's father for his consent, the young man sensed distress behind Birck's kindly blessing.

"After the young man left, Birck protested to his wife, but she said, 'Everything has been arranged. Do not embarrass our daughter further by talking openly about her trouble to Kenan.'

"And so the marriage took place with much rejoicing. And when it was time for Aleta to provide the fiertha, she closed her eyes and stood as she had seen her mother do. But it was Pearl, standing in the last row of the marriage guests, who truly compelled the providers.

"But the Sea Mother, who had come to the wedding, as she always does, saw the deception. She was enraged.

69

"Even as the providers herded in huge schools of fish, the Mother sent six of her demon fish, the huge torsios with their hundreds of wicked, pointed teeth. They tore the nets from the hands of the girls standing there and knocked them off their feet. But they did not hurt these girls, for they were not part of the crime.

"When Pearl saw this, she fainted with fear. The guests began to mutter that the talent-weakness had taken the mother because she had been the one really providing the fiertha.

"Aleta put her hand before her eyes and pretended to try again for the providers. After a moment, she murmured, 'I am too tired,' and she feigned a swoon as well.

"While Birck and Kenan attended to their women, Kenan's parents feasted the guests on the other dishes which had been prepared. But the supernatural appearance of the torsios made everyone feel that this was a cursed occasion, and they all left early, looking over their shoulders at the sea.

"And that was only the beginning. For when Pearl recovered, she went down to the beach for the daily catch. She didn't return till dusk, and she was pale. Alarmed, Aleta ran to support her. 'Mother, what's wrong?' she cried. Pearl turned her face to the girl and Aleta shivered, for she saw madness in it.

" 'I've lost the talent.' The two women began wailing.

"Kenan and Birck came running. Confronted with her new husband's bewilderment, Aleta confessed all.

"Birck and Pearl turned their faces from the young man, for they were ashamed of their deception now. Furthermore, they were certain he would spurn Aleta when he knew the truth, and they couldn't bear to see her disgrace or her sorrow.

"But Kenan's love was not written in sand to be washed away so easily. He drew Aleta into his arms, saying, 'You should have told me your secret, my love. If you were an eldrin wandering the shores, I would have eaten seaweed for my fiertha.'

"With love like that, their story should have had a happy ending. But it was not to be.

"The priests came and arrested Aleta and her mother for the crime of pretense. The next morning they were bound and sent to the Mother for judgment. The Mother is not kind to those who are fools for love. The Mother did not send them home again."

As the teller's voice sank and fell silent, conversation broke out all around the circle. Sand shuddered at the gruesome ending hinted at. Wrapped in her damp blanket, her stomach now pleasantly full and warm, she pondered the story she'd just heard. The parallels between Aleta's situation and her own were obvious. She glanced quickly around the circle of listeners, searching for any glimpse of temple robes.

Sand hugged her knees to her chest and wished for the solitude and serenity of her niche in the rocks. She fingered the shell-inlaid hilt of the knife Monarri had given her and plotted escape.

The crowd around the bonfire began to disperse. Here and there small groups of men continued to talk, voices raised to accentuate a point, and lowered in agreement. Young women left together, their soft voices and quiet laughter filling the Midisle clearing like nightbird calls.

Sand rested her forehead on her knees and closed her eyes. Berran was chatting to the man beside him, but the sound of his voice began to fade. She was dozing when he stood and pulled her to her feet. "Time to go."

"Go where?" She blinked at him.

"Somewhere where there's a dry, warm bed. Are you interested?"

They passed close by the storyteller. Berran halted. He

crouched beside her and took one of her delicate hands in his own. "That was well told, Jaunta. We are fortunate to have your skill."

She turned her sightless eyes on him. "Thank you, Berran. I am fortunate in my audience."

When he released her hand, Sand thought she saw the glitter of a fleck in the teller's palm.

Once they had moved beyond the edge of the firelight, the starlight illuminated the path between the Midisle huts. Here and there a lamp shone out of a window like an answering, earthbound star. Berran stopped at last before a small, peaked dwelling. "Here."

Chapter Seven

The door opened before they reached it. Sand squinted in the sudden light.

A woman's silhouette moved into the frame. "I heard you because I was expecting you. When I saw your companion in the circle I thought you might wind up here tonight, Berran." All Sand could see of her in the doorway was her rounded figure and the dark aura of short, curly hair around her face.

Berran propelled Sand over the doorstep. She stood in a low-beamed room. A toddler sat on the floor, arrested in the act of raising his wooden cup to his mouth. His sleepy eyes regarded her steadily, as his chubby, tanned hands clutched the steaming cup of milk possessively.

The room was sparely furnished, but color blossomed everywhere. Beautiful blankets were hung on racks, thrown over chairs, and one was even used as a tablecloth. A fire burned like a beacon of welcome.

This was the first building Sand had entered for weeks and she felt confined, but not unpleasantly so; as if the room were cradling her, rather than imprisoning her.

The woman touched Sand's cheek with her own, startling Sand by the intimacy of the gesture. No Midisle woman had touched her like that since her nursemaid had been sent away when she was ten. "Be welcome in my home," the woman told her. "I'm Jinnange."

"My sister," Berran added.

"And I'm Sand," she stammered. "Thank you." Not sure of why she was here, she wasn't sure of what else to say. "It's a lovely house," she added after a moment. "I've never seen so much color in one place." She waved at the blankets.

"I'm a weaver. I store what I weave at home until I sell it."

"You made all these?" Incredulous, Sand moved to touch one. Thick and soft. She touched another and another, drinking in the rich, pebbly surfaces as they yielded to her fingers. "They're beautiful."

Jinnange smiled. Moving to a chest, she opened it and shook out another blanket. "While we're on the subject, let's replace that damp one you're wearing."

She held up a blanket that shaded softly from turquoise to a deep marine blue. It exuded a faint scent of jinnange flowers. Though Sand longed to wrap herself in its soft, dry folds, she clutched her own grubby brown throw.

"This isn't mine," she began. "A friend lent it to me."

"Then we'll make sure it's washed and mended in the morning, so she'll be pleased by its return," Jinnange countered firmly. At the continued uncertainty on Sand's face, she added, "This is a weaver's house, child. No one is going to take your cloth from you."

Slightly ashamed, Sand unwound the mildewed blanket from her shoulders and Jinnange laid it over the window ledge. Berran turned away and swept the child into his arms. He threw him into the air, shrieking with laughter.

74

"Bedtime for you, little Kemahl. Hang on!" Fastening the little boy's hands around his throat, he climbed to the loft, wearing the child like a giggling cape.

Sand held the new blanket. "This is so beautiful and I'm so dirty. Is there somewhere I can wash?"

"Surely." Jinnange showed her a washbasin in one corner and indicated the pot of water on the fire.

"Excuse me a moment." Jinnange turned toward the ladder. "I should give Berran a hand." The weaver climbed to where childish protests and squeals of delight were drowning out Berran's deep voice.

Sand slipped out of her grubby shift and sponged herself as clean as she could. Dipping her head in the basin, she washed her hair. Finally, she rinsed her shift, wrung it out, and hung it in the back window where the night breeze would dry it.

Standing near the fire, she held the blue blanket open and let the heat dry the water droplets on her skin. Through the hiss and crackle of the fire she caught snatches of the upstairs conversation. She heard "raeth daughter" several times and something that sounded like "priest hunt."

Then Jinnange's answer sounded clearly through the faintly smoky air of the hut. "Don't fret, Berran. We'll make a home for her here; as much of a home as she wishes."

They climbed down the ladder and Berran faced Sand. She felt his intense gaze. He turned to his sister and kissed her. "Thank you again, Jinny. Good night. Good night, Sand."

Alone now with this kind-eyed woman, Sand added her thanks to his. "It feels so good to be clean again," she continued, reveling in the impact of the warmth, the soft blanket, the sweet woodsmoke, and her clean skin.

"Would you like something to eat?"

"No, thank you. I've eaten tonight. But if you offered me a bed, I would say yes gladly."

Jinnange banked the fire, extinguished the lamp, and led her upstairs to the loft.

On a soft mattress Sand lay awake for a brief moment, listening to the gentle breathing in the darkness around her. Then she closed her eyes and added her own breath to the rhythms of the night.

❂   ❂   ❂

Someone was tugging at her hair. She protested incoherently, rolling away from the source of annoyance. The tugging continued. She opened her eyes. Kemahl's brown ones stared into her own.

"Mama says to wake you up."

"Mmmm." She blinked at him.

"There's lactus for breakfast," he confided. Shiny pink streaks on his cheeks showed that he'd already thoroughly enjoyed his.

"Thank you. Tell your mama I'll be right down."

She waited till his tousled head disappeared below the level of the floor and then she rolled out of bed and stretched. Wrapping Jinny's blanket around herself again, she negotiated the ladder.

Jinny greeted her and handed Sand her white undershift, dry now and warm from the sun in the window. Sand pulled it on.

"Did you sleep well?"

Sand moved into the square of sunlight from the window. "Mm-hm. Wonderfully. I didn't get much sleep during the rain the last few days." She folded the blanket and laid it on the chest.

"Lactus fruit?"

"Yes, please. Where do you find ripe ones so early?"

"This is the first one this season. It's from the house grove." Jinnange laid a generous slice in front of Sand. "It's not particularly early, though, for a first. The winter festival is only four weeks away."

Sand hid her surprise. She hadn't realized how many weeks had passed since her wedding day.

Jinny wiped Kemahl's face. She held on to his wrist with one hand, while he strained away from her. "Did you make your bed yet?"

He shook his head.

"Then upstairs you go. You can go out as soon as that's done."

He sulked all the way up the ladder.

"Would you like some khar?"

"Very much." And when Sand held the steaming mug in both hands and took her first sip, she closed her eyes in bliss. "I'd forgotten how good it tastes."

Jinny laughed, delighted with her evident pleasure. "Why don't we sit outside? It's a fine morning. I'm afraid there won't be many more this year."

They sat on the doorstep. The winter sun gilded everything with a crisp beauty. On the stones of the path two tiny lizards sunned themselves, occasionally catching a dizzy fly. Sand stretched her legs out in front of her and leaned back against the sun-warmed boards. Turning her face up to the sun, she thought wistfully of her rock. Today she could have gone swimming with M'ridan.

Keeping her eyes closed, she sent out a silent call. She'd never tried to speak to him so far from the sea and she strained to reach him.

His lazy reply delighted her. "I hear you, little cloud of silt. Where are you?"

She opened her eyes and looked around her, showing

him all she saw. The sea was beyond her gaze and she felt his twinge of anxiety over that. "I can't swim today."

"Too bad, mudball." She felt him roll over in the water, turning his other eye to the sun. "It's a lovely day for a swim."

She bade him goodbye regretfully, with a final promise of "Soon."

Sand turned her head to find Jinny regarding her with a peculiar expression.

"I'm sorry. Did you say something?"

"About five times." Jinny didn't know whether to be offended or worried. "Did you fall asleep again?"

"Yes," Sand lied. Then she padded it with the truth. "I'm sorry. As I told you, the rain made it impossible to sleep until I found some shelter during the night before last."

"You weren't living in a house of any sort?" Jinny was incredulous.

Sand shrugged. "It was summer."

Jinny laughed. "I ask you something and I cannot guess what you are going to answer. Your life is a marvel to me. What are you going to do now?"

Sand shrugged again.

Jinny pursed her lips. "Haven't you thought any further ahead than the next second?"

Chastened, Sand shook her head. "I haven't needed to before now." She sighed in frustration. "Jinny, you don't know me or my family. Maybe you could look at my situation with unclouded eyes and judge and advise me fairly."

"That's a serious responsibility."

Sand grinned. "Then I promise to disregard your advice."

Jinny laughed. "Go ahead and tell me. I'll do what I can."

So Sand told her the story from the time of Tamin's unwanted proposal to her being found underneath Terent's boat yesterday. When she finished, Jinny sat silent for some time, her hands holding her cup, her elbows balanced on

78

her knees, her eyes focused on something other than the view before them. Finally she stood up abruptly and said, "I must think and I can't think properly when I sit idle. Come."

They heated water and washed the brown blanket that Monarri had given Sand. As it hung to dry, they mended the tears and darned the worn spots. Sand had to ask for instructions and Jinny demonstrated absentmindedly. While Sand strained awkwardly over the holes she worked on, Jinny flitted around her, her needle dipping gracefully in and out of the cloth like a hummingbird's beak. She even hummed to herself as she worked.

When they were finished, Sand stuck her needle in the cork beside Jinny's. "You're so fast!"

"I've been doing mending since I was Kemahl's age. I should be."

Sand stared at her own hands. "I've never done anything like this before."

Jinny stared at her. "This is the truth?"

Sand nodded her head.

"What do the raeth do all day, then?"

"Oh, the men have lots to do. They make arrangements with the fishers, go out with them on the boats, take the raeth women's catch to Midisle, collect beach rent, oversee the lactus groves. There's always something to do if you're a raeth man."

"But the women do nothing?" Jinny couldn't hide her astonishment.

"They use their talent, of course. That's very draining. Otherwise, they're pampered. The raeth women run the household, order the meals, play with their babies, visit with each other, oversee the servants. They spend a lot of their day playing with hairstyles and planning what they're going to buy at the next festival."

Sand didn't want to talk about her escapes to the ocean

and the languid afternoons with M'ridan. Jinny would either think she was lying or would believe her and be awed.

Jinny frowned. "We must decide what you're going to do now." She wondered if Sand would ever again have enough empty time to be bored. "I don't think you completely understand your situation." She paused for a long moment, sighing. "I don't know a tactful way to say this. Do you know that those who serve the Mother are hunting you?"

Sand remembered Berran's mysterious words overheard the night before. Her throat tightened. "I guessed."

Jinny kept her eyes on Sand while she imparted the rest of the news. "They say you are a pretender who tried to cheat your fiancé out of a huge bride-price. If they find you, you'll be returned to the Mother for her justice."

Sand's shoulders relaxed slightly. "I'd rather not have to go through with it, but it could be worse."

Jinny quirked an eyebrow at her.

"I really do have the talent, though I denied it at the wedding. I could easily get the providers to bring me back to shore."

"As long as the Mother hasn't taken your talent away."

Sand shrugged once again. "She hasn't yet. Why should she? It was *my* mother who wanted me to marry Tamin, not *the* Mother."

"You'd be an outcast."

Sand snorted. "I have made myself an outcast."

Jinny sat back and stared at Sand. Every time this girl spoke she opened up the hidden world of raeth life to her. Like every Midislander, Jinny was fascinated and repelled by the privileged raeth. And now she held power over this raeth daughter. She didn't intend to exploit it, but it was a heady feeling. "I have to get to the weavers' house now, but we should talk more. Will you stay with me again tonight?"

Sand hesitated. "I would like that very much. But I'm imposing on you . . ."

"Not at all." Jinny grimaced. "Kemahl is very sweet, but a little adult conversation is sweeter still. I wouldn't invite you again unless you were welcome. But"—she shot a sideways glance at Sand—"if you're worried about feeling indebted, you could earn your place here by helping out at the weavers' house."

Sand felt a sudden surge of panic. "I don't know anything about weaving."

Jinny laughed. "Nobody does when they start. You won't be expected to do the weaving. But there are lots of simple chores to help with."

Sand tried to hide her reluctance. "If you think I can be useful, I'll gladly come."

Jinny lent her a tunic to wear. Kemahl ran in front of them clutching a green-striped turtle.

As they walked Sand said slowly, "What I don't understand is why you want to get involved in my story. Why does Berran want me hidden?"

"It's a little complicated. Don't be offended, but it doesn't have much to do with you personally. Protecting you is a way of opposing the priests and the raeth; they're behind this search. Many Midislanders have come to believe that there is no good reason why the raeth should own all the beaches."

"But they're the ones who can use them," Sand protested, surprised.

Jinny snapped at her in response. "We can all use them! Why do the Midisle fishermen rent beaches from the raeth? Because we need them! According to the priests' stories, we are all descendants of Bedjar and Calleby—why are some of us privileged raeth and others lowly Midislanders?"

Sand answered this rhetorical question. "But the raeth women have the talent."

"That's all garbage! Priestly lies! I know of raeth women who have barely a whisper of talent; they can only call one provider three times a year when the sun is in the right place in the sky and their hair is dressed right! Other raeth women can practically speak to the providers the way I'm talking to you. If the priests banish women with no talent from the beach entirely, why don't they make the weak talents live farther inland, or just give them an eighth of a taell of beach for their family? And there's no difference between our men at all! Raeth or Midislander, they're just the same. The only difference is what family they were born into."

Afraid another question would be taken as a challenge and draw Jinny's wrath toward herself, Sand changed the subject carefully. "Do you really think you can keep me hidden? Midisle is a big place, but someone is sure to notice me and mention it."

"I don't think so. Berran doesn't want you turned over to the priests and is spreading that word. No one is going to oppose him. Many Midislanders agree with him that things must change. And those who don't are still dependent on Berran and the boatyard; that is more important to them than currying favor with the priests."

Sand considered all this for several minutes while they walked. But as they neared their destination, she asked wide-eyed, "Aren't you afraid of the Mother? You are opposing her rule."

"Sand, I'm not even sure I believe in the Mother sometimes. But I definitely believe her rules are made and enforced by men."

They approached a building with a porch running all the way around it. Large windows in all the walls showed enticing glimpses of richly colored yarns hanging from the rafters.

Upon entering, Jinny was temporarily deluged with

friendly greetings and teasing. But as the weavers noticed Sand, they fell silent, waiting. Unconsciously she put a hand to her cropped hair.

Jinny laid a territorial, protective hand on Sand's arm. "This is Sand," she announced. "You may have heard, she's staying with me."

The circle of faces relaxed ever so slightly. They waited for more of an explanation. Eventually, however, they realized they weren't going to get anything but that. Piqued, they turned back to their tasks, ignoring both of them now. Gradually the volume of sound in the room returned to what it had been when they entered. Spinning wheels hummed, looms shuffled, people's voices rose and fell.

Jinny squeezed Sand's arm sympathetically, but made no verbal comment. Beckoning, she led her around the room explaining all the equipment: looms for weaving, wheels for spinning, vats for dyeing. The clean scent of the sea swept in through the windows, gently moving the hanging fabric.

"These are the tubs where we soak the bark and roots. Then we dry them over here in the sunlight. These scoundrels tease them into batts of fiber." Three teenage boys looked up from their work and grinned bashfully as Jinny teased them. "This is where we wash and dry the goats' fleece. Here we card and spin the different fibers. Sometimes we add whisprain fluff to the yarn as well, for softness.

"Sometimes we dye it first, and then weave it. Sometimes the cloth is woven first and the dyes are painted on afterward."

Sand looked up to where Jinny pointed. Over her head in the rafters hung hundreds of skeins of yarn in a vast range of hues. She kept her face upturned, soaking in the color.

Jinny led her to an old woman sitting beside a spinning wheel.

"This is Gelya." Raising her voice a little more above the noise of the weavers' house, she spoke, "Gelya, this is Sand. She's staying with me."

The spinner lifted her lined face and greeted Sand quietly. Pale eyes regarded her, the color of mist drifting over the lagoon at dawn.

"Gelya, Sand would like to work here today, but she knows nothing of fabric. Would you mind showing her how to card the fibers and how to power the wheel?"

Sand waited anxiously through a very long pause. Finally the old woman's mouth twisted into a wry smile. "Of course not. I would be happy to teach your guest."

"Thank you." Turning to Sand, Jinny said, "You're honored. Gelya is our most experienced weaver."

"I will listen accordingly," Sand promised.

Jinny left them together. Gelya shook her head, smiling still. "And Jinny is our most experienced diplomat."

Sand seated herself cross-legged on the floor beside the spinning wheel. "Oh?"

"She worded that so that I should spend some of my time teaching you, thus doing you both a very great favor."

Sand flushed. "I will try very hard to help."

Gelya chuckled. "Of course you will. That's the part that Jinny didn't state aloud, so as to save my feelings. She knows that the Lactus Festival is only four weeks away, and I have just five blankets to sell." She held out her hands. They were calloused from a lifetime of weaving, but more than that, the joints were swollen and the fingers curled in toward the palms. "It's very difficult for me to card the fibers these days. And until my carding is done, I can't spin. So I can't weave."

"But won't anyone else help you?"

"Of course they would." The pale eyes glittered at her with a momentary flash of enraged frustration and pride.

84

"But if I take someone else's help, that's taking time they should be spending on their own cloth."

Sand blinked at her vehemence. Finally she replied softly, "You make it difficult to do you any favors."

Gelya paused a heartbeat, then began to chortle. "We'll get along fine, girl. Hand me those carding combs."

She showed Sand how to card, incorporating the silky whisprain fluff into the comb. Then she took the soft mat of fibers Sand produced and showed her how to spin them into yarn. It looked so easy as the fibers slid gently between Gelya's gnarled fingers, twisting in the air and coming out the other end as an even, plump strand.

When she seated Sand at the wheel, however, Sand realized that effortlessness is born only out of long practice. She couldn't remember to keep her other hand spinning the wheel evenly. She couldn't get the knack of letting a consistent chunk of fibers spread out between her fingers. Her yarn had huge lumps in it and then thinned out until it broke.

Sand stood up, shaking her head. "I have the strength for carding. I will stick to the task I'm better fitted for."

Even the carding got tough. After an hour her shoulders and forearms began to ache. She stretched and walked around, then returned to her chore for as long as she could before she had to stretch again. But the intervals between stretching became shorter as the afternoon wore on. When Jinny finally came to take her home, Sand greeted her in relief.

"I hope you can come back," Gelya admitted, when Sand bade her good night. "She's not fast," she told Jinny, "but she's careful. And this is as much as I could card in a week by myself. Thank you both."

"Kemahl! We're going."

Sand was conscious of the gaze of many eyes as they walked through the weavers' house to the doorway, and didn't realize how uncomfortable this made her until she got outside and a huge exhalation exploded from her lungs.

"They don't like me," she stated quietly to Jinny.

Jinny paused. Finally she admitted, "It's not a personal sentiment directed against you. But as I explained, we Midislanders have no reason to love the raeth."

"How do they know I'm raeth? My hair is cut."

Jinny burst out laughing. "Who else could you be? Merkin? You appear in our midst, you have obviously seen sixteen or seventeen summers, but no one has ever seen you."

Sand pondered her way through the implications of this. "You mean every Midislander knows every other Midislander?"

"Well, not really. There are a few thousand of us, after all. But I know most Midislanders by sight and name at least. As well as most of the raeth men who come to the Midisle market. An unfamiliar face is usually raeth."

Sand's mind reeled at the idea of knowing thousands of people. She counted quickly in her mind. She couldn't have met more than a couple of hundred people in her entire sheltered existence in her father's domain. As they reached the main road, Jinny turned in the opposite direction to the one they had come from. "Where are we going?"

"To get some dinner from the market before we go home."

Chapter Eight

Kemahl pattered on ahead of them. This was obviously a well-known route for him.

Jinny asked Sand questions about her experience with Gelya, and smiled at the enthusiasm of her answers. But underneath the easiness of their exchange, Sand felt herself becoming more and more apprehensive as they approached the rows of stalls ahead of them. Not only would she be encountering more Midislanders, but there was a good chance that raeth men would be there who might recognize her. Finally she broke off in mid-sentence and asked, "Jinny, are you sure it's a good idea for me to be going to the market with you? It's so . . . open and unprotected." She glanced quickly over her shoulder.

"I think it will be all right. Those from the temple always buy their dinner during the day, so there shouldn't be any priests here now. And as long as you're with me, no one will challenge you. Everyone knows Berran's sister." She said this matter-of-factly, without a trace of pride or self-consciousness.

"Hey there, Kemahl!" A fisherman stepped out from behind his stall, his white-toothed smile gleaming like a beacon from his tanned face. Sand recognized him as one of the men who'd been on the beach yesterday when she'd been found. She dropped her eyes to the ground.

Daulo picked Kemahl up and tossed the giggling child into the air. "How's my little man?"

"Daulo, I have a turtle!" Kemahl informed him, when he could finally catch his breath.

Daulo set him down gently. "Let's see."

"Not here!" The little boy shook his head at the obtuseness of adults. "He's guarding the weavers' house tonight."

"Good thing you warned me, little pal. I had planned to steal myself a new blanket this very night."

"You'd better not!" Kemahl's eyes gleamed. "Cause he'll do this—" He launched himself at Daulo, his head lowered like a battering ram.

Daulo sidestepped him at the last possible moment, caught him around the waist, and swung him upside down in the air. He trapped his flailing feet, cuffing his ankles together with one big hand.

Kemahl shrieked and wriggled, completely delighted.

"What price can I get for this fine boy?" Daulo sang out.

Around the stalls people looked up from their conversations and smiled. Sand glanced at Jinny and saw that she was smiling, too, though she looked away to hide it.

Daulo dumped Kemahl gently on the ground, and when the child came up fighting, he put one big hand on the top of his head and easily held him at arm's length. "How are you, Jinny?" he asked after a moment's silence.

"Same as always, Daulo."

He flinched at her tone, bright and sharp as a fish knife.

"Have you any scallops?"

"Got some big ones," he said, lifting one tray so she could see underneath.

She picked out fifteen and was about to pay for them when Berran sauntered up. "Hello, Daulo."

Berran was a tall man, but Daulo topped him by four inches and seventy pounds. The fisherman smiled a greeting in return.

Berran hooked a brotherly arm around Jinny's neck and looked down at the package in her hand. "Mmmm, scallops. My favorite."

Jinny chuckled at him. "You're about as subtle as a bael nut on the head, you know that?" She turned back. "Ten more scallops, please." She paid for them and, with the briefest of goodbyes, strode away from the stall toward the edge of the water. Sand, Berran, and Kemahl trailed behind. Looking back, Sand saw Daulo gazing after them.

"Why can't we invite Daulo to dinner, too, Mama? Ow!" Berran had grabbed for Kemahl's chubby arm and half missed, pinching him by accident. He rounded on Berran and struck out at the source of his pain.

"Sorry, sport." Berran avoided the blow and swung Kemahl up into his arms. Sand heard him murmur something to the little boy and Kemahl pouted back over his shoulder. Jinny walked on ahead, calling back, "Come on, Kemahl. Don't you want to visit the shore tonight?"

They didn't stop till they covered the distance to the water's edge. Jinny stood a small distance apart from the others, staring down at her feet, watching the waves roll up to them and back again.

Berran crouched down, sharing Kemahl's discoveries of bright stones and beautiful shells.

Left to her own thoughts, Sand closed her eyes and concentrated. The lowering sun beat warmly against her eyelids, making them glow red in her vision. She slowed her breathing and felt out across the waves. At the edge of the reefs a pod of doraado were playing. They acknowledged her presence, and when she made no effort to compel them, they returned to their game. She tagged along quietly, enjoying the easy slide of their bodies through the water.

They moved closer to shore. When they broke water a short distance away, Jinny grabbed Sand's arm.

"Look!"

"Mmm-hmm."

Jinny stared at her. "Did you bring them here?"

Sand shrugged. "Not really. They sensed me here and came closer. They're very curious animals, you know."

"No, I don't know. I don't know anything about them. I've probably seen the providers up close only two or three times in my entire life."

Jinny had finally managed to startle Sand as much as Sand had been startling her all day. "You can't mean that!"

Jinny shook her head, her eyes fixed on the doraado dancing in the evening sun. "Where would I ever see them? I've worked in the weavers' hut all my adult life." Her tone changed, expressing yearning now in every register. "They are so lovely."

Wordlessly Sand took her hand and tugged her into the shallows. Jinny tried to hitch up her skirt, but as they waded deeper she gave up.

"Are you crazy?" Berran called, pitching his voice to reach them but to go no farther.

"Mama!" Kemahl's voice traveled, shrill with fear at his mother's odd behavior.

Sand closed her ears to all this. She reached out to one of the dolphins.

The doraado was young and friendly and curious. All Sand had to do was suggest she come closer and accompany that suggestion with a sense of welcome. The doraado slipped through the water like a shuttle through a loom. She slid between Sand and Jinny in a surge of water. She swam back slowly and lay rocking on the surface within arm's reach, watching Jinny through her small, wise eyes.

"What should I do?" Jinny whispered.

"Cup her chin in your hand and rub it back and forth. They love that. But be careful with your fingernails. Their hides are easily scratched."

Jinny followed her advice. A moment later the doraado flipped her hand into the air. She clicked several times and slid closer.

"She has an itch on that side," Sand told her. "Just use the palm of your hand and rub hard. Not there; farther back. That's it."

Alight with joy, Jinny whispered, "Her skin is so soft. Like the softest tanned goatskin. Even softer."

Suddenly the dolphin slid her whole length under Jinny's hand and dove. She surfaced a small distance away, and after a series of whistles and clicks and one cough that sent a cloud of vapor into the air, she dove again and disappeared.

"What did she say?"

Sand lifted her hands, palms upward. "I just get impressions. Sensations. I wonder sometimes if that's because they talk so quickly. To them, we talk in slow motion."

Jinny was glowing as they waded back into shore. She picked up Kemahl and hugged him. "Did you see Mama touch the provider?"

"I did," snapped Berran. "And anyone else could have, too." He rounded on Sand, who belatedly looked up the beach to see if anyone had noticed. "What possessed you! Didn't Jinny warn you about the priests?"

She nodded dumbly.

"Are you trying to light a beacon fire signaling 'I'm here'?

91

And if you're bent on your own destruction, must you implicate my sister?"

Sand's eyes filled with tears. "That's why I did it. I wanted to thank her in a special way."

Berran rolled his eyes. "Some thanks! Of all the snail-brained ideas—"

"Berran, that's enough. Everybody's busy in the market, the raeth are mostly gone for the evening. No one is here from the temple." Jinny put a comforting arm around Sand. She was still smiling softly, her mouth holding new secrets in the corners. "I will always remember that. Thank you, Sand."

       ❖   ❖   ❖

As they neared the stalls, Sand surreptitiously glanced around to see if anyone was staring at their group. Only Daulo had his eyes on them.

Kemahl ran ahead calling, "Daulo, did you see my mother touch a—"

Daulo scooped him up, covering his mouth in the process, twirled him upside down, and blew air onto his exposed tummy. Kemahl screamed with laughter, and Berran, beside Sand, sighed with relief.

"Thank you, Daulo," Jinny said in a low voice when she got near enough. Then she added, "I think I'll need more scallops."

"Sure. How many?"

"As many as you can eat for dinner."

His head snapped up. Sand saw such hope flame in his eyes that she turned away, embarrassed for him.

Daulo measured what he saw in Jinny's face and then he picked out the requisite number. "I won't charge you for these," he said, grinning.

Berran lifted Kemahl up and sat him on his shoulders. Crowing delightedly, the child began hammering on his chest with his heels and clenched his fists in Berran's thick, dark hair.

"Come with us," Berran directed Sand. "They can catch up."

As they were leaving the market, Sand saw Coral's husband at another stall. She looked away, feeling ice water sluice through her veins. She tried to console herself by thinking that perhaps he hadn't seen her or recognized her with her short hair and her new clothes. She wondered if she should tell Berran, but he was already so cross with her. If he forced her to leave his sister's house, Sand didn't know where she could go.

As they arrived home, an urgent bleating greeted them from the lactus grove behind the house.

"Come on, minnow." Berran swung Kemahl down from his perch. "You're going to hunt up some bael nuts for me."

"I know where the biggest ones are!"

"That's what I want to hear. I'll milk the goat." Berran called over his shoulder, "You put on some hot water." He looked at Sand's wet, bedraggled tunic and shook his head. "And get some dry clothes on. I swear you *could* be merkin. Every time I see you you're soaking wet." A few moments after his disappearance, the bleating stopped.

When he came back into the house with a bowl of milk in his broad hand, she was sitting before the fire coaxing it into a blaze.

Dusk was gathering like lint in the far corners of the room by the time Jinny and Daulo came in. Even so, Sand could see the high color in Jinny's cheeks. Her step had more sway and rhythm to it.

They found Sand, under Berran's amused tutelage, mixing onions with ground bael nut, herbs, and milk, while Berran poured the first batch she'd made onto a flat skillet.

93

They sat down to dinner a short while later. Jinny had cooked the scallops in a creamy sauce and she spooned this over the spicy pancakes. After the initial noises of appreciation, the conversation died away.

Sand felt uncomfortable in this intimate gathering, so she, too, was silent. Only Kemahl continued to chatter, not caring if the adults responded.

Finally Berran set himself to drawing Daulo and Jinny into conversation. With skillful and patient questions he asked about this season's fishing and preparations in the weavers' house for the Lactus Festival.

Jinny told him how much Sand had helped Gelya. Meeting his eyes, Sand saw his approval. Feeling the ache along her shoulder muscles, she reflected that she had truly earned it.

Sometime during the meal the rain began. The patter of drops on the thatching increased to a roar and fell away to a dripping, then rose to a roar again. Daulo shook his head. "I hope this blows over before morning. Life is terrible for a fisher in the winter."

After they had finished eating, Berran rose and pulled down a jug from a high shelf. Pouring a little brandy into five mugs—even Kemahl got some mixed with his milk—he raised his in a toast. "A proposal," he said. "To old friendships renewed"—Jinny and Daulo looked anywhere but at each other—"and to new friendships begun." He said this last directly to Sand.

They all drank. Over the rim of her mug, Sand regarded Berran. She noticed for the first time how sawdust powdered his eyelashes and streaked his hair. If she was always wet, he was certainly dry.

"Another toast!" cried Jinny. "To my new housemate! That is"—she looked quizzically at Sand—"if you consent?"

Startled by her first words, Berran had stared at Daulo.

Even more startled by the end of her speech, he turned to Sand.

Flustered, Sand blurted out, "I'm honored. But are you—"

"No buts!" Jinny insisted. "To Sand! A long and happy friendship between us."

Daulo looked surprised as well, but after a moment he lifted his glass and drank the toast. Only Berran had a sour note to add. "Being a permanent houseguest is not necessarily the best way to promote a long and happy friendship." Sand noted that he did not drink to the toast at all.

They talked for a little longer. The spoonful of brandy in warm milk had the desired effect on Kemahl—within a few minutes the little boy laid his head on the table. Berran carried him up to bed. When he returned, he didn't sit down again. Picking up Sand's mended brown blanket, he shook it open and held it out to her. "We're going for a walk."

"In the rain?"

"In the rain," he insisted.

Squatting down beside Jinny, Berran took one of her capable weaver's hands between his own. He spoke to her in a low voice. Twice she tried to interrupt him, but he silenced her.

Finally he stood. He bade Daulo good night, and with a hand on Sand's shoulder, he pushed her out the door into the storm.

Chapter Nine

They walked without speaking through the buffeting wind. Sand knew they weren't just going for a walk; Berran had some specific destination in mind. Eventually, they passed between what looked like whale skeletons rising above her head in the darkness. Glimmering faintly in the rain ahead of them was the outline of a large building. Berran opened the door to a small lean-to attached on one side.

Once she was inside and the cold rain no longer stung her skin, other senses began to dominate. The air held the clean scents of wood and glue. Berran kindled the banked fire, picking out scraps of lumber from a barrel and stoking the flames with them. The fire blazed high, shedding both heat and light, illuminating the details of the room. Besides the hearth, the room contained a bed, a chest, a small table, and two chairs.

"Sit down," Berran invited, still playing with the fire.

Her wet blanket began to steam as the air warmed. She

unwound it from her shoulders and he absentmindedly took it and hung it near the blaze to dry.

Pulling a chair closer, she sat and held her hands out before her. Soon her skin felt hot to the touch and the heat crept inward to her bones. In all the time this had taken, Berran still had not spoken about the reason for their being there.

"You have something to say to me, Berran?"

"I? No." He shook his head.

Surprised, she waited, but he added nothing further. She spoke quietly: "You mean you dragged me outside on this awful night and brought me to this little shack for no reason at all?"

"No, of course not." He frowned. "I suppose I have a great deal to say to you, though that wasn't the reason I brought you here."

"Well, what was the reason? And what is this place?"

"This is my house." His voice held neither pride nor apology. "Through there"—he indicated a door behind her—"is the workroom and outside is the boatyard. As for my bringing you here . . ." He paused several heartbeats and seemed to search for the right words. Finally he shrugged. "You are to sleep here tonight."

"Here? Why can't I stay at Jinny's?"

"You can. But not tonight. Though I am against it, I will not prevent you from staying there after this night. I meant to find you shelter there for a night or two, not to burden my sister with a fugitive."

"I'm not staying here."

"Why not?" He allowed a note of amusement to creep into his reasonable tone.

"Because. Because it's not . . . not suitable."

He raised an eyebrow.

She pressed her lips together.

"Sand, there's nowhere else for you to go that would be dry. It's just for one night."

"But why?"

He sat down opposite her in the other chair. "It's not really my story to tell. However, Jinny has asked you to stay and I suppose by guest rights you deserve to know." He sighed deeply.

"Four years ago, Jinny was very much in love with a fisherman called Thrane. He is a giant of a man, fully as tall as Daulo. In fact, he and Daulo often fish together still and are good friends in many things. The Lactus Festival's night of masks arrived. Of course, Jinny was not supposed to know what Thrane would be wearing. But as sometimes happens, he had promised to wear a brown robe she had woven for him and to stand by a certain house and wait for her.

"Jinny got there a few minutes early and found him just arriving. Taking him by the hand, she squeezed it and greeted him.

"He laid a finger across her lips to remind her that that night no words could be spoken.

"They feasted and drank together, and when the dancing began their feet flew. I'm sure that Jinny had decided already that if Thrane wanted her she would go with him." Berran broke off his story at the sight of Sand's face. "What's wrong?"

Sand dropped the hand which had been pressed against her lips. "Weren't you furious with her?"

He frowned. "No. Why would—" His face cleared. "Perhaps you don't realize that a Midisle girl has many freedoms that a raeth woman does not?" She shook her head.

"A woman's family in Midisle has no power over her choice of partners. Of course, they try to raise her lovingly so she can make wise choices."

Sand shook her head as if to clear it. She wondered why

she'd never heard of this before and then realized she had. The way Berran described a woman's choice gave it a noble sound. He had given her a glimpse of unexpected freedom. But her mother referred to these free Midisle women as beasts with no self-control. Sand realized now that their self-determination, in fact their total control over their own destinies, had terrified her mother.

"Raeth women would never be allowed to do that," she whispered.

Berran shook his head. "No, of course not. Their talent is too valuable. People can't help treating it as a commodity: something to be bought and sold."

"I'm sorry," she said finally. "I think I interrupted you. You were saying—"

"By the end of the evening they knew they would spend the night together. But when Jinny awoke the next morning she discovered that she was with Daulo, not Thrane. She was furious, of course, and mortified by her mistake. She discovered also that Thrane was with another woman that night. This might have been dismissed as the same kind of unfortunate mistake that she'd made, except that Thrane's lover was several inches taller than Jinny and built quite differently." Berran's teeth flashed in the firelight. "Furthermore, there was the matter of Thrane's brown robe, which Daulo had been wearing. Daulo adored Jinny, but had never pressed his case because of his friend's interest. Jinny never asked whether Daulo had borrowed the robe from Thrane knowingly or not. Nor did she ask whether his arrival at her meeting place was by accident or design. She was sure, however, that he knew from her greeting who his partner was.

"The whole mess might have blown over, except that Thrane married his new love at the summer festival, and that Jinny bore a child: Kemahl. She feels she's been cheated on every side and has ignored Daulo since that night. Until now."

The fire was burning low and Berran peered through the growing shadows at Sand. "Do you understand now?" he pleaded with her. "They've had four years of misery and tonight they have a chance to talk over what went wrong and to sort things out. It's the sheerest irony that Jinny suddenly has a houseguest, making privacy more difficult. And you are partly responsible for their new openness toward each other. If it hadn't been for that stupid stunt you pulled on the Midisle beach this evening, Jinny wouldn't have been so receptive to Daulo. Now you must give them tonight alone."

She nodded slowly, musing, "It's odd. There are so many loveless marriages among the raeth. You'd think there must be a better way. But it doesn't sound like the Midisle way is any more successful."

Berran shrugged. "I don't know."

"How did Jinny get pregnant?"

Berran grinned. "The usual way."

Sand blushed. "You know what I mean!"

"Jinny cannot eat the sentranthus weed, and so had no protection. One mouthful and her throat closes up; she can't breathe."

"Poor Jinny! That's awful!"

They sat in the dark without speaking after that, the silence broken only by the soft crackling of the embers and the uneven tattoo of the rain.

Berran stood finally and banked the fire. "I'm going to bed," he told her.

"Where shall I sleep?" she asked.

"With me."

She gasped. "I can't."

He snorted. She glared into the belly of the fire while the slither and rustle in the dark behind her told her he was undressing. She heard another more weighty whoosh from the blankets and a breeze of displaced air ruffled her now-dry hair and fanned the embers to flame for a moment.

Berran's breathing soon settled to a deep, regular rhythm. Sand sat in the chair for a long time. Outside, the rain had faded away, to be replaced by a biting wind. The room grew steadily colder. Once she tried to build up the fire with the bits of lumber from the barrel, but the wind caught the smoke in the chimney and forced it back down the flue in a choking cloud.

She stared through the dark toward the bed, wondering if he'd waken if she just crawled in under the edge of the covers.

"Raeth daughter, are you going to sit up all night?"

"I . . . um . . ."

She could hear his smile as he said, "Get into bed. I don't bite."

She stumbled through the darkened room and lay down on the far edge of the bed. He reached out an arm and pulled her under the blankets. For a moment she resisted, and then she relaxed as she began to warm up. He smelled of woodsmoke and lumber.

"Better?" His deep murmur tickled her ear and reverberated in his chest against her back.

"Mmm-hmm," she agreed, already drifting off to sleep.

◦   ◦   ◦

When she woke, Berran was brewing a pot of khar. "Good morning. Khar?"

"Yes, please."

He poured two mugs. "I'll get some milk."

The moment he left the room she slipped out from under the blankets. She tried to smooth the wrinkles from

101

her shift, but to no effect. As she moved her arms, the stiffness in her shoulders made her wince. She stood close to
the fire and reveled in the heat on her skin.

"How do you feel?" he asked, returning.

"Stiff." She rotated her head on her shoulders, exploring
the aches. "Carding is much harder work than it looks."

"I'm sure you made it worse by letting your muscles
stiffen in the chill last night."

She flushed. "Berran, I want to say thank you. I'm afraid
I'm prudish. Raeth daughters are very sheltered. When you
offered to let me share your bed, I was afraid you meant . . ."
Her apology ground to an awkward halt.

He waved it away, saying simply, "I know. Come; I'll
show you the boatyard before work begins."

She sipped at her khar as they wandered the yard,
inspecting the boat frames.

"Do you know your way to the weavers' house?"

"I think so."

"Then I'll probably see you tonight. Thank you again for
giving Jinny this chance, Sand."

As she left the boatyard she felt exposed. She realized
this was the first time she'd walked through Midisle un-
accompanied. She turned her face resolutely toward the
weavers' house and checked her urge to look behind her
every few seconds.

As she walked, she compared Berran to Tamin. Remembering the light of conquest in Tamin's eyes, she reflected
that he could never have spent such an innocent night with
her.

With the force of a blow the realization struck her that
men were very different from one another. Ever since she'd
been small, her mother had stressed the idea that men—
especially Midisle men—wanted only one thing from a
woman. She had been so wary of them collectively that she'd

102

never considered them as individuals before: some shy, some brash; some trustworthy, some wicked. Just like women.

Jinny met her at the door to the weavers' house. The color bloomed in her cheeks and her blue eyes sparkled.

"Are you all right, Sand? I'm sorry about last night—"

"I hope you're not sorry! Did things . . . ?"

Jinny nodded.

"I'm glad you'll finally be happy."

Jinny laughed. "I don't think it's that simple. I'm not the easiest person in the world to live with. Neither is Daulo. But now we have a chance, at least. Kemahl needs his father. He's getting to an age where he must learn how men behave."

They sat on the porch of the weavers' house and talked till the sun climbed high. Finally Jinny stood. "Come. Gelya was asking for you."

Sand winced. "I don't know how useful I'll be today. My muscles are so sore."

But once her muscles had been exercised awhile, the stiffness left them. She began to work faster. Gelya kept a thoughtful eye on her and made a point of not spinning too quickly, so that Sand could keep her supplied with carded fibers.

Later in the afternoon, Gelya told Sand to practice spinning again while she took up two knitting needles. She worked at fantastic speed. Sand spun the same clumpy yarn as before. She finally put her chin in her hand and threw a tuft of unspun fluff in the air, watching it float back down to the basket.

"What's wrong, child?" Gelya's blue eyes rested on Sand as her knitting needles moved.

Sand shrugged. "Why don't you let me do something useful instead of wasting my time and your yarn with this mess." She pulled a sample of her spinning off the bobbin to show its shapeless, uneven line.

Gelya shook her head and glanced down at her stitches. "Child, no practice is ever wasted. You'll never get better without it. And while that yarn is not great for weaving, it's wonderful for knitting."

To illustrate, she picked out two thick needles and a strand of the lumpy yarn and began casting on stitches. Before Sand's fascinated gaze, she knit a small length and held it out for inspection. The uneven texture of the wool made a thick, springy fabric. Sand looked up, astonished. "It's lovely."

Gelya chuckled.

"Could you show me how to do that?"

"By the Sea Mother's green hair! Don't you know how to knit?"

Sand shook her head. "Our servants used to knit, but I never learned how. Now it's appropriate for me to learn how. And I really want to."

Gelya gave her a cool look and Sand realized that this was the first time she'd admitted, in so many words, that she was raeth. But Gelya didn't comment on her ancestry. She merely said, "Everyone should be able to knit for themselves. Here, I'll show you." She gave Sand two needles and a length of wool. She patiently demonstrated the stitches over and over. Sand tried to imitate every movement of Gelya's gnarled hands, but she got dizzy watching their speed and precision. Then she'd get tangled.

"Child, child!" Gelya remonstrated when Sand complained. "Don't concentrate on my speed. I've been knitting for a hundred seasons; you've been knitting for half an hour! Find your own speed. Look at the way the stitches lock together, each one joined to those around it. Learn to recognize the different stitches in the cloth, once they're off the needle. You've got to understand the way they fit together or you'll get nowhere."

Under Gelya's patient tutelage Sand learned how to knit

and how to set up a loom. The two of them spent three more days carding and spinning, and then Gelya began to weave her blankets. Sand continued to card and spin. Gradually she learned to make her strands of yarn even. It was a proud day for her when Gelya began to add Sand's work to her loom. Gelya made her a gift of all her early, lumpy yarn and two knitting needles.

During this time Sand fell into the habit of getting up very early each morning. She would make her way down to the Midisle beach by half-light, the morning mist stirred into swirling patterns by her passing. She climbed out to the end of the rocky arm which encircled the cove of the Midisle beach. From this vantage point she could see the massive coral temple, but could not be seen by the Mother's servants. Creeping down to the water's edge on the seaward side, she submerged her feet in the cold seawater while calling to M'ridan.

The winter was progressing and her feet were often numb by the time M'ridan joined her. Sometimes she would slip into the water beside him and go for a short swim.

M'ridan found the psychic shock he received as she entered the water very funny. "It's like the punchline to a joke," he explained. "It's a surprise, even though it's expected."

She relished the way her skin tingled afterward. She felt awake and alive in every nerve and pore of her body.

M'ridan was fascinated by her new life. She gave him mental pictures of the weavers' house and of the boatyard. She also showed him her new friends. Once she brought her knitting and showed it to him. He touched it with his tongue and pronounced it very odd. He said it reminded him of nets, and she caught a quick glimpse of members of his pod tangled in mesh prisons. Sometimes she just lay on her belly on the rock, reaching out as far as she could to rub M'ridan's skin.

When they parted, she would return through Midisle in the slanted rays of early morning. Jinny looked askance at her wet hair, but she never asked any questions.

Though Sand sensed that this phase in her life was as transitory as her life in Monarri's cove had been, she enjoyed it thoroughly. Her work in the weavers' house gave her tremendous pride and satisfaction. The weavers now welcomed her as gladly as they welcomed Jinny each day.

In Sand's whole new way of life, she found Berran the only unsettling note. He often dropped in at Jinny's home in the evening to chat and share a mug of khar. He was genuinely delighted by Daulo's moving into Jinny's home and didn't refrain from showing it.

But with Sand he seemed distant and harsh. While out getting some lactus fruit one evening, she overheard him talking to Jinny.

"Jinny, I'm worried that Sand's presence here is a burden on you."

Sand ground her teeth. Just when she was beginning to feel she was useful, there was that word again.

"Of course not! Don't be silly, Berran. She's hardly ever here except for meals and to sleep."

"But surely you and Daulo would rather be alone . . ."

"Daulo adores her. So does Kemahl. And so do I. If anything, she's more of a help than an imposition. She's made herself invaluable to old Gelya. What's gotten into you?"

"I just feel responsible. After all, if it hadn't been for me she wouldn't be here. And with you and Daulo . . ."

"We have plenty of privacy. The girl gets up so early every day that she's exhausted by suppertime and goes to bed as soon as the dinner dishes are washed. Daulo and I have all evening alone together. Every night. Except when you drop by." She punched his shoulder playfully.

Sand entered the room and handed the lactus fruit to

Jinny. "If you don't mind," she said, "I think I'll go to bed now. I'm not hungry and I'm very tired."

"Of course, Sand. Are you feeling unwell?" Jinny searched the girl's face.

"I'm fine. Just tired. Good night, everyone."

Sand tossed long into that night. Jinny's praise of her was a healing balm, but each time she recalled Berran's words they scraped her raw again.

After that night she made doubly sure that she gave Jinny and Daulo a lot of time to themselves. Her feelings toward Berran underwent a subtle change. She found herself listening in the evenings for his step in the doorway. Yet when he did appear, she would excuse herself and go to bed. She wanted to prove that he hadn't made a mistake in bringing her to Jinny's. She just didn't know how.

One morning, five days before the festival, Jinny spoke to her as they did the washing together.

"Has Berran done something to make you dislike him so much?" she asked. She kept her eyes on the grass stains she was trying to scrub from Kemahl's tunic.

Sand stayed silent a moment, trying to frame her answer.

Interpreting her silence as reluctance, Jinny added quickly, "I don't mean to pry. If I am, please forgive me. It's just that I have been where you are now and I wasted four years of my life afterward being bitter about it. If I could be so bold as to offer advice to you raeth—"

Sand made an involuntary warding-off gesture at the name "raeth" and Jinny abruptly broke off her speech.

Sand felt mortified at Jinny's misconception of the night Berran had spent with her. "Berran's done *nothing*," Sand answered, trying to imbue the last word with all the shades of meaning that she could. "It's not that I dislike him, Jinny. I . . . I don't know what to think of him. I know that he dislikes me. I'm wary of fostering that."

Jinny dropped Kemahl's tunic and turned, open-mouthed, to Sand. "That's not true! He doesn't dislike you! He—"

"All right, then, the word 'dislike' is too strong. But he doesn't trust me and he regrets that he brought me here. Nobody in Midisle truly likes or trusts me, and . . . and . . . oh, Jinny . . ." Sand's eyes were full of bright tears. "Jinny, I'm so happy here. You're so good to me and I feel as if I'm truly a help to Gelya. I don't want to leave here."

Jinny pulled Sand to her and held her with wet, soapy arms.

"You heard what Berran said to me that night." It was a statement and Sand nodded in confirmation.

"No one wants you to leave here, Sand. Berran is over-protective of me. But even if he was completely set against you, this is my house and your presence here is a treasure and a solace to me. I want you to stay forever."

"I want that, too." Sand clung to her, letting go much of the sadness she'd been holding in her heart since her mother had betrayed her. The two women rocked back and forth together.

Chapter Ten

"I wish I could stay here to help you, Jinny." Sand slung another blanket over the ropes stretched to display the weavers' wares. The early sunlight saturated the dyed hues until the blankets throbbed with color.

"Don't worry, Sand. Everyone in the weavers' house will take a turn with the goods. None of us will be overworked."

Wistfully Sand slid her palm over one of Gelya's blankets. "It would be fun to know who buys the things I've worked on." She looked over at Jinny. "You've put so much into all of these. Don't you want to know who's going to buy them?"

Jinny laughed. "It's interesting, I guess. But they are only my work, Sand, not my children. It doesn't really matter who buys them."

Sand imagined Tamin or her mother buying one of Gelya's blankets, and she clenched her fists. "It matters."

"I wish you could be here today as much as you do, Sand. But surely you can see it's best if you stay away. This clearing will be full of priests and raeth in an hour or so. After all, your banishment won't be for long. Once the masking starts, you can move about as freely as any of us."

"I know." Sand sighed. She stepped back from the rows of blankets and examined them. "There. That's the last one. Don't they look lovely all together, Jinny?"

Daulo's voice interrupted their admiration. "Excuse me, pretty woman. Are you for sale?" They turned to find Berran and Daulo behind them. Daulo was jingling the coins at his belt. Jinny smiled at the young giant with her heart in her eyes. "Sorry, sir. I'm taken already, and completely happy about it."

Berran laid a hand on Sand's shoulder. "I have come to escort you home. It's time."

"All right. Jinny, good luck. I hope every one of your blankets earns you a hundred flecks."

Jinny laughed. "I hope so, too, but since I'm only asking thirty flecks apiece, I think it's unlikely. We'll see you at dinner."

Berran guided Sand quickly through the gathering people. "You'll be all right alone today?"

"Of course!" She frowned up at him through the hair falling over her forehead. "I spend a lot of time alone. Why worry about me today?"

"Whoa! I didn't mean to offend you, raeth lady."

"Don't call me that!"

His blue eyes sparkled with the fun of teasing her. "It seems so unjust that you can't enjoy the fair when you've worked so hard to get ready for it."

"I'll be fine. I'm going to Monarri's to gift her for the festival tonight. She'll probably be here at the fair, but I can leave it at her house."

They were now pushing outward through the crowd. Here and there Sand saw the long hair that marked a raeth woman. She kept her eyes nervously on the faces coming toward her.

They walked in silence until Berran cleared his throat uncomfortably. "I have something to ask you, Sand."

"What is it?"

"What will you be wearing at the festival tonight, and where will you meet me?"

Sand stopped in her tracks and looked at him, speechless.

"Well?"

"I think I know what your questions mean, but I don't want to presume. And I don't want to answer until I'm sure of what you're asking."

Berran flushed, and looked away uncertainly for a moment. "I'm asking you . . ." and he bent forward and found her mouth with his own. Sand stayed perfectly still at first, but then his unexpected ardor sent the blood surging through her veins. As he felt her respond he wrapped his arms around her and gathered her to him.

Her ears started to roar, as they did when M'ridan took her too deep for too long.

She squirmed out of his arms. If she stayed there another moment she'd surely drown. She turned away so as not to have to meet his eyes.

And she saw Tamin. Separated from her by the flood of festivalgoers, he stood poised like a gull hanging over a fish. Many people passing on their way to the fair had glanced with tolerant amusement at the young lovers embracing. But Tamin's face held nothing but hatred and vengeance. For a moment they both stood frozen with people swirling around them. Then Sand placed one hand on Berran's forearm and tugged at him urgently.

"Can we get away from here? Tamin is behind me."

With an arm on one shoulder, he guided her away. She didn't dare turn around, but the urge to do so was so strong she had to lock her neck muscles in place, staring straight in front of her.

"Do you think I dare go back to Jinny's place?"

"Where else would you go?"

"But what if he brings the priests there?"

"I thought you said you weren't going to stay there today, anyway? Aren't you going to the raeth child's cove?"

"Yes, but not for the whole day."

"Why don't you look and see if he's following?"

Sand searched the people thronging the roadway, but she couldn't see Tamin anymore. Still, she felt a prickle, like a spider skittering across her shoulders.

She shrugged. "Maybe I'm just imagining things. I don't see him, but I feel he's there."

She was afraid that Berran would scoff, but all he said was, "I'll take you to Jinny's to pick up your gift and then I'll make sure you're safely out of Midisle before I go back to the fair. How's that?"

Sand took his hand in her own and squeezed it. "Thanks, Berran."

A moment later he continued. "I don't want to push, but you haven't answered my question yet."

Sand looked squarely into his eyes. "Berran, to be honest with you, I don't know. It's a new idea. Will you be at Jinny's for dinner tonight, before the masking?"

He nodded stiffly.

"Can I give you my answer then?"

He jerked his head once more. They continued on in an uncomfortable silence. When they arrived at the house, she ran upstairs and tucked Monarri's gift into the pocket of her tunic.

They walked past the empty houses of Midisle, past the storyteller's fire circle. Sand stole a sideways glance at Berran, wondering if he was remembering the first night he'd brought her here. But his face could have been one of the pieces of wood he worked with, for all the emotion it expressed. When they reached the final clearing, he indicated the track wandering through the trees. "This will take you to the beach. I'll see you tonight."

He turned and strode away.

She turned away herself and ambled along the path, lost in contemplating his behavior. The path narrowed and widened again. The heavy, sweet smell of jinnange blossom hung everywhere, brought out by the warmth of the winter sunshine. Gradually the fragrance was punctuated by breezes carrying the clean salt tang of the ocean. Eventually she reached the edge of Monarri's cove. Life had been so simple here. Now it seemed so complex.

Suddenly she felt sure that someone was watching her. She shaded her eyes with one hand and gazed nonchalantly over the sea to her left. Slowly she swung her shoulders and looked over the sea to her right. Finally she turned a little more toward land and scanned the beach and the edgewood behind her. She saw nothing. A moment later, a chill breeze danced past her and ruffled all the leaves. It was impossible to tell whether anything moved. A cloud crossed the sun, and the day took on a leaden cast. Sand shivered.

She jumped down onto Monarri's beach and quickly hid herself among the trees. She looked behind her. The beach was empty and silent except for the waves and the wind spinning the grains of sand in tiny circles.

She turned her back to the shore and followed the path to the house Monarri shared with her grandfather. It squatted, lost, in the overgrown lactus house grove. Under the eaves, the porch was gray and gloomy.

"Hello," Sand called uncertainly. "Hello! Monarri?" She waited, but no answer came.

She stepped up onto the porch, intending to leave her

gift inside the door, when the old man appeared in the doorway.

Sand squealed in alarm. She pressed her fingers against her lips.

"I'm sorry," she choked out. "You startled me."

Monarri's grandfather made no reply. His eyes looked toward her, but she sensed he wasn't seeing her. Struggling to fill the silence, Sand held up a small knitted bag.

"I just came by to gift Monarri for the Lactus Festival."

Still the old man said nothing.

"I guess she's in Midisle today at the fair? Well, I'll just leave this here for her. Will you please make sure she gets it?"

Sand was beginning to wonder whether he was walking in his sleep, when he finally spoke.

"You return to the Mother, mer-daughter."

"Pardon?"

"Back to the Mother. Soon. Her mark is upon you."

Sand shuddered. Returning to the Mother was a euphemism for dying.

"Yes, well . . . thanks. Please make sure Monarri gets this." Sand dropped the small bag on the porch.

The old man didn't respond.

Trembling, Sand strode from the hut. Somewhere on the path between the house and the beach, the sun cast off its cloudy cloak. Immediately Sand's spirits lifted a little. She began to feel ashamed of the fear she'd shown. After all, he was just an old, old man who probably didn't entirely know what he was saying.

She climbed the rocks out to the end of the point. Her niche was dry this morning and washed completely clean. The only thing that marked her previous habitation here was the black circle where her fire had burned every night.

She settled her back against the sun-warmed rock and

glanced up at the sun in the sky. Almost noon; lots of time before she had to be back for dinner. Berran would expect her answer in a few hours. Her heart fluttered.

For the first time, she confronted what agreeing to meet Berran would mean. Unbidden, a physical memory returned to haunt her: the feel of Berran's skin against hers as they slept.

A spray of water drenched her in a shocking cascade. M'ridan surfaced and grinned at her.

"Happy to see me, little mudball?"

"M'ridan! I'm always glad to see you. Though I wish you had a less spectacular way of announcing yourself."

"Why are you here?"

"I had a gift to bring to my friend Monarri. And then I wanted to do some thinking, so I climbed out here. It's usually so quiet." She splashed him with her foot, laughing.

"You were thinking about mating," M'ridan commented.

Sand blushed deeply. M'ridan caught some of the rush of embarrassment. "Why are you upset? It's time you found a mate. We talked about that during the warm season." Then, without giving her specific images or using laborious mindspeech, he gave her some of his memories of the mates he had shared with. She was caught up in the tender memory of a sensation of gliding gently through the water, embraced and embracing. Sand felt an echo of that warmth she'd felt a moment before. Their minds joined, they began an upward spiral, circling like two doraado swimming together.

And then Sand began to resist the new intimacy that M'ridan was opening to her. She felt she was in danger of losing her edges, the boundaries that defined her as separate from the rest of the world.

Sand clenched her hands. "M'ridan, I'm afraid."

"Silly mudball." Now, interspersed with the memory of his loves were memories of leaping and sunshine and the

115

fierce joy of flying through the ocean. The self-annihilation she sensed was now shot through with freedom. She stopped resisting him and suddenly felt deeply connected not only to him but to the whole world. She felt for a moment she could never be lonely again.

Sand slowly opened her eyes. M'ridan was watching her. Though his face wore its characteristic smile, for once he seemed to have no joke at the ready.

"That is mating," he stated simply. "Come swim with me, mudball."

She stripped off her tunic and slid into the sea in one fluid motion. She barely noticed how cold the water was, and she swam lazily over to M'ridan and slid her arms around him. Laying her cheek against his velvety skin, she hugged him.

They hung on the surface for uncounted time, buoyed up by occasional unconscious flicks of M'ridan's tail. Finally he nudged her in mindspeech. "Tell me about your mate."

"He's not my mate! At least, not yet."

"Tell me about him, anyway." He pushed her with his blunt snout.

So Sand gave him images of Berran. Standing tall before her in his carpenter's apron, his blue eyes intense as the summer sky. Berran sitting before Jinny's hearth fire with a cup of khar balanced on his knee, laughing at Kemahl. Watching her with his non-committal, weighing expression that unsettled her so badly. After a moment's hesitation, she gave him the sensation of Berran's warmth against her that night in his home.

"You are already mates."

"No, no! We only slept beside each other."

He splashed her impatiently. "Being mates has nothing to do with the physical. It is the caring for each other that makes it true."

116

"Not in my world, M'ridan. On the island, mates are defined by the physical—who you share your body with; who you share your home with."

He ejected mist through his blowhole by way of comment. "Do you want this man that way?"

"I don't know. That's what I was thinking of when you joined me. I don't know if I should."

"Why not?"

"Because the physical is not enough."

"You have shown me that you feel more for him. Think again."

Sand pondered carefully. She remembered Berran's story of Jinny and Daulo the night of the Lactus Festival. She remembered her own wedding. She remembered all the plans for it and the preparation and the scheming that her mother had done.

"Because . . ." she began, stammering a little. "Because I am a raeth daughter and we do not give ourselves casually."

M'ridan snorted.

Sand hugged him tighter as her doubts became clearer to her. "And we give ourselves to our wedded husbands only in a marriage bed. And our husbands are always raeth, not men of Midisle. But I am not raeth anymore!" she continued excitedly. "I am an apprentice in the weavers' house. I am a woman of Midisle, and I may agree to meet any man I choose at the festival tonight. And I choose to meet Berran!"

M'ridan slipped out of her arms unexpectedly, submerging her. Sand came up gasping with laughter.

"When a doraado has seen five summers pass, he is expected to find his own place in the sea, and not always stay with the pod. I think you have reached your five summers, Sand."

He boosted her onto the rocks to get her tunic and rose

on his tail in farewell. "May you find love and happiness." His images had a ritualistic tinge to them, as though they were part of a doraado blessing.

"Thank you," she answered solemnly.

His sleekness disappeared below the surface. "Goodbye, mudball."

Chapter Eleven

Sand strolled slowly back to Jinny's house. She paused in the doorway to watch for any loitering figures, but this end of Midisle, so far from the square, seemed deserted.

By the bars of sunlight on the floor, she judged the time to be mid-afternoon. The day had turned out unusually warm for winter. As she climbed the ladder, she felt the air growing stuffier, rung by rung.

She uncovered the two small windows at either end of the loft and then leaned her elbows on the sill of one and gazed out.

Turning her head, she caught a movement out of the corner of her eye. Something had just disappeared around the corner of one of the neighboring houses. She waited for whatever it was to reappear, but nothing moved. She stepped back into the room, out of sight, and sat down on her pallet. It was probably just a goat, she told herself, but for the first time in several hours, she remembered Tamin.

After a moment's hesitation, Sand went over to the hole in the floor and pulled up the ladder. Feeling more secure, she lay down again and dozed.

She tossed in her sleep, her dreams full of threat and ominous presence. Finally she awoke from one final nightmare of Tamin holding her head beneath the water while she choked and drowned. Sitting up with a start, she shivered in the heat of the loft. A breeze blew in through the open window and she greedily drank in the verdant smell.

She heard footsteps enter the house below and she froze.

"Sand?"

"Jinny!"

She lowered the ladder and climbed down quickly. Jinny looked at her in puzzlement. "Is anything wrong?"

Sand flushed. "This is going to sound foolish, but I didn't feel safe until I'd pulled up the ladder. I saw Tamin this morning and it upset me, I guess."

"Poor Sand! And you spent the day all alone worrying about it!"

"It wasn't that bad."

Daulo, Kemahl, and Berran came in at that moment. She tried to catch Berran's eye, but he wouldn't look at her. In a moment the house was bustling as they joined in preparing the dinner. Tonight excitement made their eyes sparkle and easy laughter burst out at the smallest jokes.

They raced to eat and clean up. Then, as they sat around drinking their khar, Sand excused herself. In the loft she donned the short blue robe that Jinny had lent her for the evening. She pulled a plain fabric mask over her eyes, obscuring her face from forehead to cheekbones. On top of that she added a headband with two spiral shells sewn like horns over her forehead and long strands of blue wool falling like hair over her shoulders.

She knelt and uncovered the gifts she had made for her

friends. She had worked diligently on them and her heart pounded now in anticipation of their reactions. She bundled them in a blanket and carried the package down from the loft. Kemahl was the first to catch sight of her. "Sand?" he asked uncertainly. The others turned to look. She set down the bundle, grabbed him, and swung him up into her arms.

"Of course, silly goat! Who else?" She twirled round and round, making them both dizzy. He shrieked and wriggled in her arms.

She turned to where the others sat. Setting Kemahl on his feet, she twirled once again with her hands in the air. "Well?" she asked. "What do you think of my costume, Berran? Will it do?"

He looked up at her question and met her eyes for the first time that evening. She smiled at him and his apparent doubt began to evaporate.

She pulled her mask and headdress off temporarily, and unwrapped her treasures. With M'ridan's help she had found a large chambered nautilus shell, and with Berran's help she had cut it in two to make a jewelry tray for Jinny. M'ridan had also searched the sea for another bottle fish and found one—a small one. Now she placed the tray in Jinny's hands. In it was a comb she had made, decorated with the iridescent scales.

Jinny was speechless at first, but finally found her voice. "Sand! This is beautiful! The tray is wonderful. But the comb—I can't take that. It's much too valuable."

Sand took the comb out of the tray and fastened it in Jinny's hair, where it glittered and shimmered, enhancing the blue of Jinny's eyes.

"The home you've given me here is also without price," Sand said in a voice pitched to reach Jinny's ears alone. "Shall I refuse it for that reason?"

Sand turned to Kemahl. For him she had whittled a

121

small flute out of a lactus reed—the kind her father used to make for her. She hung it on a braided cord about his neck and he immediately picked it up and blew such a piercing note that the adults clapped their hands over their ears.

"Couldn't you have made him a flute out of wool?"

Sand looked at Berran quizzically. "I don't see how that could work."

"That's the idea."

Jinny chuckled, and Kemahl, duly chastened, began exploring his new toy with reduced energy.

Sand gave Daulo and Berran each a thick, springy vest she had knit from her lumpy yarn.

One after another they brought out the gifts they had made or found or bought for each other.

Jinny gave Sand a green tunic she'd woven for her and Daulo gave her a bracelet of meril stones. Worn smooth by the ceaseless fingering of the Mother, they were scratched and dull when dry. But when they were wet, they gleamed with colored luster. "For the only mer-daughter I know," he said shyly. Sand hugged him and kissed his cheek.

Berran stood behind Sand and put something around her neck. When she looked down she found a small doraado hanging against her breastbone on a leather thong. It was carved from aged gray wood and polished till it looked just wet from the waves.

"Berran!" she whispered, exploring it with her fingertips. "Thank you. Oh, thank you!"

He seemed satisfied by what he read in her eyes.

Finally Jinny and Daulo rose. "Excuse us," Jinny said. "We should go and mask as well." When her face was turned from Berran, she threw Sand a gay smile.

They were alone now but for Kemahl. Berran stood. "I must go home to dress as well."

Smiling at him she asked, "Where shall I meet you?"

He crossed to her and took her face in his hands, tipping it back to kiss her.

"Oh, Sand, I'm so glad. I spent all day thinking about this morning, thinking I'd been too blunt, or should have asked you sooner to give you more time, or shouldn't have asked you at all but taken the luck the gods sent me. I'm so glad," he repeated.

"Where will I meet you?" she asked again.

"In front of the market stall where Daulo sells his fish," he instructed. Bestowing a last kiss on her forehead, he released her. "Don't be late."

Time seemed suspended while she waited for Jinny and Daulo. Kemahl was put to bed, and Gelya, who was staying with him tonight, had to be welcomed and settled in.

Finally the three of them stepped into the clear, star-sparked evening. When they reached the clearing, Jinny squeezed her hand and whispered, "Good night."

Then Sand was alone, wading through the crowd. She barely noticed the people she passed; they were merely landscape, obstacles in her path. Her mind was already across the square in front of Daulo's stall.

Behind her three figures followed, drawing ever nearer. The crowd parted uneasily to let them through.

❈   ❈   ❈

Berran stood motionless before Daulo's stall. The more his mind fidgeted, the tighter he reined his limbs. Only his eyes darted restlessly among the crowd closest to him. At the sight of every tall, slim girl who drew near, he tensed. Then, as he realized his mistake, his breathing would steady, but his eyes returned to their restless search.

Off to his right in the crowd there was some kind of commotion, but he ignored it. Tonight he had eyes and ears and thoughts only for the raeth daughter.

He waited. And waited. The priests mounted the dais in the center of the square and blessed them all. Then the drums started and the dancing began. Still Berran waited. Finally he realized she wasn't coming. His heart started to pain him and his mind began to coat it with alternate layers of rage and excuse, as an oyster coats a grain of sand. One moment he thought, She never meant to meet me. The next minute he wondered, Maybe she misheard me. Maybe she thought I said to meet somewhere else. The vacillation became torment, until finally he began to move among the crowd, searching for her. Berran was masked in white tonight. If Kryphon took on human form to watch the festival, surely he could be no more beautiful than this. Many girls smiled their invitations to him as he passed. Their smiles faded wistfully as he ignored them.

He crisscrossed the square four times looking for her. He passed Jinny and Daulo twice. He paused, on the verge of asking if they knew what had happened to Sand, and then strode away angrily. He felt sure she was deliberately making a fool of him. He would only be a bigger fool to advertise that fact.

Finally he became convinced that she was nowhere to be found. But perhaps she had fallen ill and was still back at Jinny's house? "Fool. Perentha fool!" he cursed himself.

He left the festival. His legs ate up the distance between the square and Jinny's house in long, furious strides. He slowed only as he passed the threshold.

"Sand?" he croaked out.

Gelya looked up, startled, from where she'd been drowsing by the fire.

"Is Sand here?" he asked, wishing immediately that he hadn't. She shook her head wordlessly. He wheeled and left.

As he walked home in the darkness, he remembered Tamin and the priest hunt. But he thrust this uneasiness down again. He was sure her masking would protect her from recognition.

He entered his own dark hut and threw himself on the bed. He lay there rigid, willing sleep to comfort him. But sleep didn't visit him that night. The darkness was full of visions of Sand: Sand standing in her shift the first night in Jinny's home; Sand tonight in her robe smiling at him with that shy glance.

"And what did you expect, perentha? Midisle men do not court the raeth daughters, remember? You deserve what you got. You're lucky the humiliation wasn't more public. Resign yourself. She's not for you."

Berran lay staring into the darkness until it grayed to a cloudy day. The wind had risen during the night and whistled in the chimney of his fireplace. He got up and made a mug of khar, which he did not drink.

The other boatbuilders began to arrive in boisterous humor. Good-natured taunts flew around the yard. Berran ground his teeth and shut his ears as best he could.

But at last someone accosted him. "And where were you, Berran? You must have chosen with all speed and left, for I danced till the end and never saw you once. Had a little tryst already set up?"

"Close your foolish mouth, Felthame, before I nail it shut," Berran snarled.

The raucous banter stopped immediately. The yard froze, all heads turned toward Berran.

Felthame's face whitened. His hands clenched. For a moment he stood perfectly still. Then he shrugged. "My pardon for prying too closely, yardmaster. I meant no offense."

Sensing that it might be wise to distract Berran, Vene began in a conversational tone, "What did you think of the other news from last night?"

Berran began measuring a plank for the deck of a boat. "What news is that?"

"That the priests finally caught the raeth girl who's been living with your sister."

"What!" Berran's howl caught Vene unaware. He was staring at him like an eldrin.

Vene stammered. "You didn't know?"

"Fool!" Berran left the boatyard at a run. The others were left wondering who the yardmaster was referring to.

Berran tore through the village, his feet pounding so hard that his head began to ache. He raced along the path through the jungle till he reached the beach where Daulo and several other fishers sat in a circle on the sand mending a net spread out between them.

"Daulo!" Berran cried out at the sight of him. Berran's face was patchy from the heat of running.

"Berran! What's wrong?" Leaping to his feet, Daulo choked out, "Is it Jinny?"

"No. It's Sand!"

Daulo frowned in puzzlement.

Berran elaborated. "Where is she?"

The lines in Daulo's forehead deepened. "What do you mean? We haven't seen her since she met you last night."

Berran charged up to Daulo's boat, which lay overturned on the beach. The men around the net gasped as he single-handedly turned it right side up and started dragging it toward the water.

"What are you doing?" Daulo cried out. He took the other side. "Let me help you at least. What are you doing?" he repeated, puffing as he heaved at the boat.

"Sand—didn't—meet—with—me," Berran told him between tugs on the boat.

"Where is she, then?" Daulo asked in astonishment.

The boat's stern rested at the water's edge. As Berran turned and looked out toward the charcoal horizon, a big wave slapped the flat end of the boat and sprayed him.

"The priests found her last night, Daulo. By now she'll have been sent to the Mother for judgment." Berran began pulling the boat farther into the water.

Daulo held on to one side, trying to stop him. "What are you doing? You can't interfere with the Mother's judgment."

"The Mother may never get a chance to judge her. Look at that sky." The very air around them seemed to be charged with a green light. "She'll be swamped and drowned before she can get the providers to bring her home."

"The Mother controls the storms, too," Daulo pointed out. "It's all part of her judgment."

Berran's voice thinned to a thread of sound, tight enough to garrote the big man. "This is Sand we're talking about. And you know better than to spout that drivel to me. We're talking about human vengeance, not the Mother's justice. Now let go of this boat, or I swear I'll kill you."

Daulo let go and looked at Berran with mournful eyes.

Berran heaved himself out of the water into the boat.

"Wait a minute." Daulo hauled himself over the gunwales, too, nearly capsizing the boat with his bulk. "You'll probably need help. This is dirty weather." The fisherman was already fitting the oars into the oarlocks. "I don't want to lose both my boat and the man who can build me another one at the same time." He glanced at Berran. "Let's go."

They rowed furiously around the island.

Moment by moment the day grew uglier. Purple clouds massed underneath black ones, and the electric-green quality of the air strengthened. At first the wind blew from the shore, speeding them on their way. But after a while it died, except for occasional hot cat's-paws of wind scurrying toward them from random directions. Once they had rounded the northern tip of Strandia, they rowed along the shore toward the temple. The priests would have taken her in a line directly out to sea from there. If she was still to be found, it would be in that direction.

Berran kept standing up on his seat and shading his eyes to look around, until Daulo pointed out to him that they'd be of no use to Sand if they drowned.

As the massive structure came into view, the wind died altogether. Once they reached a point directly in front of the temple, Berran looked out to sea, to his right and to his left, but nowhere could he see any sign of a lone boat. He wondered if there was any chance she hadn't been set adrift yet and turned toward land.

His scalp prickled. Where they lay in the water not a breath of wind stirred the surface. But on land, the leaves of the lactus trees were saluting with their pale undersides in a line which moved toward them across the island like the silvery blade of a drawknife. And behind that line came a rainstorm so dense it obscured everything beneath it.

Berran sat down abruptly, trying to seem indifferent, but Daulo had already seen it. Daulo pulled on his right oar till they turned toward land and then began pulling for all he was worth.

"What are you doing?" Berran cried out.

"Saving our lives" came the terse reply.

"But what about Sand?"

Daulo kept up his frantic stroking while he turned his head to glare at Berran. "Sand is in the hands of the Mother, as are we. She will be judged for her actions. We are about to be judged for our presumption. If you don't want your body to feed the fish this morning, Berran, you had better start using those oars." He turned back to his work, pulling with even more vigor.

Berran hesitated a moment longer, looking out to sea, and then he reluctantly grasped the two oar handles. Under their combined force the boat shot toward land, into the teeth of the storm.

Chapter Twelve

Sand was sure she'd never been more frightened and miserable. She was cold and wet and her wrists were chafed raw from the rough rope. The little boat she lay in already had two inches of water in the bottom. She couldn't see over the gunwales and she was so bruised from her earlier attempts she didn't have the heart to try again. Occasionally, however, a big wave would roll the boat and she could see all too clearly what lay beyond. Terrified, she'd wait for it to send her to the bottom of the sea. But her craft bobbed along on top of the waves through the driving rain like a cork.

She had no idea which way the storm was blowing her, nor how far she'd already traveled. She knew she must be long out of sight of Strandia by now. The idea terrified her.

Twice she had tried to reach out to the providers, but to no avail; her concentration wobbled violently. Storms had never before kept her from making her catch, but then she'd always been standing safely on shore.

For the first time in her life she felt the vengeful gaze of the Mother directed on her. Though she was not guilty of the crime she'd been accused of, perhaps the Mother was punishing her for all the rules she *had* broken.

The priests had certainly looked implacable in the dim light of dawn. Two novices walked her from her cell through the temple courtyard to the seashore. The small group assembled there had turned to face her, but after one quick glance around the group she fixed her eyes across the choppy surface of the water on the horizon, lest they see her tears of fright and humiliation.

She recognized most of them. The priest and priestess who had tried to marry her. The two priests who had captured her last night—one older than the other. Tamin, of course, who was the only person not looking at her—for fear of meeting her eyes. Then there were the boy and girl who had brought her from her cell. Finally there were two older novices standing beside the two boats at the water's edge. The young woman's face was set in harsh, determined lines and she stared defiantly at Sand.

The older priest, named Alesk, turned to the marriage officials. "Is this the girl?"

"Yes," they chorused.

He turned back to Sand, and she met and held his eyes.

"Sand-bel-Anemone, you are charged with the crime of pretense. You accepted the bride gift of Tamin-bar-Iola, under betrothal to him and without revealing that you had no talent—"

"That's a lie!" Sand cried out.

Alesk raised one thick white eyebrow and transfixed her with his gaze. "You did tell him?"

"No, no—you misunderstand—"

He raised his hand. "I'm sorry. I should not have allowed you to speak. This is not a trial, Sand. You have convicted

130

yourself by your actions. Your trial will be conducted by the Mother alone.

"Sand-bel-Anemone, you are sentenced to be cast adrift in a tanth. If you return to us, your name will be cleared of all stigma." He did not talk about the possibility that she would not return.

"Here is lactus fruit to eat, to sustain you. You will have a few minutes before your hands are bound."

Sand turned her face from the fruit, thinking she would surely be ill if she so much as smelled it.

Alesk drew close to her and whispered, "Build up your strength, daughter. Have hope. The Mother can be merciful."

While Sand doubted the Mother's mercy, she knew that she would need all her strength. She couldn't afford to have no reserves when it came time to compel the providers.

She accepted a slice of lactus fruit from the girl novice and took a bite. Her stomach churned like the sea before her and then settled. She swallowed and took another bite.

While she ate, the old priest spoke to the two acolytes beside the boat. He had a hand on each of their shoulders and they looked at him with reverent seriousness.

When Alesk turned back to her, the piece in her mouth wasn't chewed enough to swallow, but she was suddenly frozen.

The young priest, Rainis, came toward her and lifted the headband from her head. She started. She had forgotten she was still wearing that silly piece of frivolity with its horns and the blue wool.

"Lift your arms," he instructed her.

She did as she was told, uncomprehending, until with a quick movement he pulled her festival robe and undershift over her head.

Sand choked out an indistinguishable word. She made a movement to cover herself and then slowly dropped her arms and drew herself up straight.

No one was looking at her except the woman novice by the boat and Tamin. The young woman just looked stern, but Tamin couldn't seem to take his eyes from her revealed body.

The expression on his face revolted Sand. Moving her tongue around the half-chewed piece of fruit still in her mouth, she spat it at him. The pulp hit his leg and oozed onto the ground.

"That's almost as disgusting as you are," she hissed, her voice full of venom.

The older priest intoned, "Naked the Mother gave you to us, and naked you shall return to her sight." His hand reached toward her chest and she flinched. "Steady," he whispered. Lifting the carved doraado Berran had made for her, he tried to pull it over her head.

"No!" she cried out, catching his hand. "It's mine!"

He pried her fingers free. "Nothing is yours unless you return." In a very low voice he added, "I'll keep it safe for you until then."

They bound her wrists behind her, so that she could not just swim ashore. Alesk guided her, stumbling, to the side of the little tanth. Pausing, he said, "These two acolytes are finishing their training with the execution of your sentence. They bear you no ill will, nor can they save you. This is their trial as much as your own; the Mother's will is not always easy to serve or to endure. Now into the boat." He gave her a steadying hand. "And may you return to us cleansed and redeemed."

Rainis looked up sharply and Tamin glared at Alesk. Sand guessed that this last was not part of the ceremony, but his own personal benediction. She gave him as sturdy a smile as she could muster and said, "I will." She sat down in the bottom of the tanth.

As Alesk looked at the proud set of her head, he felt his heart might break. The two novices climbed into the larger rowboat and pushed off. The boy looked sick.

As a mark of respect, those left on shore waited till the two boats were a small speck on the surface of the choppy sea. Alesk turned away first, casting a worried look at the sky. "Raza and the Mother have obviously not reconciled their differences yet. Would that the girl had been found another night and sent out on a brighter, clearer morning."

"It's all part of her pattern," Rainis assured him.

Alesk glared at him wearily. "You are little more than a novice yourself. Learn to answer me with your own original thoughts instead of priestly catch phrases and you will have shown at least some semblance of growth." He limped back toward the temple.

Rainis stared after him, enraged. "Old fool," he swore, turning back and searching the surface of the sea. "It *is* all part of her pattern."

The motion of the tanth being pulled behind the rowboat was abominable. In painful syncopation, first the rope between the boats would yank her forward, then the waves they battled would seesaw the boat up and smash it down. Sand struggled to a sitting position twice, but both times she was knocked down again. Resigned, she lay there rolling painfully back and forth. Seeing nothing but the dangerous sky above her and the heaving sides of the boat, she soon felt queasy. Trying to ignore it, she turned her thoughts to Berran, as she had done so many times through the long night in her tiny cell in the temple. She wondered if he had heard what had happened to her or if he thought she had just run away from another wedding.

An especially big wave smashed the boat. Her ribs and the ribs of her tiny craft made painful contact.

The sound of the novices' oars changed rhythm for a few strokes and then stopped altogether. She struggled to sit up once more, gritting her teeth.

The young man looked green now, and she wondered if it was the choppy sea or the gravity of his task that made him so sick. He concentrated on untying the line of the tanth from the stern of the rowboat.

Before casting her adrift, they introduced themselves. "I am Cowrie," the girl told her.

The young man mumbled something and Sand spoke over the rising wind: "I'm sorry; I couldn't hear you."

"My name is Morven." He stared at the line in his hands.

The girl nudged him.

"We give you our names freely so that you know we bear you no malice. We do only the will of the Mother." He stammered out the last sentence, white around his lips.

Sand might have felt sorry for him if she hadn't already been feeling so sorry for herself. She looked away.

"Good luck, raeth," said the girl. She elbowed the boy, and when he didn't respond, she tugged the line from his hands and threw it overboard.

"May the Mother deal mercifully with you," Sand heard the boy call out as they drew away.

She watched them until another huge comber knocked her down.

She lay there staring at the strange clouds.

That was when she'd made her first attempt to contact the providers. Closing her eyes, she began to breathe more deeply, trying to achieve the state of mind where she could lay her consciousness over the water, feeling the life beneath her.

But the boat tossed and pitched. She couldn't make her breathing deep and even, because each time she tried, it was beaten from beneath her ribs.

Suddenly she was truly terrified. Until that moment she had been humiliated and unhappy, but she'd never doubted her ability to get back to shore. The new fright pushed her queasiness to a deeper disturbance, and despite the pain, she flung herself to a sitting position and just managed to lean her head over the side in time.

"I knew I shouldn't have eaten the lactus fruit." The next big wave knocked her down again. Then the rain began. For the first few minutes, Sand lay with her face turned skyward and her mouth open, trying to wash away the bile. The cool droplets refreshed her flushed face. But in a very short time, she began to shiver and to weep.

The rain increased and the wind picked up speed until it howled around her. Lightning flickered high in the clouds. She contemplated the very real possibility of being struck.

Finally there came a break in the storm. The wind died a little and the rain slackened.

Mustering herself, she tried again to reach for the providers, but she had lost the inner calm that a raeth woman draws upon. She couldn't even begin to reach out of herself; to be so still in her mind that she could sense the life around her.

Sand had no idea how long she'd been in the tanth. It could have been half an hour or half a day. She was still shivering. If she hadn't been so frightened, she would be ravenous by now. She tried to relax, to still her body, but the shivering continued spasmodically whenever her concentration waned.

Sand realized that every movement now was a thief of her limited resources. With no food, no sleep last night, and the cold now stealing the heat from her, she wouldn't have attempted a catch, much less saving her life by holding a pod long enough to drag her back to shore. Wherever shore was.

Sand grew furious. This new heat licked along her bones, driving the paralysis of fear from her body. Damn the Mother! This wasn't fair. How could she be expected to save herself under these conditions? Other islanders—truly guilty ones—were abandoned on sunny days with an onshore breeze to blow them back in to land, suitably chastened. Sand wasn't even guilty of her crime and she'd been put to sea during one of the worst storms she'd ever seen. What kind of just trial was this?

She squeezed her eyes shut, afraid she would go mad from the tension between her immobile body and her furiously spinning mind. She desperately needed to *do* something. And then Sand remembered a dangerous game she had tried only twice before, as a very young talent; something that her tutor, Teacki, had warned her sternly against. She visualized her anger as a sea hawk and then attached her consciousness to its legs like a leash. While in this state of frozen control she stilled her body's shaking, saving even that tiny amount of dispelled energy for a later time. "Now fly!" and she flung the hawk into space.

This was a journey to a hot, black dimension. Unlike her sensing, this state of mind took no notice of her physical surroundings. In fact, as long as she could hold this image, her physical body was a mere container whose comfort or pain did not affect *her* in the slightest. Her anger flew, fueled by her consciousness. Every time she felt its wings falter, she fed it a piece of her rage. She fed it on the injustice of her trial, the sight of Tamin greedily watching her, her mother's heedlessness in the face of her protests against marriage. One by one she pried memories of wrongs done to her from her mind like snails from a rock and fed them to the angry bird.

Finally she had nothing to feed him. She felt empty and sluggish. There was no more passion in her, no more will. And she realized why Teacki had not wanted her to pursue this path; it burned up more than it gave back. She was devouring herself and could not replace the fuel she burned.

Slowly the hawk wheeled lower and lower. Sand began to wonder, in a kind of stupor, what was going to happen next. She grew frightened at the thought of what lay below her in the blackness. The sea hawk weakened. Its great wings faltered. She clung to the bird's legs. Its outspread wings caught the air and slowed them, but without her anger to fuel it, its bones melted beneath her fingers. She looked up at the gray-brown underfeathers of its wings. Before her consternated gaze its form grew blurry, then transparent, and then simply disappeared.

Sand's consciousness plummeted through the inkiness, dropping like a clam from a gull's beak into—

Into her body. She opened her eyes with a jerk of her head that rocked the boat. The blackness was only slightly less intense with her eyes open, but she knew all too well that she had regained consciousness. Her bones ached, her skin hurt in a thousand places, and the sea raged around her boat. Night had fallen.

Sand started to shiver again. Though the rain had stopped, the wind had not. It howled around her, spinning the little boat on top of the waves. She lay there half submerged in water—there must have been at least five inches in the bottom of the boat. She shuddered. If the boat had foundered while she flew, there would have been no body to fall into when she returned. She wondered briefly where her consciousness would have landed, and then shut the thought out of her mind.

A new fear possessed her. What if the tanth had a small leak and she was slowly sinking? After a moment's panic, she turned her head sideways and took a small sip. Rainwater, with only the faintest hint of salt. Her heart returned to a more normal rate of speed.

To give herself something else to concentrate on for a time, Sand worked on curling up tight and wiggling her tied wrists under her feet until finally her hands were in front of her.

Sand pulled herself up to a sitting position and looked out across the water. She squeezed her eyes shut and then opened them to make sure they *were* open. Vertigo gripped her. She saw nothing. With a new prickle of fear, she wondered if she'd gone blind.

Eventually, however, a set of clouds swarmed across the sky above her, and she could see the flashes of lightning they tossed back and forth. Reassured, she tried to marshal her concentration and reach out again.

She'd never tried to call the providers at night before. She knew from M'ridan that doraado never really slept for long periods of time because they needed to breathe the air every few minutes. But they drowsed during this time, dreaming. She wondered if they could hear her at night or whether they would weave her calling into their dreams.

She drew her concentration tight and realized, to her horror, that she didn't have the resources to manage a thorough search. And if she couldn't search, she certainly couldn't compel.

In despair she lay down, letting the waves rock her back and forth. Her hair moved like seaweed in the bilge. Finally she remembered what M'ridan had once told her: that he always knew where she was—when he bothered to think about her.

Honing her thoughts to a piercing arrow, rather than a broad net, she cried out "M'ridan!" in mindspeech. No reply.

She was far too miserable to sleep, so she lay under the dry, lightning-charged clouds and every so often sent out her call.

She had no idea at what distance M'ridan could no longer feel her speaking to him, but she was soon convinced that she was out of his range. She kept calling anyway. Now

138

and then she turned her head and took a sip of the water she lay in. "Sand soup," she said out loud, a little hysterically. The sound of her croaking startled her. She cried out again in mindspeech—not because she believed he would hear her, but as an effort in concentration.

Dawn crept into the sky by painstaking degrees. The clouds were a less menacing color, but the wind still drove them across the sky.

Sand gave up calling sometime around mid-morning. Each time she called now, she felt her limbs grow heavier. She even stopped shivering—she had no energy left for it. Her arms and legs and back grew numb where they lay in the cold water, and the parts of her that were exposed stung as the wind chafed them. She tried tensing and relaxing her muscles, but she was so tired and so stiff. Gradually she sank into a stupor. She lay unblinking, examining her memories one by one. She supposed that this was her life passing before her eyes, as she'd heard sometimes happened to people before death.

"Mudball?"

She thought about M'ridan. She remembered the last time she'd seen him—was it only two days ago?

"Mudball?"

She blinked and her eyes stung.

"Mudball? Little Sand?"

"M'ridan!"

She sent out a call and felt a little more strength leave her.

"Hush." His mindspeech had a soothing, whispery feel to it. "Don't yell—I can hear you. You are far from your shore, little one."

"Are you here?"

"No, but I'm coming. Now whisper to me."

Sand struggled to gather her straying thoughts. Keep it

to a minimum, she told herself. "I'm in a tiny boat. I have no oars and no food. I don't know where I am. M'ridan, I'm very weak. I can't talk to you much longer."

"Don't talk, then. Just wait for me."

Sand turned her head and sucked in a sip of water. She had held back from drinking too much, but her bladder was already starting to register the pressure of what she *had* drunk. She didn't want to foul her only source of nourishment until she had to.

Time was suspended for her again. She should have asked M'ridan how long it would take him to get here. But that would have been another unnecessary question. She simply waited.

She drifted before the wind. The rocking sensation of the boat no longer left an impression on her; it had become natural, like her pulse or her breathing.

Finally she felt a thump on the boat and a new rhythm to its movement. It stopped weaving from side to side as the waves moved it. Waggling its stern a little, it settled into a straight course, moving directly under the clouds.

"M'ridan?"

"Right here, little mudball." The sound of his mind voice was as comforting as the touch of her mother's hand had been after a nightmare when she was young.

The tanth stayed on its new course for some time. She hung between consciousness and coma.

Eventually she felt the boat return to its previous duck-like waggle. "Sand." His probe was gentle. "Sand, this isn't fast enough. It will take us forever to get you to land at this rate. Sand, you have to do what I tell you. You must trust me."

"Why are you talking to me as if I was a baby?" she asked him crossly.

"Good girl! I didn't know you had so much fire left in you. Now, drink as much of your water as you possibly can."

At the very thought, her abdomen threatened to burst. "I might as well," she decided drowsily.

She turned her head and drank long, full gulps, pausing now and then for air. "That's all," she told M'ridan finally.

"Wait a few minutes," he told her. She did. "Now drink some more. As much as you can."

She drank again, but less this time.

"Can't drink any more," she mumbled to him.

"Now you've got to sit up," he commanded.

"Can't."

His inner voice took on a strident urgency. "You *must*. Do it, Sand. Don't say you can't. If you want to live you must do as I say. Now sit *up*!"

She struggled up with infinite slowness and excruciating pain. Finally she was sitting, hunched over.

"Lean to one side of the boat," he ordered.

Sand slowly shifted her weight to her right. The gunwale on that side dipped alarmingly near the water. Before she had time to think or question, the bottom of the boat received a huge blow. It overturned, catapulting her into the sea.

She panicked. Below the surface, she kicked her legs frantically, unable to use her hands. Her head broke the surface and her legs churned to keep her there.

"M'ridan!" she cried out. "I can't swim! My hands are tied!"

The next moment, a slick gray form flowed beneath her and bore her up. She jerked forward. Her wrists, rubbed raw under the rope, stung in the salt water.

Sitting astride this sleek shadow, she looked around her. Behind her the tanth floated upside down, looking like a giant sea turtle, half submerged. In the ocean around her, slim dark-finned ovals kept breaking the surface, followed in a moment by their tail flukes.

"M'ridan, you're not alone!"

"I couldn't do this alone, little mudball. There are six of us. All young males from my pod in the glory of our strength. I regret you couldn't stay in the boat, Sand. But even with all of us pulling, we couldn't get you to land fast enough. We must swim."

She thought of protesting, pointing out how weak she felt, how cold the water was, but then she gave up. What choice did she have?

She laid herself along the body beneath her, clinging with her hands to the fin and with her knees to the flanks. Down and up again, they stayed close to the surface, their backs rising and falling like the chest of a sleeping child. Soon Sand's breathing tied itself to their rhythm.

But Sand weakened quickly. She began to slip off. "I'm so tired," she moaned to M'ridan. "I can't hold on." Her legs and hands were numb from the cold. The slick back beneath her shook her off, but only for a second.

"Hold your arms out" came the authoritative voice in her mind. "Make a loop with them."

She did as she was told, and M'ridan inserted his head through the ring. His flippers stopped her sliding any farther along his back and he began to swim again, a little lopsidedly, with her hanging to the right of his dorsal fin.

The long nightmare continued. Her wrists hurt cruelly where the rope bound them, but that was the only thing enabling her to hang on. She concentrated only on breathing in when her head broke the surface, and out when they dove again.

Night fell once more, and they swam on and on. The clouds began to break up a little, showing her the stars swimming in the sea above.

At unknown intervals they would pause and a new doraado would shoulder the burden. Then they'd be off again.

The sky began to turn gray. It can't be morning already, Sand thought groggily. But it was. The sun came up slowly in the clearing sky, making the doraado backs black silhouettes on the silvery surface of the sea.

They paused again to switch bearers. But when the new doraado head plugged the space between her arms, she felt the rope slip over her hands. The fibers had absorbed so much water that they had stretched enough to free her.

She floated on her back, moving her arms and legs only enough to keep her from sinking. If I live through this, she promised herself dully, I will never again complain about being tired.

One of the doraado lifted her out of the water on his back, but they didn't begin swimming again. She looked down at her hands resting on her thighs. Her wrists were a sickening sight. As she watched, blood welled out of the raw flesh and trickled down across her hands and legs, mixing with the water droplets on her skin, starting out as a red trickle and ending as a pink zigzag stream. She was desperately thirsty again.

"M'ridan?"

"Hush, little mudball, little podling. We're deciding what to do with you."

The discussion went on for some time. Sand began to wonder if the other five were sorry they had come. She knew the idea that they might abandon her now should frighten her, but somehow she couldn't muster enough energy to care whether or not she died out here. At least she'd be free of this agonized body. She imagined her consciousness flitting through the universe as easily as a doraado through water, and found the image enticing.

M'ridan sensed her slipping away from him. "Sand. You will hang on. My pod has done this for me and for you and it has been a hard task. You will not give up now."

143

"No," she whispered back to him. She had so little left of what it takes for mindspeech that even this one tiny word drained her.

The doraado beneath her submerged gently, leaving her on the surface. "Float like this." M'ridan sent her a picture of her on her back with her arms held away from her torso. She did as she was told.

She felt herself lifted partway out of the water. She turned her head to left and right. On either side of her swam a provider. She lay supported on their side flippers.

"When one of our brothers is wounded or sick, this is how we bear him so he can breathe the air," M'ridan told her. "When our babies are born, this is how we lift them to the surface, to breathe their first breath. You are now comrade and podling. We bear you in honor and love."

Sand wanted to thank him, but she had nothing left. She sank back into unconsciousness, her body limp, her mind unreachable. As they headed toward land, those behind tasted her blood in the water as distinctive and carrying as woodsmoke in the air on a clear day. They kept watch for torsios. The doraado would protect her as long as she breathed, but they knew it was too late. They could not bring her to the nearest land before she bled to death in the water.

Part Two

The Continent

Chapter Thirteen

The woman lying on the bed looked about forty years old, though Renellus knew she had barely seen twenty-five summers. Her hair was matted against her sweat-slicked forehead. But her fever had broken and her eyes were clear and followed him around the room.

"Now you listen to me, young woman," he scolded her kindly. "It was all very well to spoil those children of yours when your husband was around to spoil you. But now that he's gone and you have the new baby, you've got to let them help you. They want to, you know. They're just not sure how. They need some instruction. They're bright, able children and you've frightened them dreadfully by getting so sick. Make sure you don't do it again."

He tucked her in gently and returned to the main room of the house, where the two young girls were attending to their baby brother as he had just shown them.

The room darkened briefly as the older son stumbled through the door. "I've brought the fish," he announced.

His ribs heaved several times while he fought for breath.

The doctor smiled and took them from him. "Thank you. That was quickly done. You must have run both—"

Finding his wind, the boy interrupted: "Doctor, they need you at the boat—the *Sea Swallow!*"

"What's wrong?"

"Someone almost drowned." His thin legs folded and he leaned against the wall. "You've got to go right away!"

"All right, lad, I'll be gone in a moment."

The doctor became a whirlwind that rushed around the house. In twenty minutes he had the fish cleaned and cooking in the bubbling pot.

He left the children contentedly blowing on the soup in their spoons, each one now in charge of a set of chores. The oldest girl grabbed his hand before he left and would have kissed it, except he scooped her up and hugged her first. "You've got a level head, little one," he whispered into her hair. "I won't worry about the others with you in charge."

His long-legged stride devoured the road to the wharves. The boy had said *almost* drowned. Surely there wouldn't be this rushed request for the doctor if someone was already dead. He wondered which of the fishermen it could be.

Once he reached the wharf, he easily picked out the *Sea Swallow* by the crowd around it. The anxious lines in the captain's weathered brow relaxed as he saw Renellus striding along the dock. "Out of the way!" Nevius ordered.

The captain gave him a hand aboard. The doctor glanced anxiously at the fishers to see who was missing. Puzzled, he did another quick head count. With an inner shrug, he followed Nevius down the ladder into the cabin. He'd know soon enough.

But the thin white face with the blue lips told him nothing about this girl under the blankets. He'd never seen her before.

148

As he checked her temperature, he asked, "Where did you find her?"

Nevius opened his mouth and then hesitated. "It's a strange tale," he said with a frown. "Best heard with a drink inside you."

The doctor lifted the edge of the blankets and reached for her wrist to check her heartbeat. He looked at Nevius with a broad question in his eyes. The captain shrugged.

The girl's wrists were tightly bandaged with strips of what had been someone's shirt. Watery, rust-colored blotches stained the cloth.

Renellus felt an artery in her throat instead. "Has she said anything?"

The fisherman held out his hands, palms up. "She's been like this ever since we found her. Except we added the bandages."

"She's freezing, and her heartbeat's almost nonexistent. Do you think there are any broken bones?"

"Oh, I don't think so. I'm not sure she has any bones, she was so limp when we found her."

"She's got bones," the doctor assured him.

The fishermen made a stretcher from two spars and a sail. Gently they lifted her blanket-wrapped body and carried her to the doctor's house. But when Nevius saw the rest of the crew trying to crowd into the cottage behind them, he let out a bellow. "Back! Out! There's no room in here for all of you!" He squared his shoulders. "I can tell the doctor what he needs to know."

With a backward glance at their fey charge, they all shuffled out again. Renellus put a big kettle full of water on the fire. He satisfied himself that she was wrapped up as warmly as could be for the moment. Pouring two glasses of whiskey, he handed one to Nevius and settled himself with a sigh. "Tell me the story."

Nevius took a big gulp first. His nostrils flared. His eyes watered. Thus primed, he began. "The sky was clear last night and the waves were finally settling. We left before dawn, wanting to get the good fishing after the storm. We had a breeze from the mainland and got a good start."

The doctor gave him a thin smile. "You're not filling out a log book, Captain. Get to the girl."

The fisherman's teeth flashed in his tanned face. "Well, we were pulling in the nets for the third time when we saw some doraan swimming toward us. The boat was almost full already. We were finishing up. We had had a very good morning. That's why I sent so much back to you with that little lad who came to the docks this morning. Wasn't that Andrius's son? Growing up, isn't he? Poor tyke, with no father." He stopped and drank again.

Renellus growled, "Nevius, the *girl*."

"Right." The captain held out his empty glass.

Biting back an annoyed exclamation, the doctor poured him another. "This stuff will kill you eventually, you know."

"I'll take my chances. Where was I?"

"The doraan."

"Oh. Yes. The doraan swam up to the side of the boat. When they got close, we could see that two of them were swimming very strangely. They were carrying something. Her." He waved his glass in the direction of the body in the bed, the whiskey sloshing dangerously.

"Nevius, if you don't hurry up and finish this story, that'll be the last drop of my whiskey you'll ever taste."

"That's basically all. The story's finished. I don't know who she is or where she came from. I'm not a particularly superstitious man, but I tell you, she gave me the shivers. I half expected her to disappear. When we made no move to take her, the doraan let her float in the water and swam a small distance away. But then they stopped to see what

150

we'd do. One of them was snapping his mouth—you know how they do that when they're annoyed? Varellus and Croius wanted to leave her there, but I've always liked the doraan. They may be fish, but they're very smart. So I finally told the men to haul her up. Her arms were all cut. Kaellus tore up the shirt he was wearing to bandage them. We'll have to take up a collection to get him a new one." He tossed the last of his drink to the back of his throat and waved the cup suggestively in the air.

The doctor rose and pointedly put the whiskey away. Still on his feet, he said, "Thank you, Nevius. Check in and see how she's doing whenever you like."

Reluctantly the fisherman parted with his glass. Just before leaving he paused, his bulk blocking the sunshine in the doorway. "I've seen how you care for your patients. Don't get too involved with this one, Doc. She belongs to the doraan and the sea. She'll have to return to them eventually."

Renellus chuckled and shooed him out. "I thought you just said that you're not a superstitious man!" he scoffed. "I'll see you later."

The doctor lifted the cauldron of steaming water from the fire. Ladling some into two small bowls, he took these over to the counter. The shelves behind his desktop were filled with small crockery jars, all marked with his hiero-glyphic handwriting. He lifted down the ones marked comfrey root, self-heal, woodsage, and borage. Taking the first two, he spooned generous amounts into a bowl and added just enough water to make a paste. The woodsage he steeped in water, making a pale tea.

He also put several spoonfuls of borage in a teapot and poured water over that.

Leaving them all to brew their various magics, he returned to the girl. He began unwinding her bandages, but had to stop when the dried blood made them stick to her

151

wounds. He soaked her wrists in a bowl of tepid water until he was able to peel away all the cloth. The blood began to ooze. Examining the wounds, he noted with relief that they seemed clean. Working quickly, he bathed them in the anti-septic woodsage tea.

Applying the thick paste of self-heal and comfrey to strips of clean cloth, he bound up her wrists again. Finally, laying a towel under her head, he gave her the borage tea, using a straw to siphon it into her mouth. Much of it drib-bled out over her cheeks and soaked into the towel, but he saw her swallow some.

Finally he began filling leather flasks with the hot water and corking them shut. He laid a single sheet over her body and then placed these warm bags all over and around her.

Renellus added two more logs to the fire and put another big pot of water on to heat. From time to time he tried to make her swallow more tea. Then he'd replace the luke-warm bags with new, hot ones.

In between, he settled down to reply to some letters from men he'd studied medicine with at the university in the city.

As the sunlight slanted through the window over his desk, he heard her stir under the blankets. She moaned softly. In a moment he had his arm supporting her in a half-sitting position. "Drink this," he commanded, holding a cup of lukewarm tea to her lips.

She wasn't truly awake, and most of it trickled down her neck and over her breasts, but she swallowed several gulps.

He went back to his letters, aglow with the belief that she would recover. He labored on through the night, warming her and forcing her to drink.

The rising sun saw her eyelids flicker open. She looked around and then closed her eyes without showing the faintest surprise or interest in her surroundings.

An hour later she awoke again, and this time she looked

at him in puzzlement. Appearing uncomfortable, she said something in a low voice.

The doctor asked her to repeat herself. She looked at him strangely and said her sentence again. With consternation they realized that they couldn't understand each other. Looking more embarrassed than ever, she indicated with gestures that she needed to relieve herself.

Gently he lifted her and carried her to the privy outside. As her body emerged from under the blankets, she saw her wrists for the first time and stared at them. She asked something, which he couldn't understand.

When he tucked her into bed, she tried a third time. He smiled at her kindly and shook his head. Resting his hand on her hair, he said, "Sleep now."

She gave him a worried look, but her eyes closed almost at once.

Renellus sat down close to the fire. He felt as though his inner eyelids were coated with grit. He was so tired he couldn't think clearly. Was it possible that her mind had been damaged by her experience and, while she believed she was speaking real words, in fact she was speaking gibberish? There were many dialects across the continent, but they all spoke the same tongue. If she was speaking a real language, she came from a place he'd never heard of.

He rubbed his eyes with the palms of his hands and banked the fire. Praying there wouldn't be any medical emergencies today, he rolled himself in a blanket and lay down on the pallet near the fire, where the girl could see him if she awoke.

❂   ❂   ❂

Sand spent several days adrift in a lethargic current. She quickly learned to trust the man with the kind face and the springy pepper-and-salt hair, but she had no idea who he was or why he was caring for her. She couldn't understand a word he spoke to her, but she had no energy to wonder why.

For almost a week, she felt completely separate from her body and her identity. Her wrists stung, but somehow they didn't hurt her. She couldn't think of who she was or where she belonged, besides here, but that didn't worry her.

Then one night she dreamed of a devouring black monster that tossed her endlessly, while sucking the marrow from her bones. She cried out for help, and finally awakened to find a dark shadow standing by her bed. She felt the bed roll her toward him as he sat down. He held her against his chest. The regular rise and fall of his breastbone and the slow, steady beat of his heart calmed her. It was so different from the wild tossing and spinning of her dream.

When he felt her finally relax, Renellus tucked the blankets around her again. "M'ridan?" he asked, repeating the sound she had shattered the quiet night with.

Sand felt the universe implode as a thousand memories broke through the shut doors in her mind. She squeezed her eyes and bit the inside of her cheek till it bled. But the tears crept out between her tight lids anyway, and her body rocked with silent sobs.

Renellus saw the tears trickling down her cheeks, catching the light from the embers of the fire. He waited a moment, wondering whether to try to comfort her again, and then wisely decided to let her remember her sorrow on her own.

Since her rescue, Sand had done little but sleep. But for the remainder of this night, her eyes closed only to unsuccessfully try to hold back her tears.

Chapter Fourteen

The doctor woke to the crackling of the fire and turned his head. Bundled in a blanket, the girl sat with her back to him. Occasionally she would lean forward and poke the fire weakly, sending up a halfhearted flurry of sparks.

Renellus rolled out of bed and padded over to the hearth. She looked up at him.

Her eyes were red and puffy. For a moment he regretted his decision to leave her alone last night with her refound grief. He smiled gently. "I'm delighted that you feel well enough to get up this morning. Let's hope you feel strong enough to eat some solid food as well."

His words plowed two neat furrows between her eyebrows. She replied. While he understood her apologetic tone, he had no idea of what she had said in her trilling language.

"You sound like a bird to me," he told her, smiling. Then he mimed it.

When she understood, she smiled for the first time. She

thought hard for a moment, her eyes far away, her head tipped to one side. With a grin she crooked a finger on either side of her head and bleated at him. Then she pointed to him. "I sound like a goat? Thanks very much!" But he smiled again.

She managed to eat some porridge and drink some warm milk with honey. Though she crawled into bed exhausted after this activity, Renellus felt heartened.

During the next few days, she began to sleep less and take a greater interest in her surroundings. Sand asked him the names of things. Before long, with a combination of mime and her new words, she could make herself understood much of the time.

In small ways she began to help around the house. When he came home from his rounds, it would be tidy, the fire burning brightly, and often something bubbled fragrantly in a pot.

The rest of the town buzzed with speculation. On all his calls the doctor was asked about his poor girl from the sea.

At the next council meeting, Nevius asked about her. They all fell silent but for the gentle sound of people blowing on their cups of chav to cool them.

Renellus stood. "She's recovering fairly quickly. As for who she is, and where she comes from, I can only guess. She hasn't mastered enough of our language to handle those questions yet." There were a few people in the room who hadn't heard that Sand spoke a different language, and they now exclaimed in surprise at this news. The doctor continued: "My guess is that she has endured a great sorrow and tried to kill herself by cutting her wrists and throwing herself into the sea. The doraan saved her. I'm not going to push too hard for answers until I feel she's strong enough to face her sadness again."

Croius stood up. "Uh, Doctor, getting back to her different language, what exactly do you mean?"

"I mean what I say. She doesn't use the words we do. When I say cup, she says 'carn.' When I say table, she says 'kherina.' Our speech is closer than I had originally thought, however. Many of her words are structured like ours, but pronounced differently."

Consternation rumbled around the room.

"Perhaps her misfortune has addled her brain," suggested the owner of the tavern where the council meetings were always held.

"That was my first theory, too," the doctor humored him. They had grown up together, and when Renellus went inland to the city to study medicine, Jayus had desperately wanted to go, too. But his father had demanded that he stay and help him with the tavern. Now, whenever a customer complained of an ache or a cough, Jayus offered his own diagnosis. And he usually offered some of his homemade brandy as well.

Renellus continued: "Her speech is consistent, however, and her wits are clear. I believe she comes from somewhere very distant."

Sound filled the air like a thick cloud. When the noise level dropped a little, Renellus said, "I have just one thing to add. If any of your women have clothes that they don't need anymore, this girl should have something to wear."

The council moved on to other matters and soon the members began to trickle home to tell their families about the strange girl and her stranger tongue.

*   *   *

Over the next few weeks, a steady flow of people moved through the doctor's door. It seemed that everyone had something they could spare for the sea waif. But instead of sending the cast-off garment over with one of the children, the whole family would come and crowd into the cottage to stare at Sand while they talked to the doctor.

At first she thanked each donor gratefully for the garments they brought. But soon she began to resent their frank curiosity. While they gawked at her and talked about her, she pretended she understood even less than she actually did. She simply said, "Thank you," like a parrot, adding a stiff, mechanical smile.

"I'm sure her mind is scrambled. You'd think with the doctor's fancy training he'd see that right away," Jayus pronounced to his wife as they left the house. "You could get a mockingbird to say thank you better than that."

As the doctor shooed the last caller out the door the next night, he laughed at her sullen face. "You've probably got the biggest wardrobe now of any girl in this town and there you sit like a grumpy walrus."

Sand understood little of this. "They *look*," she complained, bugging her eyes out in imitation. "To them I'm a strange animal. I have no . . . hurtings?"

"Feelings," the doctor corrected, and she nodded.

"You're new." He shrugged. "And different. Very few new and different things come to this little town on the coast, so far from the city." He worded the thought simply and spoke it slowly. She grasped his meaning, but continued to scowl into the fire.

When she arose the next morning, however, she looked at him shamefacedly. "I'm sorry of what I said. They try to be kind."

She dressed slowly. Renellus noticed she took great interest in the fabrics of her new clothes.

"You know about cloth?" he asked her.

She flushed. "Only a little. I am just learning to make it.

But like this . . ." She fingered the light fabric. "I have never seen it."

"What would you like for breakfast?" he asked her, and laughed when he heard her answer.

"Bread and cheese, please." Sand loved the cheeses made from cow's milk and the puffy yeast breads made from milled grains. Her bread, she'd told him, was made in small flat cakes and the only cheese she'd ever had was from goat's milk.

With the morning meal over, Renellus suggested, "Shall we go for a walk to the sea today? Are you strong enough for that?"

She turned her face to him, with eyes like lit lamps.

He took her down the main street to the harbor. The townspeople stared at her and murmured among themselves, but she ignored them.

They turned left at the harbor and took the narrow street that passed the boat houses and the fish market. They felt only a slight breeze, but high above them the clouds raced across the sun and out toward the flat blue horizon. One moment the street before them looked quaint and cozy in the sunlight. The next moment a pall would fall across their view and in the gray light the old warped buildings looked sinister and askew.

As they walked on, the spaces between the buildings became larger, and eventually there were no more buildings. A narrow sheep track led them through the scrubby meadows that bordered the ocean.

The doctor forged his way through the grasses that waved their seeds above his head. Sand followed him. Her impulse was to rush past him to the water's edge, but he suddenly hunched over, blocking her way, and began to curse violently.

"What's wrong?"

"Damn burrs!" He had stepped in a mass of creeping

tropical vines and his sandaled feet bristled with the nasty brown things.

"Sit down. I will pull them."

"Not here!"

With a grin, she agreed that might be a bad idea.

Stepping over the plant with great care, she slipped her arm around him and nestled her shoulder under his. He hopped down to the beach, leaning on her as much as he could.

As he flopped down, sprawling his length on the sand, the sun came out, washing them with heat. He put his head back and closed his eyes.

Her shadow moved swiftly across his face and down the length of his body. She knelt by his ankles and began pinching the burrs with her fingernails and pulling them out one by one. At last she sat back with a sigh.

"Finished?" he asked.

"You can't tell?"

"Still stings. But thank you." He smiled at her and rubbed her back with the palm of his hand. For a moment, she closed her eyes and leaned against the pressure of his hand, arching her back like a cat. Then she pulled away. Curling her legs up, she wrapped her thin arms around them like cords. She rested her chin on her knees, keeping her eyes fixed on the strand, where the water never ceased caressing the beach.

"What's wrong?" Renellus asked, feeling her withdraw from him as surely as if he had seen her stand up and walk away.

She shook her head. A moment later she picked up a handful of dry sand and let it slide through her fingers. "What do you call this?"

"Crysage. Unless it's from black volcanic rock. Then we call it crysak."

She looked at him with eyes full of a pain he couldn't fathom. "How many names do *you* have for sand?" she asked softly. Hefting another handful, she said, "This is what my name means in your language." It trickled through her fingers.

They sat in silence for a long time. Twice Renellus licked his wind-dried lips to say something, and twice he shut his lips on the words.

Finally Sand spoke. "You never asked me from where I came."

"I thought remembering might do you harm."

Sand looked at him over her shoulder and smiled. "If my ocean time did not hurt me, how can thoughts?"

"Memories can be very powerful. And I would argue that your trial by seawater hurt you very badly."

Sand frowned. "I feel fine now. Tired sometimes, but fine."

Renellus waited a moment, then asked, "Do you want to tell me where you came from?"

Sand looked out toward the sea again. "I want to tell you." Her voice was so low that the doctor had to strain to catch her words. But he dared not move closer for fear of startling her.

And so, in her lilting accent and stumbling in his language, she detailed her story for him. Partway through, she turned to face him. He had to school his face not to divulge his doubts. Without too much trouble, he could believe she came from an island far out to sea. The mainland fishermen never had to go far for their catch, since fish thronged the coastal waters. There could be a hundred inhabited islands there, if they were far enough beyond the horizon. But when she began describing her communication with the doraan—or the doraado, as she called them—he began to think she was retelling some legend of her people.

It was obvious that her culture was more primitive than his own. Under the kind of intense stress she'd endured, he could understand how she might have come to see her trial as a religious experience. The doraan had been known to

161

help shipwrecked survivors to land before. How easy, he reflected, if you believed in a sea goddess, to cry out for help in the dreadful situation she'd been in. And if help came miraculously, to believe it was in response to your cry.

His heart was more stirred by pity at the barbaric way her people had treated her.

Sand was nearing the end of her narrative. Renellus encouraged her with sympathetic noises at the appropriate times, thinking it could only help her heal to share this horror with someone.

Suddenly her stream of talk broke off. Sand staggered to her feet and ran to the water's edge. Following the direction of her gaze, Renellus saw several black-finned backs break the surface and disappear, over and over again in lazy slow motion.

Sand didn't make a sound: not a cry, not a word, not a whimper. The doctor felt his scalp prickle. For a long time the doraan circled in front of them, playing gracefully. Frozen at the water's edge, she stood like a tree growing there. Only her hair moved as the wind lifted it in sections from her shoulders, twisted the ends together, and let them fall again.

Then she cried out. One long, keening note that raised bumps on the doctor's arms. She flung herself into the water, ignoring the cold, forgetting her clothes. She thrashed into the sea, going deeper and deeper, until finally only her shoulders and head remained above the water.

Renellus found himself knee-deep in the sea without any recollection of getting to his feet to follow her. Sand stopped then, and he paused in his pursuit. He had to squint into the sun to keep his eyes on her, and the waves washing against the shore behind him obscured any sound Sand might be making.

Finally the group of black ovals straightened into a line and moved down the coast. Her head turned and she watched them till they were indistinguishable from the shadows of the waves.

Still, she didn't turn back toward land. "Sand!" Renellus called her, but she didn't move. Cursing heartily with every inch the cold water climbed inside his clothes, he plunged after her.

She seemed oblivious to his splashing and his voice. Finally he reached her and turned her to face him. She moved like a drowned body. At the sight of her bleak face, he caught his breath. Whatever doubts he'd had about the truth of her story disappeared in that instant. "Sand."

She didn't see him. Though her eyes were wide open, she didn't seem to be focusing on anything but some inner pain.

"Sand!" He grabbed her by both shoulders and shook her. Nothing flickered in those empty green depths. He cupped his hand and splashed her face with the icy water.

She blinked. Once, twice, and then her eyes focused on him. "I wish I died," she said, and dissolved into tears.

Renellus dragged her back to shore. He pulled her up onto the beach, forcing her to put one dispirited foot in front of the other, again, and again, and again.

He could feel the violence of Sand's weeping as she shuddered beneath his arm. High up on the beach he let her fling herself down onto the sand. After the worst of the violence had drained from her, she began talking in her own language in broken, hiccuping sentences. He heard the name of her deity several times and assumed she was praying. He sat quietly, waiting.

But he misconstrued Sand's fervent words. She wasn't praying; she was cursing. For the first time, since she had fed all her rage to her internal hawk as she endured the ocean trial, she felt anger again. "Damn you, Mother! Damn you, damn you! How could you do all this to me? Wasn't it enough to almost kill me? What is it that you want of me? What have I done that you should punish me so? Was it so wrong to refuse to marry a man I didn't want? Goddess, I hate you!" Another passion of weeping claimed her.

The doctor stretched out on the sand beside her. Sitting up on one elbow, he laid his other hand on her head and stroked her hair with his fingers. She rolled over and wrapped her arms around him, pressing her cheek against his chest. He waited, smoothing her hair with his palm, until finally her crying ceased but for the occasional convulsive sob.

As the wind sent the last cloud scudding over the ocean, the sun beamed down on them in a dedicated fashion. Their teeth chatttered. Renellus propped her up and began to unlace her clammy shirt. For a few moments she sat hunched over, unmoving, and then she began to help him with cold fingers. She suspended her clothes on the rustling sea grasses to dry. Meanwhile, the doctor stripped off his own tunic, trousers, and boots. Dressed only in their damp underwear, they nestled into the sand, and the wind licked the moisture from them.

Now and then an especially strong gust of wind would drive stinging sand against their skin. Renellus let Sand rest and warm herself silently for a while, before he asked, "Will you tell me what's wrong?"

Sand rolled her head to the left to regard him and shrugged, scratching her shoulders against the sand. She stared at the sky again. Finally, when he had given up on her answering him, she said, "I cannot talk to the doraado. I cannot feel them. When I tried to talk to them, a pain came to my head and everything is black. I wish I died in the storm."

Renellus moved to shelter her from the wind with his body. Looking at her skin in the bright sunlight, he said,

"Sand, you must listen to me. Do you remember how bruised and cut you were when I first met you?"

She nodded.

"And do you see how you're almost healed?"

She raised her arms and stared at them. All the bruises were faded, the scrapes were gone, and even on her wrists only the deepest cuts still had scabs. She let them drop. She nodded.

"I'll be honest with you. I don't know anything about the way you talk to the doraan. But didn't you strain your talent to its fullest limits during your terrible time on the ocean? To dangerous limits, in fact?" Sand nodded again. "Perhaps you've strained whatever faculty enables you to talk to the doraan, and you just haven't given it enough time to heal properly."

She looked into his face, the blood rushing to her cheeks.

He continued: "For instance, I speak to you with my voice. If I talked too long, too loudly, it's possible I would strain it. Then I would find it difficult to talk for some time after that. And if I tried to talk or to shout too soon, I could do further damage. But if I speak a little, or not at all, my throat will heal in its own time and soon you would never know anything had been wrong with it."

She looked into the sky. "I'm frightened to believe you. You might be wrong. But I'm more frightened not to believe you. If I don't have my talent, life will be too lonely to live."

"Nonsense!" he said heartily. "I don't know anyone with a talent like yours. We get along fine without it."

"How are you not lonely, then?" Her eyes fixed on his. Hers were wells filled with yearning.

He thought for a long time and then answered her a little sadly, "Sometimes I am very lonely. I have always thought that's simply a part of being human. That's why I became a doctor—to try to feel more connected to people.

165

To feel that my presence in this life matters to someone."

She continued to gaze at him, her eyes bright with unshed tears; sorry for herself and sorry for him.

Overwhelmed with pity and the urge to comfort her, he leaned over, pulled her to him, and kissed her lips. She didn't move or respond, but he felt a surprising response in himself and began to kiss her with more urgency.

For Sand, this physical echo of what she'd felt with Berran was more disturbing than enjoyable. She put a hand on his chest and pushed him away. "This does not feel right. This will not make either of us feel less lonely."

For a moment he was angry that she had broken the flow of what he was feeling. And then he realized that she was right. He had no answer for her. He stroked her hair in mute apology.

When the heat of the sun's rays had raised a thin film of sweat on them both, he sat up. "Let's go for a swim." He pulled her to her feet and down to the water's edge. Still hanging on, he plunged into the water, tugging her along with him. She stumbled in the thigh-deep water and submerged for a moment. He flung himself in as well. When he came up gasping, he found her laughing.

"What's so funny?"

"The shock of the cold. It's like the punchline to a good joke."

He shook his head. "You're a strange one, Crysage."

She looked startled. "Please don't use your own language to name me. When you do, I feel like someone else. And I already feel too strange and sad."

For the rest of the day Sand stayed silent, and her despondency continued day after day. Renellus longed to heal what hurt her, but he understood that what she needed could not be given to her by any human. She'd have to find her own answer.

After two days, the doctor had a flurry of calls to respond to, and each day when he returned, he would find Sand gone from the house. She would come back later, sunburned and complaining of a headache. Renellus had brewed her birch bark and wood betony tea for three nights in a row, before he realized what was causing it. In the middle of pouring out the water, he turned to her. Boiling water splashed onto the floor and steam rose from the flagstones. "You've been going to the beach every day!"

"So?" She lifted her chin, eyes blazing defiance.

"Little fool! If you strain yourself now, you may never communicate with the doraan again!"

"You don't know! You said you know nothing about my talent!"

"That's true—but I know about the human body. I know if you break a bone and don't let it rest and heal that you'll never walk properly again. If at all. I know that if your voice gives out on you and you keep on trying to talk and shout and yell, if you ever get your voice back, it will always sound as if you have barnacles in your throat. How important is this to you?"

She closed her eyes and thought of the enveloping tenderness of M'ridan's persona. "The most important thing in life."

"Then can't you wait a little?"

She nodded slowly.

"I'm sorry. This is partially my fault. You have nothing to do here and you're bored. No wonder. Tomorrow I'll find you something to work at while your mind heals."

The next morning he began taking her on his rounds with him. When the townspeople opened their doors to the two of them, they looked askance at Sand. But because she was there with the doctor, they all opened their doors wider and allowed both of them into their homes. For Sand's part, she sat silently near him and watched him work. Sometimes he would ask her to hold something for him, or to stir some mixture into a paste.

But her silence at the bedside was merely the balance for her chatter outside. The moment they left a house, she would question him about the treatment he'd used. She'd ask why one mixture differed slightly from another, though they were both for the same illness, but for different patients. And she was fascinated with his herb lore. In the evening she'd stand, leaning against his worktable, taking down a bottle, uncorking it, pouring some of the contents into her hand, sniffing it, studying it, putting it back, and returning the bottle to the shelf. Then she'd begin with another bottle.

Then a day came when he had no patients to visit. That morning he took her to the house on the hill overlooking the bay. The baby lay in a cradle on the doorstep, where the oldest girl, Ivea, crooned to it. Chellius and Bavia were running about farther up on the hill. Renellus found their mother kneeling in the garden, planting for spring.

She brushed the hair out of her eyes as she rose to her feet to greet them, leaving a streak of dirt on her forehead.

"Gaia, this is Sand. Maybe you've heard about her? Our sea child. I've brought her to give you a hand. I see you're right back at work again, while your wild animals run about as they like."

"But I feel so much better . . ."

"Well, you look terrible." Sand stared at him. He was normally so gentle and kind with his patients. "You're thin and tired and you look fifteen years older than you should."

Sand looked away, embarrassed for the woman, as the doctor scolded her like a naughty child.

"Now, Sand has nothing to do, and you have far too much. It's making you both ill. I thought you could trade her some chores for some of her idle time and you'd both be better off."

He left the women staring shyly at each other. Before he rounded the road out of sight he turned back to look. The two younger children were racing down from the heights to investigate the stranger.

Sand's days fell into a new rhythm. In the mornings she'd go out with the doctor, if he had patients to visit. In the afternoons she'd help Gaia. With the two of them working, they'd expanded the garden to half again its original size. The house was turned inside out and back, and Ivea was busy with her knitting needles while Bavia and Chellius squabbled over who got to use the spindle. Wood for the fire was stacked high beside the door, and even the over-grown weeds around the well had been scythed into respectability.

When Renellus saw the new order in the little cottage he was delighted with his strategy. Sand's progress made him even happier. As she moved about his house in the evenings, she exuded tranquillity. She spent hours watching the fire or studying herb lore, and she fell asleep as soon as she crawled into bed. Her nightmares visited her less and less often. Even her painful thinness began to round with developing muscle.

Gaia invited the doctor inside during one of his visits for a mug of chav. She, too, looked plumper, and the high color in her cheeks was the glow of good health, not the flush of fever. Renellus looked around him as he bounced the gig-gling baby boy on his knee and congratulated himself on the successful marriage of his two problems.

Chapter Fifteen

The wonder of Sand's arrival was beginning to wear off by the time a new visitor arrived in Cliffport. An apprentice starwatcher from the university brought grave news that stirred up the sleepy town like a stone dropped into a silted pond.

Walking along the street toward the tavern, Renellus could hear the gathering from several buildings away. As he opened the door to enter, the smoke in the low-beamed room stirred uneasily. His eyes burned as he threaded his way through the crowd. He bought a tankard of ale for each hand from Jayus, so he wouldn't have to struggle back for a refill, and settled himself where he had an unobstructed view of the stranger. The starwatcher sat staring into his ale, oblivious to the people examining him. His youthful countenance contrasted strangely with his stern expression. It wasn't until he blinked, and Renellus saw the effort it cost him to raise his eyelids again, that he realized how exhausted the young man was. Dark circles banded the skin under his eyes and his clothes were so dirty and travel-stained that no amount of washing would ever get them completely clean again.

When the room couldn't possibly hold any more, Jayus yelled for silence. The lad from the city stood on his bench, swayed, caught himself, and began to speak. The other patrons hushed only when they realized that he was talking and they weren't hearing.

". . . and it's been three hundred and twenty summers since it last neared our sun, by city records. Now it's coming again, and I've been sent to warn you to get your boats well out into the ocean, and your families, animals, and valuables well inland."

"What?"

"What did he say?"

"Why?"

Noise erupted in the room as people started asking those around them what he'd been talking about.

The young man rubbed the back of his wrist over his pale forehead and blinked twice. This time he held up both hands for silence and waited till there wasn't a sound in the smoky tavern before he started again.

"By the records of the city and our own observations, we know that a traveling star is approaching our world. You can see it in the sky at night now if you look toward the spiral constellation. This same star has been visiting our sun and retreating again every three hundred and twenty years, approximately. Sometimes it passes close to our world, sometimes farther away. This time we think it will be very close.

"Over the next few weeks it will become larger and brighter every night. It's huge, larger than this world, and as it passes close to us, it will exert a strong pull, disrupting the forces that hold this world together."

171

The tavern was utterly silent. Finally someone called out, "What does that mean?"

"In the past it has meant earthquakes, high seas, floods, tidal waves, and storms. The severity of these depends on how close the star passes."

Waves of sound beat against the walls of the tavern again and the youth wearily lifted his hand for quiet. "I have spent the last weeks riding up the shore to warn all the coastal towns and hamlets of what is to come. You must take your families, animals, and valuables several miles inland and your boats out into deep water."

His listeners began asking specific questions. The evening broke up very early as the council dispersed to go home and tell their families and neighbors the news. The young man sat down again while the people filed out past him. He supported his chin with his hand and his eyelids drooped. Every now and then, someone would stop by his table on the way out and ask him a question, so he was unable to fall asleep.

Finally the tavern was nearly empty, and still the messenger sat there. The doctor approached him. "Excuse me, my name is Renellus."

The starwatcher's eyes opened slowly and he struggled visibly to focus on the outstretched hand before him. He raised his own and grasped it. "Petrius."

"Well, Petrius, you've certainly poked a stick into this wasps' nest! Normally my fellow townspeople are very hospitable; strangers are such a rarity that we fight to entertain them. But I'm afraid you've given them so much else to think about they've forgotten you. You look as if you could use a bed—I've got a spare."

At the word "bed" Petrius pushed himself to his feet. "You just spoke the charmed word."

Sand stood as Renellus entered with the stranger. The

172

doctor introduced them briefly and then showed Petrius where he would sleep. The young man slid out of his clothes and lay down immediately.

Renellus asked, "What time must you be gone in the morning?"

Petrius smiled blissfully. "Tomorrow there is no time that I must be up. With this town I have given my last warning. Another apprentice was doing all the towns from here north. I can sleep late tomorrow. Oh, blessed sleep!" And he stretched like a cat beneath the covers. "That is"—he paused, embarrassed—"with your permission, my host. Forgive my manners. If it's inconvenient, please wake me and I'll be on my way."

"Never mind that. Sleep well. I'm sure you've earned it." The doctor laid an extra blanket over him. The young man was asleep before he finished pulling it up to his chin.

Renellus sat before the fire with Sand. Shoulder to shoulder they talked about the news, and then the doctor announced he was going to bed.

"I'm not sleepy yet," Sand told him. "I'll just sit here for a while."

She stared into the fire for hours, feeding it twigs and sticks. When she finally stood to go to bed, she saw the stranger's eyes sparkle in the firelight. She moved to stand beside him, and whispered, "Are you all right? Can I get you something?"

His eyes looked through her and she realized he was not completely awake. But he whispered, "Thirsty," so she fetched a mug of water and watched his throat move as he gulped it down.

With no sound other than a rustle of covers, he lay down again and closed his eyes. Sand stood beside his bed a moment longer, watching, and then turned away and made a bed for herself on the sleeping couch.

The starwatcher slept late the next morning, and the other two moved about the cottage quietly, so as not to wake him. Renellus watched Sand's pale, set face with concern. "Is something wrong?"

"I think so." Her forehead puckered between her brows. When the starwatcher finally awoke, they gave him breakfast and chav, and Sand hovered nearby as he ate. When he was finished, she sat down beside him and began questioning him in her charming accent.

Petrius looked at her in astonishment. "Where are you from?"

She said self-consciously, "It is where I am from that I must talk to you about. The doctor has told me of your warning to these people. I come from a far island—"

"Really? How amazing! My old teacher would be so pleased. Andronius has always maintained there are other places over the sea, beyond the horizon, if we would just sail far enough to find them. Would you travel to the city with me to tell them about your island?"

She shook her head. "I want to return home as soon as I can. But the doctor told me of the warning you bring. What I want to know is, what will happen when your storms begin, far out in the ocean?"

"What's the highest point on your island?"

Sand looked at him blankly.

"I mean, is there a mountain? Or hills and cliffs as there are here?" He pointed through the window.

She shook her head. "My island is very flat."

"Then I'm afraid your people are in terrible danger. You see—" He looked around him and pulled a charred stick from the fireplace. Crouching down, he began drawing on the flagstones. "This is a side view of the ocean. Here's the bottom, rising toward land. For an island, it rises and sinks again on the other side. Here's the normal surface of the

174

water. Now, when something cataclysmic happens on the ocean floor, a wave of force emanates from it."

Sand was confused by some of the unfamiliar words he was using, so she concentrated all her focus on the drawing before her.

Petrius drew an explosion on the bottom of the ocean and then a curve moving away from it through the ocean. "This wave runs along the floor of the ocean. Far out to sea, where the water is very deep, the wave will seem to be only a big comber, perhaps the height of a man's chest. When the wave reaches land, however, and the ocean becomes shallower, the wave is pushed farther and farther above the surface. If there is a quick rise from deep ocean floor to the land, the water will stand higher than the tallest tree." He drew his curve once more, the same size as before, but now it was positioned near the island and the curve towered over the flat bump. "And then it runs far up on land and crashes down, destroying everything there."

He looked at Sand to see whether she'd understood him. Her complexion was ashen. "How can they be saved?" she asked.

"Someone must warn them. If they take their boats, their belongings, and so on into deep water, the only thing they might have to contend with is storms."

Sand clenched her hands in her hair and groaned. "How will they know? They can't know!"

Petrius stared at her. "Surely someone will take them the message."

"I'm sure they would," she agreed, "if only they knew where to take it."

With Renellus's help, the young man learned the story of Sand's exile. As he heard of the loss of her talent, his face lost some of its gravity. "I think you'll find that things are not quite as desperate as they may seem. There is a new department at the university. They study and help to develop gifts like your talent. Let me send a message to my teacher and he will visit their college and persuade them of your urgent need. The College of Telepaths will understand. For if we can't get a message to your people, they are doomed."

Even as he was speaking, he began rummaging in his knapsack for pen and paper. Borrowing ink from Renellus, he began his message to the city. Sand brought him another cup of chav and hovered nearby as he wrote.

After half an hour of intense scribbling, the young man folded up the sheets and sealed them with some gum. Renellus took the letter and the two men left the house for the docks, in search of transport for it to the city. When they returned, Sand asked, "How soon will you hear back?"

Petrius stared into space as he calculated. "Four days at a minimum for it to get there, and four days back. And probably two days in between to make arrangements. It can't be any less than ten days, and maybe more."

Sand chewed her lip in an agony of frustration. Petrius tried to reassure her. "I don't expect anything to happen till long after that."

Time never passed as slowly for Sand as it did in the days that followed. At first she stopped going to Gaia's house and began haunting the shore again, watching the black backs of the dolphins as they frolicked in the bay. She didn't dare try to compel them. If she strained something now which had been healing, and if that prevented her from finding M'ridan and her island, the blood of all her people would be on her hands.

After a couple of days at the shore, however, she found the waiting intolerable. She began to spend the days at Gaia's again, where she worked like a demon, chopping

176

wood, weeding the garden, clearing more land, and entertaining the children. Each night she returned to the doctor's, wolfed down her supper, and fell asleep while the sun still slanted in through the doorway, too exhausted to worry.

The ninth day came and Sand didn't go to Gaia's for fear she'd miss the man from the city. Exasperated, Renellus told her, "He's coming to see *you*, Sand. If you're not here, he'll wait."

But she couldn't settle to the idea of being anywhere else when the man arrived. She spent the day cleaning Renellus's home, but at every footfall or hoofbeat on the road outside, she flew to the front door.

Night fell and no one had arrived. Sand went to bed early with "Tomorrow, tomorrow, surely tomorrow" chanting silently in her head. But the next day passed and the one after that. By noon of the twelfth day, Sand alternated between depression and frenzy.

"They're not coming," she announced that night during supper, which she didn't touch.

"Don't be ridiculous—"

"Of course they're coming—"

Petrius and Renellus paused to disentangle their retorts, each indicating that the other was to continue.

Petrius began again. "Of course they're coming, Sand. Even if they didn't want to come out of scientific curiosity, which they will, they would come out of moral obligation. Your island will be the answer to many academic questions and the beginning of many new questions. Academics are addicted to questions. They won't be able to stay away. And they will feel obligated to do all they can to save those lives."

But Sand turned away, feeling his assurances to be hollow.

The next morning, she paced up and down constantly,

unwilling to leave in case the city men did arrive, and yet miserably certain they would not come. In exasperation, Renellus marched her down to the wharves and put her into Nevius's hands. "Take her out and keep her busy," he pleaded.

Until they were well out to sea, she was pretty much ignored. As they drew away from the dust and the town smells of Cliffport, homesickness consumed Sand. The faintly spicy scent of the clean sea air and the stronger smell of the fishing boat itself made her long for Strandia with all her being.

Once they were far enough from the mainland to catch the wind, the canvas sails snapped open and crackled as the wind bellied them full.

She felt the pitch and yaw of the boat's deck beneath her and heard the water bubbling past the hull and the gulls keening behind them. Her hands gripped the rail. Below, flying before the bow spray, doraado played in the water.

Once they were well under way, Kaellus and Croius brought her chav and questioned her as she drank it. They had been on the ship the day she'd been found and hadn't seen her since. Nevius came and sat with them awhile. Even at this hour he carried the scent of strong drink about him like perfume.

He chucked her under the chin as if she were very young and asked, "What's wrong, doraan-sa? You look like a catfish that has lost its whiskers."

"I'm very worried. My people live on a small island far out to sea and don't know about this traveling star." Once started, she poured out the whole story to him: about the doraado, and how she couldn't talk to them anymore but couldn't get home without their help. Collecting her courage, she reached out and grasped one of his leathery, calloused paws in her own slim hands.

"Captain, I know Petrius thinks you should take the big

boats into deep water when the time comes. Couldn't you start early? If you left now, provisioned for a month, isn't there a chance you might find my island? The doctor says the city men are coming, but it's been so long. I'm sure something has happened to prevent them."

Nevius gave her a kindly look and, withdrawing his hand, laid it on her shining hair for a moment. "Well, we'll have to think about that, doraan-sa. Wait and see. Don't you worry too much about the city men. They'll come in their own time and then we can see what's to be done. We'll wait for them." He turned to supervise two of the young men letting out the nets.

Sand let her protest die unspoken. Helplessness and anger washed through her. She could see Nevius had no intention of listening to her any further. She wanted to scream at him, to hit him, to find some way to convince him, but she knew nothing she could do would touch him where he would listen.

She was tired of living to other people's schedules. She was tired of waiting for the city men to arrive, tired of waiting for her talent to heal, tired of always reacting to other people's decisions instead of making her own and acting on them first.

She felt a grim fury begin to seep into her. She sat perfectly still, remembering rage and experiencing it once again. And then, one of the young fishermen turned and offered to show her the boat. Rising, she told him she would be delighted.

He took her from stern to bow and back again. She insisted they let her help them with the sails. She asked about the sheets and the rudder and the anchor. The sailors showed her how to coil ropes so they didn't tangle, and so they could be undone with one twist. They showed her different knots and different uses for them.

She helped them haul in the catch, and when that was

179

finished, they did some maneuvers so she could see what directed the boat's movement. Nevius even let her take the helm for a while.

And the whole time that they were preening and showing off for her attention, she was burning each and every piece of instruction she received into her mind, scoring it deeply.

The more interested she seemed, the more the fishermen told her. She combed every inch of the boat with them, asking questions about this line and that wooden peg.

And when they finally returned to town, she helped them dock the ship and fold the sails away, noticing how they attached to the yardarm.

So overriding had her new purpose become that she didn't remember the man from the university until she stood before the doctor's cottage in the twilight. She stepped lightly over the threshold and glanced quickly around. Renellus and Petrius were sitting alone at the table with a block of cheese and a loaf of bread in front of them. Fresh cups of chav steamed between their fingers. They turned as her shadow fell into the room.

"What did you bring us for dinner?" Petrius smiled at her.

Renellus took the net of silver fish from her hands and turned her so the last of the sunset's light fell upon her face. His own face lit up. "That's what I was waiting for. Your eyes are sparkling again and your cheeks are as pink as cliff roses."

She smiled at him obliquely and turned, afraid he might see the new purpose behind the sparkle in her eyes.

She helped them clean the fish and cook dinner. She was quiet, but the doctor didn't worry; her step had bounce once more and her movements were light and deft again.

After dinner the two men announced they were going to the council meeting at the tavern. Sand said, "Good night. I'll be asleep when you get home." She hugged Renellus tightly before he went out the door, to his surprise.

He hugged her back. "Good night, Sand."

She waited till she could no longer hear their footsteps on the road outside. She cleaned the dinner dishes. And when she was done, she filled a small sack with some of the clothes she had been given, and on top she set a wrapped package of cheese and dried fruit, some leathery figs on a string, and a small loaf of dense bread. She went through Renellus's medicinal herbs, filling small packets and adding them to her bag. As she tucked the last one away, her heart twisted within her and she paused for a moment, gazing into the smoky fire.

She wished she knew how to write as Petrius did, for she'd have liked to leave a note for the doctor apologizing for the terrible thing she was doing and thanking him for all his care. After a moment's thought, she returned to his medicine shelf and pulled out the bottle of heartsease. She thrust it under her pillow. Renellus had once told her with twinkling eyes that it was for broken hearts. She hoped he'd remember and understand.

Checking to make sure the street outside was empty, she tucked her sack under the bushes growing outside the door.

Sand changed into dark leggings and pulled on a black tunic. She tucked a small knife into the sash around her waist. She even laid out her sandals, so that she could just swing her feet down into them and silently lace them up.

Then she lay down on her sleeping couch and pulled up the blankets around her chin. Despite her certainty that she was too excited to sleep, she immediately did.

She woke up several hours later, when Renellus and Petrius came in at last. Fully clothed under the blankets, she was bathed in sweat. She paled at the thought she might have tossed her blankets off in her sleep and given the whole plan away.

The two men bumped around the cottage in the ember

light and finally lay down. Soon the noise in the room steadied to the deep, even pulse of sleepers' breathing.

After waiting a long time, she sat up and slid her feet into
her waiting sandals. Just as she tied the second one on,
Renellus moaned and turned his face toward her. His eyes
flew open. She sat frozen. But his eyes were focused on his
dreams, and after a moment, he turned his head the other way.

Sand stole quickly from the house. Outside, there was a
fresh breeze blowing from inland and the sky was heavy
with cloud. Not a star showed, and except for the occasional
lit window, the world was a black pit.

She felt around under the bush till she found her sack.
Not allowing herself even one last look, she shouldered the
bag and strode along the road as quickly as the inky blackness allowed.

Twice she had to crouch beside a wall as a townsman
passed her, returning from the tavern. She ducked her head
so her hair hid her pale face, kept her eyes and mouth shut
and her hands tucked into the sleeves of her tunic.

As she passed the tavern, she chanced a glimpse inside
and saw it stood almost empty but for Nevius and a few
other fishing boat captains dawdling over their whiskey as
Jayus swept up around them.

Finally the soft tap of her sandals began to echo lightly.
Crouching down, she felt the roughness of sun-weathered
boards beneath her.

All around her the darkness was filled with the soft slap
of waves and the sonorous snores of wooden boats rocking
against the wharves. Occasionally one of the ships creaked
as it strained against its mooring rope and then nuzzled up
against the dock again.

Sand crouched quietly for a few minutes, listening
intensely. She rose, as assured as she could be that she was
the only creature awake at the waterfront.

She pulled off her sandals and leaped lightly onto the deck of Nevius's boat. Tucking her sandals and sack out of the way, she looked around. There were only four other ships tied up here that were a possible match for the *Swallow's* speed. The other small sloops and rowboats could never catch the brig. She crept to the nearest competition and eased herself on board.

Feeling her way, she climbed the rigging. Once she reached the yardarm, she had to find the ropes that looped below the yard. Slipping her feet onto them, she inched outward, away from the mast. Then, clinging desperately with one hand, she dug through the many folds of the bound-up sail to where it was attached by short pieces of rope to the yardarm. Pulling her knife from her sash, she sawed through the fibrous stuff until, with a muffled click, the last strands parted and her knife touched wood. She slowly slid her feet farther out, found the next rope, and began again. Only the farthest ties at one outside end of the yard did she leave untouched. She couldn't stomach the idea of swaying thirty feet in the dark over the stone wharf.

She descended and made her way to the next ship.

She had barely started aloft when she saw lanterns swaying along the street toward the dock. She heard men's voices arguing and laughing and singing. She scampered up the now-illuminated rigging and perched on the yard, feet dangling, arms around the solid mast. The small knot of men arrived at the dock and then split into five different groups. Two men boarded the ship she was on. A solitary figure staggered over to the *Sea Swallow,* and as his voice rang out in a bawdy chorus, she recognized Nevius.

The two men below her conversed for a few minutes as they stumbled around the deck, stowing things away. Sand hung in the air above them, afraid to breathe, desperately trying to invent some plausible excuse should she

183

be discovered. Eventually they clambered down below-decks without even a glance skyward. She let out her breath in a long, slow hiss. She sat immobile for a few moments longer, considering her next move.

She had hoped she would get this part of the night's work done before anybody boarded the ships. But she had only two choices—abandon both her plan and her island or proceed, but even more quietly than before. She turned and once again began the arduous work of sawing through the ties while balancing on the thin rope beneath her feet.

By the time she hauled herself up the rigging of the fourth and last vessel, three hours had passed since her arrival at the docks. She could sense the night slipping past her with the fluid speed of an eel. She tried to hurry, but as she forced her hand beneath one of the myriad folds of canvas, she overbalanced, slipped, and fell.

She clawed at the canvas and grabbed the rope she'd been standing on with one hand as she fell. Agony spiked through her shoulder and she dropped her knife to grab the rope with the other hand as well. The knife fell away from her in apparent slow motion, and she clenched her eyes and teeth against its landing. It hit the bare deck and bounced. The clatter was even worse than she'd dreaded.

Immediately she saw a line of wavering light around the edges of the hatch and knew it would only be seconds till she was discovered. Gritting her teeth against the searing pain, she swung back and forth and flung herself outward just as the hatch banged open.

Her body cleft the night water like a spear. She let herself drop a long way beneath the water before she started back up, searching for the underside of the boat. Hand over hand she crept along the hull. Seaweed writhed beneath her hands. Her lungs almost burst before she reached the surface. But when her head broke water, she subdued the urge to gulp air. Instead she sipped it quietly.

She hugged the waterline, barnacles scraping her chest. Nearby boats reflected the light from lanterns on the deck above her. She heard voices but couldn't catch what they were saying. Before long she began to shiver and she clamped her jaw shut to keep her teeth from chattering noisily. Finally the men above went back to their beds, apparently without discovering the source of the noise.

Quickly she swam to the nearest skiff and hauled herself over the gunwales. Panting, she flopped down in the bilge and the fish scales. She began to shake violently.

When she'd caught both her breath and her courage again, she climbed onto the wharf and padded back to the *Swallow*. The boat seemed to be waiting for her, rubbing itself against the wharf like a cat. She climbed aboard. All was quiet but for a distant rhythm like waves breaking on a shore. Nevius was snoring in the hold below.

She sat down on a coiled rope and rested her forehead in her hands. After a moment she rummaged in her bag and drew out her packet of herbs. Clutching them tightly, she climbed down the open hatch. The cabin below was filled with a dim golden light. The captain had passed out without extinguishing his lantern. Not by even the faintest twitch of an eyelid did she disturb his sleep.

Finding his cache of whiskey was easy; he had half a bottle beside him on the floor. Into this she measured spoonfuls of valerian, catnip, and eyeweight. Corking it again, she gave it a vigorous shaking. When the liquor turned from clear gold to dusky amber, she poured out a quarter of it into a cup and knelt by his bed.

"Nevius. Nevius!" She called him several times, becoming progressively louder. She shook him.

Finally he opened his eyes, trying to focus on her. Sand spoke in a rush.

"Nevius, the doctor sent me with this for you. He says you drank too much in the tavern tonight. He says you'll feel terrible tomorrow unless you drink this."

His whiskery face was turned to her, but his eyes were cloudy. He raised himself onto one elbow and drained the whole draught at once. He slumped back and closed his eyes. He had never really wakened, but now he passed quickly into deep unconsciousness. Concerned, she glanced at the bottle. As she climbed the ladder, she offered a quick prayer for Nevius to the Mother. She hoped she hadn't given him too large a dose.

And in case it hadn't been big enough, she closed the hatch behind her and latched it.

Calling to mind everything she'd learned about the boat, she hoisted the small jibsail. Casting off the mooring ropes was the trickiest part of doing things alone, but she did it from the bow first and the stern last, so the boat was already half-turned out to sea.

Sand loosed the stern line and, holding it tight, leaped back onto the boat; then, with one hand on the wheel, she payed out the line. Gradually the boat moved away from the wharf, and when she had sailed a half taell from shore she caught the wind. The jib bellied out and Sand felt the wheel begin to resist her slightly. She heard the water faintly burbling past the hull, and behind, bubbles glistened in the slight wake.

Far across the land behind her most of the stars had already died. Only a few bright familiars remained and one whose presence overshadowed theirs.

Kryphon was returning and his golden cape streamed out behind him.

Part Three

The Sea

Chapter Sixteen

Sand had been sailing for half an hour before she realized how lucky she'd been. Except for the knife, everything had gone smoothly. Even Nevius, snoring in the cabin below her, was a reassuring thought. If she really got into trouble, he was there to get her out.

She wondered what the penalty was for this crime. "They won't catch me," she resolved. She started at the sound of her own voice.

Far behind her now she could see the houses north of the town clinging to the cliffs like barnacles to a rock bathed in rosy light. A moment later the sun climbed over the rim of the world and dazzled her eyes. Resolutely she turned and looked out to the far and empty horizon before her, where twilight still lingered. A shiver rattled her, and to dispel its melancholy effect, she tied the wheel and went forward to rig the mainsail, whistling as she did so.

Aloft in the rigging, as she undid the knots that bound up the great mainsail, she glanced back once more. She thought she saw one of the ships rowing out of the harbor.

She clambered back down, and with two yanks on the downhauls, the great canvas sail opened with a whoosh and a snap. She adjusted the angle to the wind and thrilled as she felt the ship begin to heel over a little. She left the four-teen different lines all tangled on the deck and returned to the helm. If anything sudden happened now that the main-sail was set, she wanted to be ready to correct it.

The higher the sun climbed in the sky, the stronger the breeze became. Sand stood at the wheel, feet braced apart and head up. Although she was beginning to feel her lack of sleep, her heart sang.

Looking at the waves all around, she cried aloud, "O Sea Mother, hear me! I am your daughter Sand, returning to you and to my people. Mother, once more I am placed in your hands, only this time it is through *my* will to achieve your purpose. For I believe now it was your plan to bring me to the continent so I could warn your children about the danger that is coming. Mother, I am yours. Please take me home."

She raised her arms to the sky and waited. Just as she was beginning to feel self-conscious, a pod of doraado surfaced and began leaping along beside her, riding her wake and her slight bow wave. They danced in the pink light of morning, breaching, sending cascades of foam high in the air.

At the same time, the breeze began to stiffen and it shifted direction. With a whoop, Sand laid her hands on the wheel again and adjusted her course to take advantage of this new wind.

Sand sailed for several hours, making good time. The early-morning sun beating down through the chill air felt good. She relished it, feeling it soak through her dark clothing.

Late in the morning, however, the air grew hot and she felt her exhaustion. She began to sway as she held on to the

190

helm and her eyes closed of their own accord. Finally she tied the helm and went below to check on Nevius, just to be moving and to stay awake.

A rush of hot, stuffy air hit Sand in the face as the hatch creaked open. She waited a moment and then descended to the square of sunlight on the floor below. Nevius was breathing deeply, but his clothes and his face were soaked with sweat. The tiny room smelled sour and stale. As she stood poised, mulling over what to do next, Nevius moaned and his eyes contorted, as though to shut out some dreadful sight.

Her heart clenched remorsefully. She glanced at her hands and wished they had more medical skill. She could ensure that he slept, but not that his sleep would be peaceful.

She picked up his doctored bottle of whiskey and debated giving him another dose. He moaned again, and began tossing his head back and forth, sending a spray of sweat in an arc across the room.

Sand set the bottle down: no more for now. She filled a pail with cold seawater and sponged his face and neck. He relaxed finally, his breathing deepening and slowing.

When she returned above deck, she left the hatch open to cool the hold. All this had kept her awake, but as soon as she resumed her post at the helm, she began to sway again.

"I'll sail till dusk," she told herself firmly, wondering if she'd ever be able to last that long. She could doze, she could long with all her being to lie down, but as long as she stood on her feet she couldn't actually fall asleep.

It was in one of her moments of drowsiness, however, that a new sensation jolted her awake.

Someone invaded her consciousness. Gradually the creaking of wood, the rippling water along the hull, the flapping of the sails, and the cry of the gulls that followed her all began to fade from her mind and she focused more and more on an inner sound.

She felt something in her mind. Not clear images, not the sense of a whole presence, as with M'ridan, but as though she could hear an animal through a barrier. First a faint scratching, and then a more frantic scrabbling. She stood frozen, eyes jammed, shutting out the distractions of the physical world while she concentrated. She waited, like a child trapped in a dark house, unsure if the person bumping around in the darkened room next door is an enemy or a friend and unwilling to call attention to herself until she found out.

She felt it getting closer to her innermost dwelling place and she cowered, shrinking away. It was as if she were back in Jinny's house and heard the intruder pause just before climbing the ladder to the loft where she was trapped.

"Sand!"

Her eyes flew open with a cry. Nevius swayed before her on the deck, his face an unhealthy color, sweat beading his forehead.

She stood rooted to the deck for the moment, the intruder waiting in her mind. She dealt with the more immediate problem.

"Sand, what's happened? What are you doing here? Where are we?"

"Uh . . ." She gaped at him. She hadn't expected him to wake up so soon. The dose she'd given him should have been blanketing his mind for another two hours at least. She began by repeating her last words to him. "The doctor sent me to you with some medicine, because you'd had too much to drink . . ."

He squinted at her. "I sort of remember that . . ." Moving forward, he took the wheel from her.

She took a deep breath and improvised. "When I came

192

back on deck I found that the mooring lines had come loose and we were floating in the harbor."

"Why didn't you wake me?"

"I tried. But you were completely passed out. I couldn't get you to stir. I was afraid to sail it back because I couldn't dock it by myself in the dark."

"You could have called for help."

"I did. No one heard me. By morning the wind had blown us so far out that I couldn't see land anymore. I put up the sails so I'd have some control."

"You could have anchored."

"I didn't know how."

He gazed at her a long time. "You know how to rig and sail a brigantine, but you don't know how to drop anchor. Very strange." At last he shrugged. "Well, I suppose you did the best you could, but I don't think much of your judgment or your luck. Let's get back to port. Where are we?"

Sand shrugged.

"Has the wind been coming from behind you the whole time?"

She nodded.

"And how many hours have you been sailing?"

"Twelve. Maybe thirteen."

He sighed heavily. "Well, it could be worse. Let's get her head around and start back. We'll have to tack the whole way in this wind. This is going to take some time."

Sand stood poised on one foot while she debated making another plea for finding her island. Then, with a mental shrug, she decided to follow his lead for a while. For the moment she was too tired to fight him, anyway. She judged that they were far enough from land that they wouldn't sight it again before dark, and by morning she'd surely think of a plan. Besides, she tried to convince herself, I am in the Mother's hands now. Perhaps this is all part of her plan.

So, under Nevius's critical eye, they came around and set the sails toward shore. He had her take down the small foresail and put up the larger jenny to catch all the wind they could. Then he set her to coiling all the fourteen lines that lay in untidy heaps on the deck wherever she'd dropped them. Finally he sent her down to the galley for some fresh water and some biscuits. Sand found she was ravenous and desperately thirsty, though she hadn't noticed it till then. She broke off pieces of biscuit and savored them one by one. Then she pulled the figs out of her sack and offered them to the captain.

He stared at her. "Odd, isn't it? Your being all prepared for this little accident?"

The blood rushed into her face so fast she felt dizzy.

He continued with his mouth full. "There are some other pretty strange circumstances in this, too. The doctor's never worried about my drinking before now. And why did you drop the mainsail? The jib would have been enough to steer by." He watched her face.

Unable to think of a convincing lie, she shrugged. Taking a deep breath, she met his eyes squarely and simply said, "I think we both know the answers to your questions, Captain. I'm sorry. I haven't slept in a long time. With your permission, I'll grab some sleep."

"Go ahead. I don't need you. When I can't sail this boat alone on a quiet sunny day, my body'll be feeding the fishes."

Sand went forward and flung herself into the hammock stretched between the two masts. Alone again at last, she rocked there.

Behind them the last brilliant shard of sun disappeared. They sailed on into the deepening twilight and the stars began to glow above them. Sand lay awake longer than she'd have believed possible. Far away the mournful cry of a lonely seabird sent ripples of disturbance across the surface of her mind, and above her the wandering star burned brightly in the heavens.

She turned her head away from that baleful, one-eyed stare and looked across the sea. Close by the ship four doraado broke the surface in a sweet, swift arc. Pink light reflected from the clouds above slid over them.

Sand's heart ached. The thought of the task she'd embarked on overwhelmed her. Suspended in a hammock between two masts, the only outcroppings on a glassy sea, she felt herself an infinitesimal mote in the universe. However she strove, surely she could make no difference in the monumental events happening around her.

And while she lay there, she caught the echo of a footstep in her mind. Instantly she was entirely focused inward, waiting for another sensation announcing the presence of an intruder. Again she had the horrific sense of standing in the dark with an enemy nearby but not knowing where. She could almost hear his breathing. She waited and strained and listened—and fell asleep.

She half awoke later to find Nevius padding around her. With a whoosh and a rattle the big jenny fell to the deck.

Sand sat up on one elbow trying to see what was happening in the dark.

"It's all right. The wind has died for now, so we'll put out a sea anchor for tonight and sail again in the morning." She saw him preparing to fold the mainsail up, so she flipped out of the hammock and offered, "I'll bind it for you, Captain."

In the dark she scuttled up the rigging, and as the giant sail scalloped toward her, she folded it in upon itself and tied the whole thing into a neat canvas package around the yard.

Within ten minutes she had slid to the deck beside Nevius again. Nevius dropped a small sail over the side. "If a wind comes up, that'll slow us down." He laid one of his great paws on her head. "You're as good as a lad. Better. Most of my crew wouldn't be as sure-footed on that rigging in the dark." He turned away and added something she didn't quite catch, but she thought he said, "I don't care what you've done."

She crawled back into her hammock, blushing with guilt. If only he knew how she'd gained her proficiency on the rigging in the dark.

When she awoke in the gray light of pre-dawn, Nevius loomed over her with a cup of chav in his left hand and the whiskey bottle in his right. He extended his left to her. As she clasped the steaming mug between her numb fingers, she thanked him. Pausing for a moment, she closed her eyes and cast about inside herself, trying to catch a sense of intrusion. If he was there, he wasn't stirring.

Nevius had already hoisted the foresail while she slept beneath it. He looked about him and grinned broadly. "It's going to be a beautiful day. The wind's shifted to the north, so we won't have to tack all the way back; we can run before it. We'll be home soon."

Sand swallowed a large gulp of the hot liquid in an effort to wake up her brain. She had to do something or by noon they'd be sailing back into port. As soon as Nevius took one drink from the bottle, he was going to realize it tasted off and she'd never again catch him that way. She'd be in disgrace, she'd have accomplished nothing, and her people on Strandia would still drown.

Even as she debated confessing everything to Nevius and pleading for his help again, something happened. On the eastern horizon, a sail appeared, glazed with peach-colored light. Nevius saw it and startled her by cheering. She turned, splashing some of her chav on the deck, and stared at the distant square.

196

Thinking feverishly, Sand suddenly cried, "A toast to good luck! Drink up, Captain!" She clinked her mug against Nevius's whiskey bottle, which he uncorked and put to his lips. He tipped his head back.

Sand counted four swallows before she leaped up and grabbed him, shouting, "Nevius, stop! That's enough!"

Interrupted, he choked. "What?" He looked around in alarm.

Gently prying the bottle from his hand, she said, "We're not home yet. A toast is one thing—let's not celebrate too energetically."

He scowled at her. Then, running his tongue around his mouth experimentally, he scowled at the bottle. "All right; if you're so eager, let's be sailing."

She climbed to the yard and untied the mainsail. All the time, however, she kept her eyes on the captain. She had already started down the rigging when he began to reel below her, clinging to the downhauls to stay upright.

She hurried to his side. "Captain, what's wrong?"

His blotched face regarded her vaguely. "I don't know. I don't feel myself."

"Why don't you lie down till the dizziness passes. I don't want to have to rescue you from a fall overboard."

She got him installed in her hammock and brought him some fresh water; he fell asleep while drinking it. Hoping he'd had enough to dilute the large dose of sleeping draught he'd consumed, and hoping still more that he hadn't had enough to poison himself, she set about doing what she had to.

First of all she bound him in the hammock like a fly in a spider's web. "Sorry," she addressed his unconscious form. "But I can't have you surprising me again."

Then she finished setting the mainsail and resolutely turned the ship back out toward the open sea. She glanced over her shoulder. They hadn't gained on her much, but they were definitely closer.

She set herself to outrunning them with every ounce of determination she possessed. All day she sailed directly out to sea, hoping to frighten them by getting so far from port. But they dogged her course determinedly, and being more experienced sailors, by night they had halved the distance between them.

Sand slipped into the galley at dusk for more chav and biscuits. She dug her packet of cheese out of her sack. Though it was greasy from the heat, it still tasted good. Going forward, she forced the still-unconscious captain to swallow another gulp of his drugged liquor.

She continued sailing on into the night. The breeze held steady and light until late. Finally it became fitful and died. Many times during the night she strained her eyes to see if the other ship still followed through the dark. The last time she tried, however, she discovered a solid gray wall rolling toward her.

A moment later the fog covered the boat. Since she couldn't even see the length of her own ship from bow to stern, she felt it would be safe to light the small lamp hanging on the mast.

Everything became eerily still. The water quieted beneath the ship. Above her the sails hung limp. Within minutes a cold, dank sweat hung from every surface, beading the ropes, oozing from the wood. The lamp pressed with feeble hands against the encroaching mist.

The silence was so complete that Sand's ears started to ache with listening. She scraped a foot against the wooden deck, just to make a noise and reassure herself that she hadn't gone deaf. Then she heard another sound: a clatter of something dropped on wood. After that, a slow, periodic splashing. She decided to douse the light. Surely, she prayed, with the fog to cover her, they would pass right by. In the morning she would elude them somehow.

But her invader finally made himself obtrusive. He wouldn't let her move. If she'd been turned to stone, she couldn't have been more effectively frozen. And while she continued with her inward struggle, the other ship crept nearer and nearer, over the glassy sea. Finally they were so close that she could see the fog begin to stir ahead of their passage. The voices were clear and distinct, though she couldn't catch all the words.

She no longer thought to escape them, but she didn't want them ramming the *Sea Swallow* by accident. She fought to cry out a warning, but her tongue was a broken clapper in the bell of her mouth. She struggled to throw off this supernatural grip that held her. The ghostly outline of a ship slid into view.

A voice on the ship called out a quick succession of orders, and the ship did a neat quarter turn and nestled up to the *Swallow* as gently as a wing to the body of a bird. In a moment the two ships were grappled together. Men leaped across the gunwales onto the *Swallow*'s deck, and moments later a cry heralded the discovery of Nevius.

She shivered as she saw a tall figure haul himself over the taffrail. Renellus made his way quickly forward. She hadn't guessed that he would be with the pursuers. Several men surrounded her quickly and held her tightly. And then the intruder released her.

She stood perfectly still, perfectly silent, watching the activity obliquely but not meeting anyone's eyes. One of the crew took the wheel, pushing her out of the way to do it.

Renellus spent a long time over Nevius's slumbering form. Finally he came aft and said, "Let her go. Sand, get your things."

"I just—"

"Get your things." His voice became even quieter. It terrified her. She hurried to comply. Renellus, who had never looked at her with anything but tenderness, had just regarded her as if she were some revolting species of squid.

Before he did anything else, he rummaged through her sack and took away the medicines she'd stolen from him. Her cheeks burned and she stared down at her hands.

"Let's go."

On the foredeck of the other ship Petrius sat with two men she didn't recognize. Renellus led her forward toward the small group. Petrius looked carefully away from her, embarrassed. An older man looked travel-stained and very weary. But the third man met her eyes sheepishly. Instantly she identified her invader.

Perhaps I wouldn't have been so frightened if I had seen him, she thought.

Physically he was small, though petit would be even more accurate. His clothes, though just as dusty as his companion's, were worn with a certain style. Finally, he was lovely. From his tangle of dark curls, past his thick eyelashes to his delicate, chiseled jaw, every feature was perfect, creating an entrancing whole.

Renellus seated himself on a closed hatch and watched the activity on the deck of the other ship.

Petrius began, "This is Sand. Sand, this is Andronius, an anthropologist from the university and an old friend of mine." The older man inclined his head in acknowledgment, his jet-black eyes drinking in every detail of her. Petrius laid a hand on the younger man's shoulder and massaged the muscle there with his thumb. "And this is Lucius."

The young man gave her a wry smile. "We've already met in a way, and I already owe you an apology. It wasn't a very good first impression. I beg your forgiveness."

His bright self-possession and physical beauty contrasted

with her shame and heightened her self-consciousness. "Please don't think about it. I'm sorry, too, for . . . uh . . ."

"For stealing a ship, drugging a man, and leading us on an awful chase before we even had time to wash the road dust from our skin." He ran a finely boned hand through his hair and grinned at the others. "You see? A minor transgression. She didn't mean to do it. She's very sorry. She'll make sure it doesn't happen again."

Renellus scowled and moved away.

"Well, I *am* sorry," she called after him softly, wishing Lucius and his pertness to the bottom of the sea. She turned back to the other three and waited. Finally she asked, "Well, what next?"

"Sleep for you first," Lucius announced. "Then, when you're rested, we're going to fix your brain. And then you take us home to this island that we're all so fascinated by."

She ground her teeth quietly. His manner irritated her.

At the mention of Strandia, Andronius brightened. "I can't tell you how much I'm looking forward to this. Vindication of my theories after all these years! When Petrius's message first arrived in the city I could scarcely believe it. I immediately began using all my influence to get Lucius—our most gifted telepath—to be assigned to this project."

Lucius ducked his head—an overtly modest gesture, which he then spoiled by giving Sand a brilliant, mischievous smile.

Andronius continued: "The university is such a ponderous institution—really, you can't imagine how difficult it was to get them to move with anything resembling speed. But finally they agreed to release Lucius from the research he was involved with. But the deliberation! The days wasted! I had to point out to them the dreadful irony of my position. My theories confirmed after thirty years, only to have the evidence scoured from the face of the earth a

201

month or two later, unless we did something. Dreadful!"

Sand wanted to yell at him, but she kept her voice quiet, her mouth set. "This is about saving lives, not proving theories. Excuse me." She stalked away from them. Lucius said something she didn't catch and the other two chuckled. Seething, she wrapped herself in a blanket and tumbled into a hammock. She retreated like a snail into the shell of her sleep.

She slept through the whole next day, oblivious to the life of the ship going on around her. When she awoke, the ship was sailing through the night once more and stars sparkled above.

She lay still, rocking in the hammock, watching the stars for a long time. Then she became aware of breathing close by. She turned her head and found Petrius sitting nearby, his back against the mast. She saw his teeth flash white in the starlight. "I love watching them, too. That's why I became a starwatcher. We know so little about them."

"Why would you want to know more? Isn't it enough just to see how lovely they are?"

"But we would never have known to warn people about the traveling star had we not been watching and wondering and making notes all these years."

Sand had to agree that this had its applications.

"Even when the information is not particularly practical, it's still fascinating. For instance, you see that broad band of smoky light across the sky where the stars are clustered so thickly? Well, we see it like that because this world is on the edge of a massive group of stars in a big, flat swirl. Because we're on the edge, when we look straight in toward the center, we see as many stars as there are grains of sand on the beach, all bunched together in the sky. A lot of them are so far away you can't see them really, but there are so many they look like a cloud. You see? Isn't that fascinating?"

Sand agreed and yawned, stretching as much as the hammock would allow her. "But I find the story we tell at home about those stars just as fascinating," she amended, "so perhaps my opinion isn't worth much."

"And what story do you tell at home?"

"Are you sure you want to hear it? What if you like mine better than yours?" she teased.

He laughed. "We truly know so little about the stars, compared to what there is to know, that if your story made more sense to me than the one I just told you, I might tell it in the city as a new theory."

"First you must understand how all this began." Sand settled back and kept watching the night sky above her as she talked. Her voice took on a resonant timbre. "In the beginning there was only the sun and the sea. The sun was Raza, Father to all the life that swam in the belly of the Mother. For uncounted ages they existed alone together. But then the spark of a new being appeared beyond the sky, growing closer and larger and more beautiful, until he eclipsed even the beauty of the sun . . ." And when the old tale of the Sea Mother scorned had been told, Sand continued: "There was once a fish that glowed pure as a pearl, and rode the waves of the Sea Mother in clusters like studded jewels about the girth of her vast belly. Lacmara it was called, and rightly so, for it was truly the milk of the sea. The meat of the lacmara was sweet and tender, and it swam in such numbers that the boats of the sons of Bedjar and Calleby would balk in the path of its passing."

She was interrupted by Lucius's dropping down beside them on the deck and laying his head against Petrius's shoulder. She paused, but he commanded, "Don't let me disturb you." A moment later he shot to his feet and disappeared toward the stern.

"But one day the Sea Mother felt the echo of Kryphon

and waves of hope swelled within her, smoothing the rough memories of his betrayal into pebbles of renewed longing. She plucked up the vast girdle of her precious lacmara and flung it high into the blackness of the sky as a beacon of her longing. And that teeming swath of lacmara swims even now across the night sky, a sparkling ribbon of hope for all who seek the amorous attention of scoundrels."

After a moment's silence Petrius said, "I like it. But I don't think I'll set it forth as a new theory in the city." He caught sight of Andronius advancing with Lucius in his wake. "I have no doubt that the city will hear of it, however."

Andronius was upon them. "You've been telling stories of your people! You must repeat them."

Obligingly she began, but he interrupted so many times: to question her, to get a torch to write by, and finally, just laboriously writing it all down, that long before she was finished she was heartily sick of him.

Even when she was done, the three men were not. They argued back and forth among themselves. Andronius seemed passionately concerned with what she'd told him, but the two young men winked at Sand when he wasn't looking. Disgusted she realized that they were arguing with him for the fun of watching his reaction.

"I tell you it's a quaint, primitive folktale, but it has its basis in fact. It will make my reputation in the college for generations!"

Lucius, with another wink at Sand, replied, "I hardly think that telling the College of Starwatchers that what they have observed to be millions of stars are actually white fish is going to enhance your reputation in any desirable way."

"Not that part, you young fool! But this interloping god, this Kryphon—don't you see, it's obviously the wandering star! It fits perfectly: the advancing and retreating, the upheaval of the sea and the destruction that follows. A perfectly charming tale," he asserted, flipping through his notes once more.

Sand tipped herself out of the hammock and went forward, seeking a place of solitude, away from these men who tore the delicate fabric of her myth and belief with every heavy-handed word. She crept out onto the bowsprit and lay full length on it. From here, the sound of their voices was just a murmur becoming one with the hiss of the waves beneath the bows and the creaking of rope and wood.

Here Renellus found her hours later, still staring out toward the black horizon and whatever destiny awaited them.

Chapter Seventeen

Lucius swept down on her the next morning as she lifted her mug of chav to her lips.

"No, no. Absolutely not." He extracted the mug from her fingers untasted. "No stimulants this morning. Who knows what queer baggage I'll be tripping over in your head, O sea child. I don't need any added distractions."

He pulled her to her feet and forward on the deck. "I wish we had somewhere more private, but this is the best we can do. Now what's the matter?"

She hadn't quite managed to hide a certain sulkiness. "Last night . . ."

"Oh, last night! I'm sorry," he apologized smoothly. "But Petrius is a great audience. He encourages me to a shocking degree. And old Andronius is just too sincere—I have to tweak him now and again."

She glared at him.

He sighed in mock misery. "No one understands me." Taking both her hands in his, he began, "Close your eyes. Now relax and let me in."

Once more she felt the disagreeable sensation of him walking through the rooms in her mind, opening cupboards, sifting through chests. "Aha! Here I am."

And now he stood before her. But openly this time, rather than hiding in the shadows where she couldn't see him. She peered at him inwardly, and the harder she looked, the clearer he became. They stood in a gray place, with gray mist surrounding them to their knees.

"Sand, is there a particular place where you often used this talent of yours?"

She thought of Monarri's cove and nodded.

"I want you to picture us standing in a place near there but not right in that place."

She visualized them in the clearing around Monarri's cottage. She looked around it with a heart so full of emotion at being on her island again that tears trickled down her cheeks. Renellus, silently observing the pair on the foredeck, noted the tears with concern.

Lucius was examining the clearing. "Your power of visualization is astounding!" For the first time since she'd met him his tone held no edge of mockery. "I've never seen anyone create an inner place so clearly."

"I don't make it. I only remember it."

"But most people don't remember things with such clarity. This is unusual."

"I have to remember things clearly or I can't show them to M'ridan," she told him abstractedly. Meanwhile, she was examining the glade with consternation. The building looked the same: neither more nor less rickety than the last time she'd seen it. But the path to the cove was completely overgrown. A fallen tree and a riot of creepers and vines blocked the way. She turned to Lucius in alarm. "I can't get to the cove. Something's happened to Monarri! This would never have been allowed to happen while she was living here!"

207

"No, no. Calm yourself. Remember this is not truly your island: it's only your vision of it. I would guess that there's something through there"—he indicated the overgrown barricade—"that you're afraid of. In other words, you want to get to the place where you can use your talent, but you stop yourself because there's something you're afraid of."

Sand wrinkled her forehead, trying to understand. "So what do we do?"

"We remove the obstructions, of course. You lead the way."

She showed him where the path should have led out of the clearing toward the sea. Indicating the tangled vines, he said, "You first."

Sand grabbed one of the vines. She was suddenly overwhelmed with the memory of Berran, mixed with reluctance and sadness. She let the vine slip from her hand.

"What's wrong?"

She tried to explain what had just happened.

"Good. Now this is what you're going to do. Grab on to the vine. Use both hands." As she did so, Berran appeared again. She tried not to look at him scowling at her. Lucius continued: "Try to break the vine."

She strained, but it was as tough as mooring rope.

"Now observe your friend. How does he look?"

Sand searched her mind for the right word. "Forbidding."

Lucius nodded. "All right. You have to change his look to welcoming. You have to concentrate on how glad he's going to be to see you, how relieved he'll be that you're not dead. And anything else you can think of."

Sand remembered the feel of his arms around her. The look in his eyes sometimes when he watched her in Jinny's home. The sound of his voice when they made plans to meet at the festival.

Lucius watched the play of emotion on her face. "Pull now!"

She did, and the vine fell apart in her hand like cooked spinach.

She smiled at Lucius triumphantly, but he just motioned her to pick up the next vine. When she did, the two priests Alesk and Rainis appeared.

"What are you afraid of?"

She whispered, "What's to stop them from sending me to sea again?" She thought of the deep black water sucking at her and shuddered.

Lucius reasoned with her. "They promised that if you returned alive you would be exonerated, right?" She nodded slowly. "Then break it."

The vine fell apart. They continued at this for hours. Some of the vines were mere tendrils and Sand could break those with barely a moment's consideration. Others were as thick as her forearm and Lucius had to talk her through those fears.

Finally they came to a huge bael-nut tree fallen across the pathway. Lucius's shoulders slumped. "I can't do that today, Sand. I've had it."

She chuckled. "That belongs here. The people who live here just can't be bothered with cutting it up." She stepped lightly over it.

He smiled wearily. "What a relief. But in any case, I've had enough."

"So what now?"

"Just let go of this place. We'll come back tomorrow."

He disappeared and Sand was left on her own. The glade behind her looked just as it had when they arrived. Although they had been there for hours, the light was still the light of mid-afternoon. Alone now, Sand realized there were no sounds. The leaves didn't rustle, the distant surf couldn't be heard or felt through the core of the island. No birds sang, no insects buzzed. All was silent and still. Sand let go of the construct, returning to the ship.

Renellus hovered anxiously over both of them, worried because Sand hadn't yet opened her eyes, more worried because Lucius had, but looked very ill.

Lucius lay back on the deck, drawn and pale, with his eyes shut. Once he was satisfied that Sand was all right, the doctor chafed the young man's wrists, pinched his earlobes, and loosened the neck of his shirt. In this instance, however, Sand was better equipped to deal with the problem. "We call this seef-tharl. Talent-weakness. He needs to be kept warm and fed. Start with some thick, sweetened chav and get me some blankets for him."

She lay down beside the supine form and nestled up close, sharing her warmth. While the doctor dosed the hot drink, Petrius borrowed bedclothes from several sailors. He laid them over their bodies and then snuggled in underneath on the opposite side to Sand. By the time Renellus returned, Lucius felt able to sit up supported by his friend's arm.

Renellus crouched beside them and offered the mug. "What brought that on?"

Lucius shrugged. "Sitting here all day concentrating with no food. Expending my energy in great lumps, trying to keep up with this rogue talent." He smiled at Sand.

"We should have stopped sooner."

"We haven't got much time. I was trying to get as far as I could today." He shook his head and said no more.

Next morning, having supped and breakfasted well with lots of sleep in between, Lucius felt ready to continue. "You should rest today," Sand warned him, looking at the black circles in the delicate skin under his eyes.

"I know. We can't afford to. We haven't got time."

Sand raised her eyebrows.

"The dear doctor is trying to keep it from you, but this is

the last day we've got to go blindly hunting. The ships are equipped with food and water for five days more. We're five days out from shore already."

Sand stared at him.

"We may have to turn back, even if you do regain your talent," he continued. "If we're too far from your island, the ships will have to get supplies before going on."

"We can't!" she protested. "We'll never be there in time to warn them and get everyone organized."

"Nevertheless, that's what will happen. The sailors are nervous enough already. Some of them would welcome the chance to go back and stay there. They've had time to think twice about going to a strange place since they've been out here. They didn't have the opportunity to consider it carefully before we left. Everyone was in such hot pursuit of the stolen brig. You're lucky the boats are provisioned as well as they are."

Sand flushed.

"Do we get to work now?"

She nodded, not meeting his eyes.

Renellus had instructions to stop them during the day at several points and make sure they ate and rested.

With the news that Lucius had just imparted, Sand was eager to begin. They had barely closed their eyes when she stood in the clearing. Lucius appeared a moment later, looking cross. "Not so fast! Your head is not the easiest place to find my way around in."

Sand was staring at the path in dismay. The vines had grown back overnight on the portion they'd cleared yesterday. It wasn't as choked as it had been, but the green tendrils snaked everywhere.

Lucius shrugged. "No worse than I expected."

"What happened?"

"You've been living with these fears for months without

211

even knowing it. They've become part of the fabric of your mind. Just because you reasoned yourself out of them yesterday doesn't mean they loosed their stranglehold on your subconscious."

Sand felt herself begin to shake with rage and frustration. "We can't go through this again."

"We have to."

"No, we don't."

"Have you got another plan?"

"Stand back." She began to swing her arms back and forth. "What . . ."

Sand collected her frustration and shaped it once again into the swift-winged hawk that had carried her partway across the ocean. With a shriek and a thunderous clap of wings she launched into the air.

"Stop!" she heard Lucius cry. "You don't know what you're doing."

Beating her wings, she rose swiftly above the choked forest. For one second she thought she saw the blue sparkle of the sea ahead; then a huge cloud enveloped her. It felt as though she was trying to fly through wet whisprain fiber. The thick air clung to her feathers and clogged her wingbeats. She shrieked again. The sound was absorbed by the clouds. Her anger reached a new pitch. She grappled this amorphous enemy with her will. Concentrating till she felt a red-hot wire searing behind her eyes, she blasted the fog around her.

"Clear! You will disappear! I don't care what terrors you hold. I'm not afraid of you or of anything. I *must* get home. You're the only thing stopping me. Now *clear*!"

As she battered the clouds with words and will and wings, she felt the oppression lighten a little. With that encouragement, she redoubled her efforts. The hot wire became a red glow filling her vision and the fog began to evaporate, rolling away in the air currents stirred up by her beating wings.

A few moments later, when the world was only a scorching molten curtain flowing before her eyes, she saw the sea sparkle below.

Sand didn't know whether she had gained her objective or not. She knew she was rapidly exhausting her resources. Flailing, she wondered what she should do now.

The moment she hesitated, the fog swirled closer to her again. As it began to obscure the opening below her that showed the sea, she thought she saw something dark break the surface. And then . . .

"Little mudball."

She hugged her wings to her body and plummeted out of the sky.

*   *   *

Anxiety consumed the doctor. As Sand and Lucius began their inner journey, the doctor sat down nearby. He studied their faces. Today he was determined to allow no mishaps. But almost immediately he saw fear settle on Lucius's features. Uncertain, Renellus moved closer, wondering whether to rouse them. While he hesitated, Lucius stiffened and cried out. The first word was "Stop," but the string that came after was unintelligible.

Several of the sailors turned at the outcry, but seeing the motionless tableau they carried on with what they'd been doing.

The doctor knelt, frozen, wondering whether he should try to wake them. A moment later Lucius relieved him of the decision by opening his eyes. He stared at Sand and moved forward as if to rouse her—then stopped short of touching her.

"What is it?"

Lucius turned his distraught face toward the doctor and shook his head. Leaping to his feet, he began to pace back and forth, watching her the whole time. As he walked, he gnawed on the side of one thumb.

Renellus grabbed him and spun him around. "By the gods, what's wrong?"

"Shh! I don't know. Maybe nothing. Maybe everything. Her mind is strange to me. I wouldn't attempt what she's doing right now, but perhaps she's been trained in this. In any case, I think it would be more dangerous to rouse her than to leave her."

They hung over Sand, watching every shade of expression that flitted over her face. Concentration shaded to effort, effort to stress, stress to anguish, and then—

And then her eyes flew open, though she obviously saw nothing. In one swift movement she sprang to the side of the ship and launched herself in a crisp, sweet arc over the gunwales and into the ocean.

Pandemonium broke out. All hands rushed to the side of the ship, heeling the boat over. The captain bellowed at them to return to their posts.

They loosed lines and threw them over the side randomly. She had disappeared, so their aims were a mixture of guesswork and luck.

And then when the sailors had begun to shake their heads, they saw dark shapes flying underneath the surface of the water and one light shape among them.

In a precise ballet, six doraado, with Sand clinging to one of them, leaped from the water and breached, spraying the sailors where they crowded the side of the boat.

"It's them!" Tears mixed with the seawater on her face. "It's him." She clung to the doraado she rode as though she'd never be parted from him again.

A murmur of wonder rose from the same men who only

214

last night had been urging Renellus and the captain to turn back.

And when Sand was finally hauled back on board, unable to stand from weariness, there were many of them who wouldn't touch her to bring her in but who couldn't take their eyes from her either.

There was a gentle bump as the *Sea Swallow* came alongside and grappled with the other brig. Her crew were goggle-eyed, not wanting to miss anything, and they poured aboard, Nevius leading the way.

Renellus picked Sand up and carried her forward to the hammock. "No more bones than a strand of seaweed," he scolded.

"You must follow them." Her limbs were limp but her will was iron. "It's close."

"Don't fret." Lucius had the hammock lined with blankets and Renellus laid her in them. He shook his head at her. "You always go too far."

The corners of her mouth turned up slightly and she murmured, "Nothing happens unless someone makes it happen." Her eyes closed and she passed out.

The sailors hung about in a respectful semicircle. When they saw her lose consciousness, another mutter ran around the deck and in a moment every man was voicing his opinion.

"We must turn back!"

"The luck of the ship is dead!"

"No, no. We must follow the doraan!"

The captain leaped onto the nearest hatch cover and bellowed for them all to shut up on pain of whipping.

Lucius meanwhile thrust his way through the gathered knot of men to the side of the ship. Below him the dolphins lay sideways in the water, grinning at him. He reached out tentatively toward them, feeling for intelligence at a distance,

215

as he had done when he pursued Sand. There. Something, though very unfamiliar.

And then in his mind there was a vision of himself standing at the edge of the ship, as seen from the water below.

He, in turn, sent back a vision of the doraan in the water.

He received a picture of the ships following the doraan, and then another clear picture of a shore lined with trees.

Thinking for a moment, he sent pictures of the sun and night sky, one after the other, several times. Then he added the feeling of a question.

Three suns blazed in his mind at once, and he raised both arms in salute to the doraan before he turned away.

The argument still raged hotly as he pushed his way to the captain's side.

"We have our guides," Lucius shouted. "We're three days from Sand's island."

Argument broke out again. Some shouted that in three days they might be caught in a storm and swept off course with no provisions. Others shouted that it was clearly their duty to follow the dolphins.

Suddenly Nevius shoved his way through the crowd. "I've never heard such sheep-mouthed bleating in all my life," he ranted at them. "This girl has got more courage in her eyelashes than you dogs have in your backbones. You want to slink back to shore? Well, I say good riddance to any so-called man who hasn't the guts to follow where this girl has the heart to lead. My boat will take her and any true men from this company, and the rest of you cowards can just sneak home."

The men before him dropped their eyes, looking anywhere except at him, and by ones and twos they slipped back to their tasks. A moment later the foredeck was empty except for the two captains, the unconscious Sand, the doctor, and the three men from the city.

216

Nevius beamed at them. "There. There's no use trying to reason with that bunch," he explained in a confidential bellow to Lucius. "They sail with their bellies, not their brains. You just have to cram some metal down their throats to stiffen their spines. They'll be all right now." He slapped the other captain heartily on the back and vaulted over the taffrail to his own ship.

Andronius was fumbling with his notebook. "Did any of you notice which sailor made the reference to the luck of the ship? These seamen retain some charming superstitions. I wonder if it's because they live so close to the elements." He tapped his front teeth absently with the end of his charcoal, blackening them.

Renellus and Lucius conferred over how to treat Sand. The captain took the helm again, muttering about mutiny. And Petrius went forward to watch the doraan charting their course in sea foam.

Chapter Eighteen

When Sand opened her eyes she could hear breakers crashing on reefs. She thought she caught a whiff of bael-nut blossom. She felt suffused with well-being and the knowledge that she had something to be very happy about. And then she remembered M'ridan.

The night sky above her glistened with stars, clear and bright. They paled toward the east, where Kryphon burned. Lifting her hand, Sand saw the shadow the wandering star cast on her blankets.

Laboriously she wriggled out of her cocoon. She crept to the taffrail and looked out toward the sound of the surf. She saw white breakers in the starlight, curling over the reefs to settle in the lagoon. Turning around, she stifled a cry. Off the other side of the boat, limned in starlight, lay Strandia. Tears blurred her vision and she leaned against the rail for support.

Renellus, hearing the noise, hurried forward. Putting his arms around her, he hugged her tightly. "Thank the gods. You're all right?"

She nodded.

"We sailed in after dark. It was perfect. There was a light breeze blowing, we could see the doraan and the reef clearly in the starlight and they led us in, neat as could be. We dropped anchor only about an hour ago."

"How long?"

"We've been sailing steadily since you found the doraan: three days."

She stood up on shaky legs. "I want to bathe."

"In the morning."

"Now. Not in the morning with everyone looking. I'll be fine."

She peeled off her tunic and, climbing onto the bowsprit, slipped down to hang from it and then dropped into the water.

Renellus's anxious face appeared over the edge of the boat above her. Treading water lightly, she waved to him.

Then, tremulously, she closed her eyes and sent out her call over the water: "M'ridan." Immediately he surfaced underneath her, so she felt the whole soft length of him. She laid her cheek on top of his head and cupped his chin in her palm. "I can hardly believe we are here again."

"I missed you, mudball."

"Where were you?"

"Never very far. I could feel you but I couldn't hear you. One morning I felt you on the ocean again, and I knew we would be together soon."

"M'ridan, you saved my life."

He butted her under her chin with his snout. Then, without warning, he ducked her under the water. She came up sputtering and heard him squeaking at her.

"Too serious. Being away from me so long has not improved you. You're too solemn."

With that criticism, he began to swim, turning like a corkscrew as he did, so that she was alternately under and above the water faster than she could keep track of. She began to giggle, swallowing some water in the process, and choked it up, still laughing. M'ridan finished his performance by leaping in the air, doing a half twist, and landing with her underneath him.

She released him and struggled to the surface, gasping for air. He slid underneath her and boosted her back into her own element.

Shaking the wet hair from her eyes, she saw the doctor poised at the side of the ship.

"I'm fine," she called, still giggling.

"Then keep it quiet," he snapped in relief. "Other people are sleeping."

She leaned down and breathed gently on M'ridan's blowhole.

He splashed her with a lazy flip of his tail flukes. "Better."

After more gentle play she climbed back up on board. Leaning on the rail, she watched M'ridan's fin appearing and disappearing as he sliced through Kryphon's bright reflection lying in a band across the sea. Feeling as boneless as a jellyfish, she crawled back into her blankets and slept again immediately.

She woke at dawn with the rest of the crew and watched the shore with uncomfortable amusement as the islanders discovered the two ships anchored in the lagoon. The beach began to fill with people jostling at the water's edge for a good view. Sand watched them, her heart full of strange feelings. Jinny was probably there, and Daulo. Berran too.

Andronius appeared at her elbow. "Who is that?"

A boat was pulling away from the temple beach with four figures in it.

"The two rowing will be novices. The two in the white robes are priests in the service of the Sea Mother."

"This is wonderful. Wonderful." He vibrated with excitement. "You must promise to translate every word for me."

Andronius's words gave her a shock. She'd forgotten that she was the only one who could speak the language. She realized she'd been counting on hanging back during this coming meeting and then making her way to Jinny's house later, unannounced.

As the boat drew nearer, her misery increased. Sitting stiffly in the boat were the same two priests who had sentenced her to judgment. When they were within hailing distance she gathered her resolution and croaked out, "Good morning."

The older priest, Alesk, recognized her first, despite her odd clothes and longer hair. Sand felt some of her tension melt away as he smiled widely.

"It's the raeth daughter."

The younger one, Rainis, added, "The pretender."

She shook her head. "*Not* a pretender. That will become clear."

Alesk said, "I'm glad to see you back again, raeth child. I've spent many uneasy nights since we set you adrift in that storm. I don't care if you'd had the talent of Calleby herself, I doubt that you could have compelled the providers to bring you back through that."

Scandalized, the younger priest croaked out a protest. Sand heard the words "Will of the Mother!"

At ease now, Sand said smoothly, "I think, when you've heard what these men with me have to say, you'll agree it was the Will of the Mother. Won't you come aboard?"

"Is it safe?" one of the novices asked, looking at all the unshaven sailors peering back at them.

Sand smiled wickedly. "What motive could I possibly have for harming the servants of the Mother who exiled me?" Rainis glanced nervously at Alesk and then back at the distant bulk of the temple.

Alesk didn't hesitate, however. Grasping the dangling ladder, he climbed swiftly and elegantly aboard, despite his flowing robes.

Andronius was poking her in the ribs with his sheaf of notes. "What's happening?" She shot Petrius an imploring glance, and he deflected the anthropologist from her side.

For the next two hours she translated back and forth as Renellus and Petrius explained their mission and the priests struggled to understand. She extended their offer of the ships, and explained that they must go deep enough into the ocean to survive the waves which would sweep the island.

The priests heard them out politely, asking questions but not committing themselves. In fact, to Sand's consternation, they didn't seem to take the threat seriously enough. They seemed more worried about the two large boats in their water, and would any more be coming?

Finally Alesk stood up and courteously excused himself and his companion. "We will certainly think about this surprising news you have brought. The Mother will tell us how to respond in her own time." He looked around him from one silent face to another. "You have come a long way to bring us these messages and deserve what comforts we can provide you. Sand-bel-Anemone, we will make arrangements for these boats to anchor along that shore with the raeths. These boats must have fresh water and bael nuts. Please tell them to feel free to fish these waters as well."

Sand was speechless for a moment. "I will not tell them that. It's more of an insult than anything else. Of course they're welcome to fish these waters! They've come to save Strandian lives and you think you're doing them a big favor by letting them replenish their stores?" She shook her head.

The younger priest, with his ready temper, flared at her.

"You forget yourself already, raeth daughter. You, who were sent to the Mother for judgment and have returned in a most questionable fashion, cannot expect us to leap to action at your least word. You do not recognize authority, but fortunately the rest of Strandia does. We shall retire to the temple and discuss your tale with the others and ask the Mother for guidance. And when she gives us her answer, we shall know how to respond to this tale you bring."

Alesk had tried to dam the flow of the younger man's words, but had finally given up. Now he apologized. "My colleague is hasty. But whether it is couched in polite words or presented bluntly, he has told you the truth. We must confer with the others and wait for the Mother's word."

Sand bit back the first retort that rose to her lips. She said coolly, "Your thanks are acknowledged. I hope the Mother gives you her answer before she rises up and sweeps you all back into her womb. She is nothing if not impulsive."

She turned away to find Lucius translating the last staccato interchange for the others. Realizing that he must have plucked the meaning of their words from her mind, her temper fragmented. Stepping close to him, she hissed, "Do me a favor. Stay out of my mind from now on until you're invited."

Alesk remembered something before he descended the ladder. "Sand-bel-Anemone!"

She turned to see him fumbling at the neck of his robe. He pulled on a leather thong and drew out Berran's carved doraado.

He dropped it into her cupped hands. Its polished sides released the heat they'd stolen from him into her cool fingers. "I promised I'd keep it for your return. I was afraid we had been the end of you, but a promise must be kept."

He laid a hand on her shoulder and pressed it gently. With the movement of his robes the air brought her a faint scent of the sweet-briny meltara cakes. As the warmth of his hand lingered and the breeze touched her and moved away, she felt suddenly, overwhelmingly, that she'd come home.

The priests receded over the water till the dot that was their boat merged with the shore. Now she longed to be there, too, and was in a fever of impatience at the thought of all she had to do before she was free.

"Captains, it's been suggested that we move to more permanent anchorage." She guided them to the little wild islands that guarded the lagoon of Strandia, and everyone spent the rest of the day hard at work. The more she longed to be in Midisle, the more jobs she found that had to be done first.

She took two sailors and a bundle of water skins to shore in the dory. She showed them how to cut the lactus reeds and collect the water within. This took a long time. Finally they rowed back to the ship, where everything was now in confusion. Every idle hand had been put to work mending the sheets and sails. Nevius and the other captain were deep in conversation. When they saw her climb over the side, they turned to her for an answer. Nevius cleared his throat. "We'd like to catch some fresh fish but we're not sure of the protocol here. Should we go outside the reef to fish, or are we allowed to catch some here?"

Sand, with one half of her mind caught up in the fantasy of standing once more on Strandia, turned to this new distraction with a sigh. Her eyes glittered. "You need fish? I'll show you how the raeth of Strandia fish. Lower your nets . . . No, no. Don't weigh anchor—do it right here. Then just tell the men to wait."

Nevius looked at her askance and the other captain looked frankly dubious, but they told their men to drop the nets over the side. Meanwhile, Sand moved to the rail. Closing her eyes, she explored her talent like a recent invalid rising for the first time. Dizziness swept over her, initially. But soon she began to work by habit and instinct, as the search began to feel more familiar.

Not far away, a small group of young doraado paused in their lazy game of leapfrog and turned toward this source of discomfort. Hunger assailed them, paired with acute distress.

Quickly they turned and sought out schools of fish. Driving the fish before them, they herded them toward the hunger. Meanwhile, they sent back reassurances: food was coming.

On deck the men saw the doraado occasionally break the surface as they swam closer. Now and then a soft word broke the silence of their waiting. Nevius, catching one comment, stepped to her side. "Sand, you know we don't eat the doraan."

Still concentrating, she didn't answer him, but she shot him a look of such scorn that his weatherbeaten cheeks burned with color. Stung, he defended himself. "They were worried you might not know."

She closed her eyes and projected harder.

A moment later the men began shouting and the boat swayed beneath her as they hauled the nets from the water and poured the silver treasure they contained onto the deck. The men fell silent and looked from their catch to her and back again. The few that were closest to her sidled away.

She waited for some word of thanks, some acknowledgment of her talent, but no one spoke. Her only acknowledgment would be their silence. Loudly she said, "Keep only what you need for right now. Put the rest back. The Mother is always bountiful." She bent and picked out several fish. One by one she tossed them down to the waiting doraado, sending her ritual thanks with them. She turned to Renellus and Nevius. Laying a hand on each of their shoulders, she said simply, "I must go for a time. I'll be back before morning. Your men are welcome to use the small islands, but keep them off the raeth's private beaches."

She moved to the bow and walked light and cat-footed out onto the polished bowsprit. Silhouetted against the hazy horizon, she paused. Then she dove.

Minutes later the watching crew saw a dolphin join up with her, and riding him, she disappeared behind the tiny islands.

Lucius turned to Petrius and murmured, "If her talent for the dramatic is as impressive to the Strandians as it is to this crew, we'll have them flocking to join us, priests or not."

❂   ❂   ❂

Sand and M'ridan took their time rounding Strandia. Every curve of the shore, every outlined tree against the sky wrung her heart with bittersweet pleasure.

M'ridan took her to the point between Midisle and the temple, to the place they had met while she lived with Jinny. As he boosted her up onto the rocks, he spoke to her in an unusually serious vein. "Be careful, mudball. I don't want to lose you again."

"You won't lose me. My name has been cleared. I'm free to walk the island." She sat and waited till the sun crept behind the horizon and the shelter of dusk fell around her. Then she climbed over the rocks to the Midisle beach. A handful of fishermen were still there, cleaning up their stalls after the market. A few latecomers picked out their dinners from the leftover wares.

She walked through them without looking to either side. People straightened as she passed and stared after her. Her strange clothing marked her as a stranger from the strange ships. She could feel the eyes on her back and it made her skin twitch.

When she moved onto the empty path to Jinny's house she felt numb. Nothing had changed. She had almost died, had fought for her life, and was now fighting for theirs. She felt years older than she had the last time she'd been on this road. She was a very different person, but this place was the same.

She began to shake as Jinny's house came into view. Her breath came in shorter and shorter gasps. Her stomach felt like a frantic caged bird. What am I afraid of? she wondered.

And then she stood before the cottage. Light streamed in a long band out the door, stretching right to her feet. She paused still, afraid to step onto that golden path. And as she hesitated, she heard Daulo's deep voice, Kemahl's childish piping, and Jinny's clear laugh ringing out.

Sorrow welled up in her. How long did it take Jinny to learn to laugh again after my exile? she wondered. A month? A week? A day? What a good thing the dead don't return, she thought. How could they bear to see that their passing made no impression, that the world continued just as sweet, just as awful without them? Had not Jinny longed for her, missed her, the way she had longed for Jinny?

She was about to turn and leave when Jinny's laugh spilled out again. Stepping determinedly onto the edge of the light, she followed it up the path and stood in the doorway.

Daulo sat with Kemahl on his lap, drying him after his bath. Jinny sat across the table, watching them, her face illuminated. They made a beautiful tableau, but Sand couldn't appreciate it.

Jinny stood up. Sand must have moved involuntarily, because Jinny's eyes were drawn suddenly to the doorway.

Sand saw the blood drain from her face, leaving even her lips pale and pinched. She gave a low moan and Daulo,

227

alarmed, followed her gaze to the door. He leaped to his feet, holding Kemahl to his chest.

Kemahl started to cry, and when Sand stepped across the threshold, the sound rose to a shriek of terror. Sand stopped and just looked at them. All desire for revenge had fled.

"Isn't anyone going to say 'Hello, Sand, welcome home'?" she asked. The trembling in her lower lip interfered with her speech.

"Sand? By the Sea Mother! Sand, is it really you?" Jinny stepped forward tentatively.

Sand waited, perfectly still. "Solid as this house."

Jinny touched her with one finger. And then, sure that this apparition was not some disembodied ghost, she wrapped her arms around her.

Speechless, they hugged for a long time. Even when they moved to the table, they continued to hold hands.

"Didn't the priests tell you I'd returned?"

"They went right from the shore to the temple and they've been closeted in there all day. There are a million rumors about what's going on, but you weren't part of any of them."

They began trading stories of what had happened, beginning with the account of the night of the Lactus Festival.

"Berran almost went crazy," Jinny concluded. "When Daulo forced him back to the island, he seemed a beaten man. Then he started openly defying the priests. He'd always been outspoken with the Midislanders, but now he became outspoken even with the raeth and the priests. They stopped blessing the boats he made. For months he's only been able to do carvings, because no one will fish in an unblessed boat."

A step was heard in the doorway. The four faces in the room turned toward the noise.

Berran stood there. "Came by for a cup of khar," he

explained as he stepped inside. His glance passed over Sand like the shadow of a cloud passing over the sea. He didn't recognize her immediately. Then slowly he returned his gaze to her.

"Berran," she greeted him.

At the sound of her voice he leaned a hand against the side of the door. He looked wildly at Jinny and Daulo. "Do you see her, too?"

Jinny's laughter bubbled up, spilling into the room, buoying them all up. "Of course. Did you think she was a ghost?"

Sand punched her playfully. "Why not? *You* thought so."

"I don't know what to think." He turned his eyes to Sand again and kept them on her as they talked long into the night. By the time Sand returned to the ships, she had truly begun to feel she had come home.

Berran walked her back to the shore in the dim blue light cast by Kryphon. "Why don't you stay at Jinny's?"

Sand shrugged. "Things have changed. They are a whole, healthy family and they're not used to me being there anymore."

"But you don't have to . . ." He hesitated. "You'd be welcome to stay with me."

She took his hand. "Berran, I thank you. But I feel my place right now is on the ships. I'm the reason these men have come here. I'm the only link they have with Strandia. They don't speak the language, they don't know us." She paused. "I have this silly fear that if I'm not there, we may wake up one morning and they'll be gone. I know in my head they wouldn't do it, but I'm afraid anyway."

"That's the only reason?"

"The only reason."

She felt his hand tense. "What about the doctor you lived with. Is he on the ship?"

She dropped his hand. "Berran, I've given you my only reason."

Chapter Nineteen

"The Sea Mother sent me a dream last night."

Alesk looked up. Little lines deepened between his brows. "The Sea Mother sends you a lot of dreams. You are certainly favored." His words were innocuous enough, but his voice was sharp with sarcasm.

"She rewards those who are worthy."

Alesk sighed.

"These foreigners are right. I saw it in my dream. The sea will wash over Strandia. We must work with the sailors and get our people out to sea."

"Rainis, I don't believe you. I don't know what you have in mind, but I suspect it's more of a scheme to enhance your own importance than to serve the island."

"May the Sea Mother punish you!" Rainis choked out.

Alesk waved a languid hand at him. "Rainis, I've lived on this island for sixty summers now. It's a good living. The sea provides us with all we need, but it's passive. I don't believe it's going to rise up and cover the island any more than it ever has. It's just not likely. The sea exists—that's all. Not a goddess. Just a body of water."

Rainis hunched his shoulders and glanced quickly out the window at the placid sea. "You mustn't say that! What about the blazing in the sky at night?"

Alesk lifted his shoulders in a weary shrug.

"How can you call yourself a priest of the Mother?"

"I don't anymore. I have been questioning for a long time. I felt I was a voice of reason and clarity among hotheads like you." His eyes rested briefly on Rainis. "But lately I've realized that you'll do what you want, no matter what I say. You'll do it under the guise of following the Mother's lead."

Rainis answered through clenched teeth. "It's no guise, unlike your priestly posturing. I do not betray the Mother. I merely serve her."

"Who knows, Rainis? In your pronouncements there is often more of your wishes than I am comfortable with hearing. You hold control over so many people—you must take care to be empty of self. You must always remember that you're merely a vessel for justice and guidance. And mercy."

"Mercy?" Rainis rubbed his ear between thumb and forefinger. "The Goddess has never been known for her mercy."

"Of course not. Because her justice is dispensed by mere humans who need to make an impression. Mercy never impresses anyone. A little cruelty, however, that's a different story."

Rainis was a simple man, the youngest son of an outlying raeth family, and hardly used to insight, never mind revelation. For a moment Alesk thought he had managed to reach him, but then Rainis shook himself and returned tenaciously to his original thought. "But I *did* dream about the island being covered with water. And we must leave before that happens." He braced his feet apart, his eyes bright, defiant.

Alesk yielded. "You may be right. When one has as many questions as I have, it is impossible to deny someone who is as sure of his answers as you are."

"Then you'll help me persuade—"

"No."

"But you just said—"

"Rainis, look at me! I am completely unconvinced of anything. I couldn't persuade a mosquito to bite me! No one will believe anything I tell them, because I don't believe anything myself."

"Then you're lost."

"Irrevocably."

Rainis growled, "But you have no right to drag innocent people after you."

Alesk agreed. "Rainis, I'm not going to publicly oppose you. However, I'm not going with you on the ships either. I will stay here as support for those who wish to stay. But I will not attempt to convince anyone of anything. That's final." He went back to work and didn't look up again, even when Rainis banged the door behind him as he left.

Chapter Twenty

Lying on the bowsprit of the *Sea Swallow*, Sand bobbed up and down, rocked side to side. If she watched the water advance toward her face and then recede, she soon felt queasy. But as long as she kept her eyes on the distant horizon she was fine.

She would have liked to turn over and watch the stars, but she didn't move. Every fiber in her body ached from the work she'd been doing on the island in the last few weeks. Once she got herself settled comfortably in one spot, she didn't move unless she had to. And lying on her stomach, she could press her hands over her ears and cling to the bowsprit by the pressure of her knees and elbows. If she turned on her back she'd have to use her hands to hang on and then she couldn't keep her ears covered. She'd sworn that if she heard one more baby screaming that night she was going to drown it—or herself.

Even if she had managed to overcome her lethargy and her aversion, there was only one star to be seen. The night sky was a royal-blue dome, completely dominated by a huge, celestial tadpole. No distant star could compete with that.

As the star had grown larger and brighter, she'd made a habit of lying on the deck at night watching it and listening to Petrius and Lucius argue. Now she was tired of it. Actually, she was just plain tired.

When Kryphon began to near their world, Petrius had started the exodus to the ships. At the beginning there wasn't enough room for everyone who wanted to join them. Each day, every able man who believed in the escape by sea labored in the boatyard, finishing fishing boats and knocking together rafts.

Many of the weavers stopped making cloth and began making anchor ropes, twisting the fibers till their fingers blistered from working with the rough bark.

Jinny, Daulo, and Berran were the biggest recruiters, and the fishermen started taking their boats from the beaches and sailing them out to join what was becoming a little floating city. Marjilee they called it: town of the waves. Made up of many small vessels lashed together, the whole town undulated in the ocean swells like a skin of fish scales laid in a net over the water.

When Rainis joined them Sand had to subdue her distaste for him. He was useful; his fanaticism touched people who had been unmoved by simple explanation.

But for every Midislander who believed in the danger there were two or three raeth who didn't. The raeth and their families referred to the floating community as Peshonetilee: town of the fanatics. The very fact that so many Midislanders were convinced was enough to persuade the raeth population that the supposed flood was unworthy of their attention.

*   *   *

For a while the momentum swelled and more and more people joined them. But the longer the star hung in the sky above them, the less dreaded it became. Sand was astonished by how quickly people accepted it as simply a new presence, no more dangerous or unpredictable than their beloved and faithful Raza. When the boats became crowded and uncomfortable some people moved back to Strandia.

But the first tides shook their complacency, and people came in hordes.

Sand was drying off after her swim one morning when something caught her eye. For a moment she couldn't place it. Then she realized that the sea had retreated. The boats which had been pulled just out of the water were now stranded. She called Petrius; he stood silent for a long time looking.

"What's happening?"

He shook his head.

That afternoon the sea crept higher and higher, till there was almost no beach left. Boats floated off their anchorages and, in some places, floundered into lactus groves awash with seawater.

That evening, when Rainis shepherded his new charges out to Marjilee, he started shouting his good news as soon as he was within earshot. "Tomorrow you must send all your shipwrights to the boatyard. With this new sign, the ranks of the believers are swelling." He seemed to take this as a personal victory.

More and more fishing boats tied up alongside, and the boatbuilders worked night and day on the rafts.

Sand worked until she was ready to drop. She helped in the boatyard, she helped in the weavers' house. And she helped feed the little town on the waves as well. Since the

235

fishing boats were too precious to be wasted on gathering food, the few talents on Marjilee spent all their time and energy compelling the providers.

Monarri's talent was invaluable. Soon after her return to Strandia, Sand had visited her cove. Monarri was sitting on a rock on the point and the sound of the waves on the shore masked Sand's footsteps. It wasn't until she called her that Monarri turned and saw her there. Her face turned fish-belly white.

"Monarri, it's me! I'm back. Safe and sound and whole."

When Monarri finally lifted her head from where she had buried it against Sand's chest, she said, "I thought I was going mad. I've imagined you here so often on these rocks. But I knew this was different. I thought my mind had snapped."

Monarri joined her on the ships immediately. She had no trade, no commitments, and only her grandfather as family. As she pitched her few belongings onto the deck the next morning, she told Sand, "I told him about the giant waves. He just said, 'Of course.' Stupid, eldrin old man!" Her eyes glittered with tears.

Monarri helped her compel the providers and so did the few other raeth women that joined the boats. But the raeth were few and none of the talents was as strong as Sand's. So most of the burden of providing fell to her.

As if this didn't take enough of her energy, she was constantly called upon to translate for those from the continent. She had finally decided to give Lucius permission to pluck the language from her mind, and he could often translate, if necessary, so long as she was awake. Sand got used to Lucius rummaging through her mind looking for the word he needed. She never became comfortable with the sensation, only familiar with it. But when she was asleep he refused to hunt for the words he needed for fear of crushing her dreams.

Because of her link with M'ridan, it was her job to check the anchor ropes, or sometimes to retie one which had torn when it rubbed on an outcropping of coral. M'ridan would hover nearby while she struggled with the task before she had to surface for air; once she was back on board, she would lie in the sunshine for a long time, soaking up the warmth while Renellus plied her with stimulating teas.

For the first week or so Renellus was at a loss for something to do. The islanders were too healthy to welcome an extra doctor. So he set himself to watching over Sand's health. Even now, as she lay on the bowsprit meditating on whether or not she could be bothered with turning over, she heard his low voice behind her. "Leave her alone. She's exhausted. Wait until tomorrow." Unfortunately, he spoke all this in the mainland tongue. Then he added all he could think of in Strandian: an explosive "NO!"

Berran's voice argued with him, this time in Strandian, which communicated no better than the doctor's tongue. "You must let me speak to her. Who are *you* to tell me to keep away?"

And so it continued; their voices growing louder and curious faces turned toward them from the nearby boats. With a sigh Sand slithered back along the bowsprit and climbed onto the deck.

"I'm awake," she said to Renellus. Turning to Berran, she said in a low, forceful voice, "Must you fight over me like torsios over a scrap of fresh meat? You humiliate me!"

"I have no interest in fighting over you," he retorted, stung. "I need your help—that's all."

Turning to Renellus she said, "He needs my help with something. I'll be right back."

When she did return, she said, "I know you were trying

to guard me, but you're fussing over me. You don't have enough to keep you busy."

"That's the truth."

She smiled. "I'll return the favor you did for me on the continent. Tomorrow I'll find you some chores."

The next morning she led him to the weavers' house and introduced him to Gelya. "This is a doctor," she began. Feeling for the most diplomatic phrase, she continued, "He hasn't much to do on the ships but fuss over me. I thought maybe he could fuss over someone else for a change. He has some treatments for the pain in your hands which are very effective." She threw this last tidbit out in an offhand manner.

Gelya's eyes flashed at her. "You've been studying Jinny's technique well, my girl, but you don't have to be tactful about these." She grimaced at the curled claws lying in her lap. "If he's got something to ease the pain or to make them more useful, he can spend all the time he wants here."

Renellus had learned only a few words of Strandian so far. But within moments he and Gelya were in rapt conversation consisting of his language, her language, and a windmill of gestures. He waved Sand a cheerful goodbye.

In the next weeks he spent every day at the weavers' hut. When he wasn't treating Gelya he talked to the others about the herbs used in dyeing. But before long the supplies of medicinal herbs he'd brought with him from the mainland began to dwindle. Each day there was a spoonful less of Gelya's medicine in the jar.

Renellus began to wander the paths around Midisle examining the plants. Many were strange to him, and others that he was searching for he couldn't find.

Sand decided to take him to see Alesk. "The priests have a great knowledge of herb lore. If there's a substitute plant on Strandia for what you're missing, he'll know what it is."

Andronius overheard. "I'd like very much to be allowed

to join you," he pleaded. "I had hoped to get more information from that young priest, Rainis, but he's the most officious young toad! If he isn't entirely too busy to talk to me, then the information is sacred to the Mother and not to be shared with us heathen."

Though Sand found Andronius unbearably irritating at times, she pitied him. With a quick glance at Renellus to make sure he didn't object, she agreed. "If you haven't got Lucius with you to translate, I don't know how much of the conversation you'll understand," she warned both of them.

"I've picked up quite a bit of it from the weavers," Renellus said in her own tongue, with a grin.

Alesk courteously met them in the temple courtyard. When Sand explained her mission, he welcomed the men. "With so many of the dedicated spreading the Mother's word, it gets very quiet here these days."

Sand returned to collect the two in the late afternoon and found them standing in the sun at the water's edge on the temple beach.

Alesk turned to her with a smile. She saw that he held a piece of bluish-purple seaweed in his hands. Its broad, flat leaves clung to his skin with clammy insistence. As she drew nearer she heard him say, "Sentranthus. It's the reason our island always has the right number of people, the right balance of raeth and Midislander. And since Sand is here to take you back, she can tell you the story of Palma and the sentranthus."

She smiled softly. "That was always my favorite story."

"I must get to supper—they won't think to leave me any if I'm not there. Doctor, I've enjoyed our time together. Please come again. Andronius . . ." They clasped hands and Sand translated the parting courtesies.

Sand was pleased to have the story to occupy Andronius as they made their way back to the ships. Otherwise he asked so many questions and stopped so often to examine things that even the shortest trip took forever.

So she began: "In a far-off time when the bones of Strandia were much younger than they are now, people cluttered the island. Lactus reeds and food became scarce and raeth fought with Midislander for room for their homes. Bael nuts and lactus fruit were eaten before they ripened. And new trees that were planted got trampled by the passage of many feet and didn't grow.

"In one raethdom lived a daughter named Palma, newly come to her talent. She was the oldest of a large family and every winter there was another baby for her to help her mother with. Sometimes she thought she would go mad from the noise and the lack of privacy. In the early morning and the late evening she used to steal from the house and swim away from shore. She'd float on her back, rocking in the waves, and watch the light waxing or waning in the sky.

"One morning she decided that it was time to swim back. But the wind had come up and it was blowing her out to sea. She swam and swam, struggling against the rising waves. As she grew more and more tired and the island drew no nearer, she began to panic. Just as she began to sink and choke, something velvety and sturdy surfaced beneath her and lifted her into the air. One of the doraado had felt her fright and come to save her.

"As she clung to its back, gulping in air, she heard him tell her how silly she'd been. She gasped as much from surprise as for air. He was talking to her! And she could understand and answer him."

She looked at the two men beside her. "Perhaps you don't realize how unusual that is. When a raeth woman calls to the providers, she sends feelings and she receives impressions. The sensation is very vague. The sharper the image she can project, the easier it is for the doraado to hear her, but it's not like having a conversation.

"However, it was almost like that for Palma. The doraado was intrigued by her and they talked for a long time. She discovered his name was K'nspekkel. When she came home late that morning, her mother was furious with her for the work she'd missed. But as soon as she had a chance she went swimming again and called to the doraado. He came to her and they played together long into the night.

"This pattern continued for weeks. Life became bearable for Palma because of her new friend. When she wasn't spending time with him in the water, she could still talk to him in her mind. She became very dreamy and often her mother had to shout at her to make her wake up to her tasks. Palma's mother went from rage at her missed duties to cold fury at something she couldn't name. She was sure her daughter was meeting a lover and before long would shame them all.

"So her mother arranged for her to marry a neighboring raeth son. When Palma found out, she was heartbroken. She swam out to sea that night crying as though in great pain.

"K'nspekkel met her.

" 'Would that I had drowned the day we met!' she moaned.

"He was shocked. 'Why?'

"She explained to him about marriage and the endless childbearing that it would entail. 'I cannot swim free with you when I am as big as a whale myself!'

" 'Then don't have children.'

"She thought he was mocking her, until he explained that by eating a certain type of seaweed after they mated, female doraado absorbed the new life back into their bodies before it had a chance to grow inside them.

241

"Palma held her breath. 'Do you think it would work for me?'

" 'We are physically closer than you think.'

"So Palma married the raeth son and her father built them their own hut on his already crowded raeth holding. For a long time Palma was happier than she'd ever been. She grew fond of her new husband. She was free from many of the duties she'd had to perform for her mother. She spent more time than ever with K'nspekkel. And each morning before she swam back to shore she ate half a leaf of sentranthus seaweed.

"Several years passed and Palma's sisters married and became pregnant. They pitied her childlessness. One day she grew exasperated with their condescension. 'I can have children whenever I want to,' she told them. 'I choose not to.'

"They didn't believe her and mocked her until finally she told them about K'nspekkel and the seaweed.

"Men have a saying on Strandia: A secret is safer shouted in the market than whispered to a raeth woman. Palma's sisters were proof of that. Before many days had gone past, every raeth woman on the island knew about the seaweed, and word of it had reached the temple. The priests and priestesses were fascinated, not only by the rumor of something to reduce the number of babies, but by the tales of Palma's ability to talk to the doraado.

"They took her from her raethdom and dedicated her to the Mother as a priestess. Then they made her ask the doraado questions. Things like the best places to dive for shellfish, where to find large schools for the fishing boats, other doraado medicines, and so on. They also asked metaphysical questions about the Sea Mother, which the doraado laughed at and gave her silly answers to. But eventually K'nspekkel grew tired of the question game and refused to answer any more of them.

"Finally they told her to ask K'nspekkel about the doraado themselves: their habits and their religion. Palma closed her eyes and sat quietly for a few moments. Then she looked at them. 'They will show you.'

"She led them all down to the temple beach, to that very spot where I found you tonight. They stood on the sand while Palma waded out into the water. Then they saw the providers. Hundreds of them—more than anyone has ever seen in one place before or since. They swept in toward the shore, gray arrows slicing through the water; waves of them rolling in.

"And then they were all around Palma, whistling, squeaking, and laughing. She staggered as one of them surfaced beneath her, lifting her off the bottom.

"She called to those waiting on land. 'They worship freedom. They show their reverence with joy. And I choose to worship with them.'

"Before their astonished eyes, the providers turned as one and began swimming back out to sea, and Palma went with them. By the time they'd organized the fishermen to follow, she'd vanished without a ripple. And she was never seen again.

"For seven days after that, not a single provider answered a raeth woman anywhere on Strandia. You can imagine how that frightened the priests with the island as crowded and hungry as it was. And then they began coming again. But they had reminded the temple that they were honoring a choice made long ago by doraado. They feed us out of sympathy and love, not as servants.

"Within two generations Strandia returned to the population it has now. The priests watch to make sure that it doesn't grow too large. But they have never again tried to interfere with the doraado or with one that the doraado love. Not until recently, anyway."

They made the rest of their way back to the boats in silence, the two men reluctant to disturb Sand's preoccupation.

Chapter Twenty-one

Sand made a special trip to her family's holding to tell them of the danger. As she trudged up the slight rise from the beach, she looked all around her. Not much had changed here in the time since she'd run away. She counted fewer fishing boats on the beach. Her mother would be cross about that. Fewer flecks to buy trinkets with at the festival.

Someone stood on the porch, shading their eyes to watch her. The person wheeled and disappeared. Sand was sure it had been her mother.

By the time she reached the door, Marris was waiting for her on the porch. He descended the steps to meet her, clasping her in a big hug, holding her close.

"How are you?" He gave her a lopsided smile. "Stupid question. How wonderful to see you, daughter." Keeping one arm around her shoulders, he walked her down to the beach.

She slid her arm around his waist and felt the muscles of his back rigid against her forearm. She could imagine the exchange of words that had just erupted inside the house. As they traded questions and answers, she too began to sense her mother's eyes burning into their shoulder blades.

"How is Anemone?"

The tendons jumped in his neck in his effort not to look back. "Fine."

Sand sighed. "Father, I came to persuade you to bring the family and join us on the boats. And to ask you to urge your beach renters to join us as well. We need as many boats as we can get."

Marris frowned. "Sand, I've heard a little about this nonsense. In fact, the island is talking about nothing else. But priests with visions are nothing new . . ."

Sand made a face at this reference to Rainis. "Him! I don't know what his motives are, Father. He persuades the credulous. But the news about the danger first came from the city on the continent." She had to use the other language for "city" and "continent," and those two words dropped as heavy, guttural pebbles into the liquid trickle of her island tongue.

They reached the beach and Sand hunted around for a stick. While her father watched, she drew diagrams like the ones Petrius had drawn for her.

"You talk about the coming danger. Danger is something that comes in its own time, like a torsio in the water. It cannot be predicted."

"But, Father, many dangers have portents—one only has to recognize them. For instance, if there's a storm coming, you know it by the sky and the wind and the feel of the air. That's because you've seen many storms and you know the feel of them.

"The problem with the coming of this star is that a man can experience it only once in his lifetime, and then it doesn't come again for many generations. But in the city is the university—a place of study. They keep records there from one generation to the next. So if a man studies the records he holds the experience of many people, for thousands of years. And the records say that each time the star has come, the coasts have suffered terrible damage."

She looked up to find an odd expression in Marris's eyes. "Father, am I explaining this badly?"

"Daughter, you have changed. You're a woman now—not just my daughter, though that you will always be. You're grown."

A sad expression crossed his face, a cloud flying across the sun, and then it was gone, as his daughter's childhood had flown before he even realized it.

"I'm convinced. But there are more people involved in this raethdom than just me. I'll let you know."

"But you're the raeth! Surely if you ordered them—"

"Sand, if you haven't realized by now that being raeth simply means having more headaches than everyone else, you haven't had your eyes open. Everyone who respects my authority resents me for it all the same. And fights me every chance they get. All I can do is try to persuade the fishermen, just as you have tried to persuade me. And *because* I'm the raeth, I must use even more tact than you have. And I can tell you right now, your mother's going to be the hardest of all to convince."

Sand hugged him. "Poor Father." She threw her stick into the long beach grass and brushed the sand off her hands and knees. "Just remember, Father, convince who you can, but if *you're* convinced, you be there no matter who else comes."

He grinned at her. "You'd make a terrible raeth."

❋   ❋   ❋

The preparations dragged on for too long. Eventually the tides ceased to impress people. Many of the fishermen removed their boats from Marjilee and returned to their homes on Strandia. Many other people chose to sleep on the rafts at night, but returned to land in the morning to do their daily work. Sand couldn't blame them. Life on the ocean's surface was anything but comfortable.

Petrius argued with the deserters every morning. "You're all crazy! Just because it's light doesn't mean you're safe. Kryphon grows pale during the day, but his strength doesn't fade."

Sand would station herself near him and translate for him, though his passionate harangues embarrassed her. One day as they sat on the deck afterward dejectedly drinking their khar, they talked over the situation.

Sand blew on her khar to cool it. Not meeting his eyes, she said, "Petrius, are we right in trying to keep the islanders here on the boats? Please don't be offended, but I can understand why they're not staying. Kryphon has hung in the sky for a month now and nothing's changed."

He frowned. "Sand, I wish I could tell you for sure, but I don't know. You can't say nothing's changed. Look at the tides."

"But nothing bad has happened—no one's been hurt. Will anything worse happen?"

He scowled. "I can't say for sure. It might not. I think it will. The records say it's probable. Who knows?"

Leaving him morose and doubting, she and Renellus went into town to see Gelya. Sand was delighted. In the weeks since the doctor had begun his treatments, she'd grown twenty seasons younger. The pain lines in her face were smoothed away and her hands moved through the fibers with ease and surety.

Renellus mixed the tea for Gelya as Sand sat in her old spot by the weaver's feet, chatting.

Sand had been made very welcome in the weavers' house since her return. She was eager for this time of emergency to be over so she could begin to build a life of quiet routine in which to explore who she truly was. With no one to hide from now and every door open to her, she was very excited by the prospect.

Sand was reaching for a handful of bark to work with, when the earth growled and shook itself like a wet goat. All the stored fiber in the rafters fell down on the people below, some landing in the fireplace and catching fire with a sharp whoosh.

All around, people were crying out in shock, righting the equipment which had tumbled over. Children screamed in fright.

Sand's eyes locked on the doctor's. His skin gleamed with pale moisture.

"This is it." She was certain. Then louder, to reach everyone in the hall, she repeated, "This is it! If disaster is going to strike, it will be soon. Maybe in minutes. Get out to the ships. Tell everyone you meet. You have no extra time. You must believe me now. Someone help Gelya to the boats."

She and the doctor sped from the house. "You get to the ship," she told him. Cutting off his protest, she continued, "There will be need for a doctor when this is over. Make sure you're safe. I'll come as soon as I can. But I speak the language, and the bones of Strandia have just pleaded my cause. If people are ever going to believe me and come, it must be now. Be safe!"

She fled through Midisle, shouting as she went. Many people wandered in the streets looking dazed. Here and there huts leaned at crazy angles. Several were on fire and people worked feverishly to save them.

"Never mind the buildings!" she yelled at them. "Your lives are at stake. Get out to sea!" She gave everyone she met her warning, but only once. She didn't stop to persuade them, she didn't wait to see if they obeyed. She told them all to tell others.

The houses of Midisle thinned and then she was on the winding jungle track that led north between all the raeth-doms. She stopped in at every fifth raeth holding she came to and gave her warning to the first person she saw. Pleading with them to tell their neighbors whether or not they believed her themselves, she sped on. As she pounded along the path she reached for M'ridan.

"Mudball."

"Have you felt it?"

He visualized for her the seabed heaving beneath him, chunks breaking away from the coral reef surrounding Strandia.

"M'ridan, I have to warn everyone, but when I'm through I'll be at the far tip of the island. Can you meet me there?"

He agreed and she found his quiet assurance calming.

As she emerged from the jungle behind her parents' home, she tried to shout, but her panting had dried her throat and all that came out was a croak. She began to cough. Like a nightmare, she thought, running up onto the porch. The most important thing I've ever had to say to my parents and I can't speak.

She burst into the main room and found her mother sitting on the floor weeping over a broken ornament. When Anemone realized the sweaty, coughing woman before her was her daughter, she scowled as if the disaster were some-how Sand's fault.

One look at her mother's set face and Sand turned from her. Grabbing a pitcher of fresh water, she lifted it to her mouth and took a gulp. "Marris!" she screamed. "Father!"

No answer. Wheeling around, she looked at her mother again. "Mother, you and I have many things we have never said to each other, things that should be said. Please get off the island. I want the chance to talk to you someday. Please save yourself." She crouched and hugged her mother quickly, before springing out the door. She had no idea whether Anemone would listen to her or not.

She raced toward the knot of men on the beach, calling as she went. Her father broke from the group and ran toward her.

"It's happening now, Father. It truly is. Please tell your neighbors two down on either side. I haven't been able to tell every raethdom. And then get out to sea fast. Take everyone who'll come with you, but go. Now!"

She spun to leave and then turned around and hugged him. Tears were streaming from her eyes. "I love you. Make sure this isn't the last time I get to say that to you."

She ran on, spreading her message farther and farther down the shore. She began to feel the tangible weight of danger pressing against her. When the earth had moved this morning she had sensed that there would be a breathing space before anything more happened to disturb her world. Despite what she'd said in the weavers' hut about minutes, she hoped it would be hours. But by now hours had passed. Raza had crept to the top of the blue dome above her head and started down the other side.

The next time she emerged from the jungle to the raeths' shore, the imminent danger struck her like a blow. The ocean floor was uncovered, a vast wet expanse of sand. Far from her across its gently ribbed surface and against the glittering ribbon of surf she saw the silhouetted figures of several people, including a child, wandering around the newly revealed ocean bed, picking up shellfish. Her skin prickled. At the same moment she felt M'ridan's presence in her mind, urgently.

"Mudball, get into the water! I'm coming for you!"

She ran toward the transition from sand to waves. As she neared the figures she screamed at them, "Get a boat! Get into the water! Do it now!"

They turned and stared. The child waved an enormous starfish at her. Sand might have been speaking another language for all they responded. For a moment she debated trying to convince them, and then a fragment of her early conversation with her father came back to her: ". . . you be there no matter who else comes."

Taking her own advice, she splashed through the shallows straight out into the sea. Ahead of her she could see what looked like a white wall rising up out of the ocean to waist height. With a shock she realized it was the reef that protected the island. Altering direction slightly, she made for a break in the wall. Soon she was moving in slow motion, fighting the resistance of the water, which was now up to her chest. Again, like a nightmare, she thought, only worse. There will be no waking from this one.

❂   ❂   ❂

To Alesk, the earthquake brought illumination. Literally. The giant coral blocks of the temple split and the wall of his cell opened to let the sunlight stream in.

His ears rang. Then the ringing grew fainter and was replaced by screaming. He looked into the courtyard. A wall had collapsed and two novices, a boy and a girl, were trapped beneath it.

The girl was already dead by the time he reached them. The boy had fainted. The screaming continued. He realized it came from one of the other priests in the temple. The man stood there keening; a demented wail.

251

"Someone get him"—he pointed to the screamer—"out of here."

No one moved. Some of the novices were simply staring fearfully at the temple walls, as if they might leap on top of them at any moment. One man was on his knees retching. Others knelt on the sand mumbling fragmented prayers to the Mother.

The boy underneath the massive block was one of the temple-born. Alesk looked compassionately at the screaming man—the boy's father.

The older priest had never felt so helpless. He had no knowledge of how to move the toppled stones. He turned a novice away from the grisly sight.

"Get me the shipwrights."

The novice stared at him, or through him.

Alesk shook the boy. He repeated his instructions and watched the comprehension flood behind the boy's eyes. Alesk pushed him in the direction of the boatyard.

Then he knelt and examined the two adolescents. Cowrie and Morven. Perhaps it would be better if Morven just died—surviving this accident would leave him with a horrible life. A part of Alesk was immediately horrified at this callous detachment. He sent another priest to the weavers' house to find Renellus. This left only a handful of the faithful wandering around the courtyard in a stupor.

"All of you! There's nothing useful for you to do here. Get back to your normal tasks, and when we do have something you can help with, we'll call you."

He kept one novice with him. He'd often seen her helping in the dispensary. She was white to the lips, but didn't seem frozen with shock like some of the others.

His agonized vigil began. While he waited for his messengers to return, he watched the bright red life leak out from beneath the stones. Finally he stopped a young novice carrying robes to the temple workshop. "Go to the shipbuilders' yard for help. I sent Gurja an hour ago but he hasn't returned."

The novice ran off on long, skinny heron legs.

The messenger he'd sent to the weavers' house returned; he'd hunted all through Midisle but couldn't find the doctor. "I could hardly find anyone. They've all gone to the ships."

The boy's eyes widened as Alesk cursed comprehensively. "Rainis and his dream visions," he spat. "The self-important fool."

Just then the last messenger panted into the courtyard. "They're all gone, not a soul left."

"Well, get a boat and go out to the ships. Tell them we need help."

"There are no boats, sir. They've all been taken. I tried to do that already. Gurja went in one of the last. They know. Those people on the ships know by now what has happened."

Alesk saw the confused misery in the two faces before him. Schooling his voice, he said, "That's all right. It's not your fault."

It was then he heard Morven. Whirling around, Alesk saw that the boy's eyes were open. He made a sound like a sigh, like a chuckle. By the time Alesk bent over him he'd ceased making any noise at all; even the faint whisper of breath in his chest had stopped.

Alesk closed the boy's eyes with his right hand. He rocked back onto his feet and slowly straightened. Finally he lifted his eyes to where Kryphon showed in the blue sky, a pale version of his nighttime glory. He lifted his arms and began the song of soul-sending over the broken bodies. The two messengers joined in after the opening lines of the blessing.

As the melody began, others flooded out of the temple to join them, providing the harmony, the descant, and the

253

deep, solemn bass notes. As the numbers swelled, Alesk felt them all bound into the music, felt the fear that pressed upon them, felt the comfort that the transcendent music gave. Felt somehow that they were singing it for themselves as well as for the dead before them.

And as the song gave its last poignant swell and died away, Alesk felt the world holding its breath.

He turned to the novices to give them some comforting words about their companions who were gone. The words clogged his throat.

Beyond the group in the temple courtyard stretched a surreal scene. The courtyard fell away to the beach, and the beach stretched impossibly far into the distance. It stopped at an enormous wall of water that hung from the sky.

In the next second, he realized it was not motionless. It rushed toward them, getting taller every second.

And then he only had time to realize that Rainis had been right—that simple-minded faith was true salvation and that their myths held the answers to his questions after all—before the water swept over him and sang its own song of soul-sending.

Chapter Twenty-two

Tension held the floating island together as much as the ropes did. New people and new boats arrived every few minutes and the crews were kept busy lashing them securely together.

The two captains watched the horizon, trying to identify the disaster before it arrived. Without exception, everyone else watched the island. Everyone on board had someone still on the island who'd scoffed at the warnings: friends, family, or neighbors.

For a long time, nothing happened. The tense groups at the boats' sides began to break into smaller clusters. People looked less anxious. Renellus even heard one woman say, "We're making ourselves look like fools again."

"By the Mother, I hope so," her husband said fervently.

Renellus felt a hesitant touch on his shoulder and a whisper. "Doctor?"

He turned and, to his surprise, found Berran behind him. "Where is Sand?"

The doctor shrugged, feigning a relaxation he didn't feel. "She said there were people she had to warn."

"Probably her damn family. Raeth aren't worth her effort."

Renellus gave him a mild glance. "She thinks they are." Then, seeing the authentic distress beneath the harsh words, he added sympathetically, "I worry, too."

"Why didn't you stop her?"

"Sand? Might as well try to stop the sea."

Berran smiled, acknowledging the truth of this.

A boat drew near with several of Berran's workers from the boatyard and their families in it. Huddled in one corner was a teenager in the grubby robe of a temple novice. He was crying.

Berran glanced at Felthame and raised his eyebrows. The shipwright shrugged uncomfortably and looked away.

Renellus came up close behind Berran as the shipwright reached for the boy's hand and steadied him as he climbed aboard.

Gurja blinked several times quickly and brushed away his tears. "Shipmaster! It's terrible—the temple wall broke when the earth shook and it fell on my friend Morven and another novice—a girl. I ran to the boatyard for help. The priests don't know how to lift the stones off Morven." He began to sob again, his thin frame shaking. "The boat-builders said they wouldn't come, they had to be here so they'd be safe. I don't want to end up like Morven. I want to be safe." His eyes were blank, focused on the horrible scene he'd left behind him. "I'm a coward," he whispered.

Berran thumped the boy's shoulder. Beginning with a silent curse, he continued out loud, "You've done what you could. You brought me word and that's enough. Staying on the island with your friend would accomplish nothing. You've been the best friend he could have." Consigning the boy to the care of Felthame's motherly wife, Berran leaped from boat to boat till he reached the outer ring. He spied Terent sitting in his fishing boat, slowly chewing on some cold fried conch strips and staring at the shore.

"I need your boat." He leaped into the bottom and lifted Terent to his feet. Renellus landed lightly behind him. "You're not coming." Berran turned his head so that only the doctor would hear him.

"I am."

Berran bunched his carpenter's muscles and half lifted, half threw Terent into the next boat over. "I owe you," he told him.

He turned back to the doctor. "Get out. It's too dangerous."

"For me, but not for you?"

Berran didn't answer.

Renellus continued to argue. "Look, we don't know how long it will be till something happens. It might not happen at all. But I can't leave them there."

"I don't need your help."

The doctor regarded him steadily. "Once you single-handedly lift the wall off those two, what are you going to do with them? Can you stop the bleeding? Can you subdue the pain?"

Berran drilled him with an angry glare, but his silence was consent. He turned away and began undoing Terent's messy knots, cursing the fat man's sloppiness. When he got to the bowlines, he found they were free already. Renellus was sheathing his knife. The sawn-off ropes floated behind them.

"I owe you." Renellus smiled.

Despite himself, Berran grinned back.

They both set to work on the oars. Berran set a grueling pace suited to his own carpenter's physique. The doctor grimly tried to keep up.

Halfway to the island the doctor glanced at their destination. "Berran!"

At the odd note in his voice, the carpenter looked, too. He shuddered. The reef stood up out of the water. The beach had grown immense. Berran had a sudden strong image of the Mother yawning, breathing in, in, in; and baring the ocean bed behind the line of coral—her jagged teeth.

Without comment, he altered their course and a moment later they shot through one of the gaps in the coral. For a moment, watching the distant floating town through the gap as they rowed, the doctor thought he saw the whole thing undulate as though a god had grabbed the corners and shaken it like a blanket. Then the town disappeared from view.

A wave obscured it. The two men watched in disbelief as it grew and grew and grew, blotting out first the horizon and then the sky.

It rushed toward them soundlessly. Renellus noticed that everything was silent. Except for a faint breeze in his ear and the creak of Berran's oarlock, there was nothing—no gulls, no shore birds, no distant surf.

When the wave hit the coral reef, sound re-entered the world. The crest began to tumble over itself, boiling, foaming, roaring.

The wave reached them and their boat was lifted high and flung toward Strandia. Berran uttered one hoarse oath and, lunging forward, grabbed the doctor, holding his body against his own. They rode before the curl of the wave for a few of the most exhilarating seconds of their lives. The shore raced toward them. A moment later the world exploded. The crest of the wave poured down on top of them, slamming them into the bottom of the boat. They were swept in high over the beach sand and hurled into the trees. The world split thunderously apart. The bow of the boat hit a tree and they were catapulted out and driven beneath the wave. The force hurled them through the underwater forest, among the writhing treetops. They were beaten by

258

branches. Berran held grimly on to two things: his breath and Sand's doctor. He tried to shield their heads from being smashed like ripe bael nuts against the tree trunks. When he felt a tree grazing the length of his side, he risked all on one chance and threw one arm and one leg around it. The water whipped him around the tree, dislocating his shoulder.

He wrapped the other leg around the tree and, clinging with his knees, let go with his now useless arm. Operating in a miasma of agony, he now struggled to hang on to the doctor with his good arm and hang on to the tree with his knees.

Renellus moved in that second. He flipped around and wrapped his legs about the tree and both arms around Berran. Berran could feel the doctor's chest as tight as iron, trying not to breathe in the sea.

Breathing was becoming more imperative each second for them, when the violent pushing of the water began to slow. For a second they hung motionless.

Suddenly the water began to flow in the opposite direction. They swung around the tree, scraping their inner thighs raw. The Mother plucked at them with strong fingers. They clung even harder, but this effort with no air made little black dots dance before their eyes. Finally the doctor's lungs convulsed without his permission and he began to choke in the water. And then their heads were in the air again, and they coughed and gagged together.

Below them the water swept out to sea, the surface moving down the tree trunks as if someone had pulled the bung from a barrel. The two men let go of each other and maneuvered themselves onto sturdy cross branches. The doctor settled Berran firmly onto his perch. Then he set about wrenching Berran's shoulder back into its socket.

"Otherwise you'll never get down this tree," he said.

Berran set his teeth against the expected agony. But after one excruciating moment the pain faded to a bearable ache.

Renellus told him, "That will hurt for a few days, till the muscles recover from the stretching they suffered."

Berran swung one leg over the branch, letting it hang down on the other side, and settled himself against the tree. He wiped the beaded water and sweat from under his eyes and over his lip and tried to steady his panting. "When you're ready, we'll climb down," the doctor suggested.

It was then they saw the second wave.

⚬ ⚬ ⚬

Sand had not yet reached the reef when a slick gray form surged underneath her and lifted her up.

"Hold tight."

They sped through the reef and M'ridan said, "We dive! It's faster."

Sand snatched a breath and he ducked her under the surface. They shot straight out toward the open sea. She knew he was sounding the bottom. Eventually he seemed to be satisfied with the depth, for he lifted them to the surface. She twisted around on his back so she could see the island.

A dreamlike sense of the unreal possessed her. Under the sunny blue sky the island lay as it always had. True, the coral reef stuck up out of the water like a jawbone with jagged teeth. It obscured her vision of the beach. But each rolling swell lifted her up to give her a glimpse of it again.

The sea seemed especially calm. She and M'ridan rocked gently up and down. One particularly heavy swell lifted her high enough to see the raeth family with the little child still poking about in the matted seaweed.

She shuddered. "When is it coming?" she muttered aloud, as they slid down the back of a comber. M'ridan must have caught the question, because he said, "That was it."

She watched in disbelief. As they wallowed in the valley

between rollers, she waited for the next one to lift them high enough to see the reef, or at least the trees on the island. It never came. The comber rushed away from them, obscuring the island, the reef. Sand could see by the disappearing clouds on the horizon that the wave was mounting into the sky.

She waited what seemed an eternity and still the island didn't reappear. M'ridan began swimming, choosing a course parallel to the reef. She kept her eyes fixed on the surface of the water where Strandia used to be. And then the treetops re-emerged—and gradually the rest of the trees—as though someone had punched a hole in the bottom of the ocean and the water was draining out.

From this distance everything looked fairly normal, though she could see trees on the beach torn up like weeds. The island seemed to be receding quickly, and she realized that the backwash from the wave was pulling them out to sea.

M'ridan picked up speed, and she saw a little boat ahead of them with a man and his family in it.

"Mudball, you must get in this boat and stay here."

"Where are you going?"

"People are drowning. I feel their terror, their need."

"I need you, too."

He snapped his beak angrily. "You are safe. This is real need." He boosted her into the boat. "Stay here. It's not over yet. I must go." He dove and disappeared.

It took her a moment to realize what he meant, and then she saw it. The water had retreated from the island. The trees and the beach were bare once more, and it was still retreating.

Once again the ocean floor was revealed, foot by foot.

She closed her eyes and reached for the familiar flamboyant pattern that was Lucius. "Sand! You're safe?"

261

"Safe. Tell everyone to stay where they are. There's going to be another wave."

"By the gods!" He cut her off and Sand slumped in her seat on the boat. She looked up to find the wondering eyes of the family whose boat she'd entered staring at her.

Lucius meanwhile raced to the captains. "Sand just reached me. It's not over."

All around the periphery of the floating town people were working feverishly to detach their boats. Some who had left others behind on the island wanted to get back and find them. Others who had good eyesight could make out struggling flotsam in the lagoon and knew they had to work fast to save them.

Sand's reputation as a prophet was established, however. When Rainis called out that she'd said there would be another wave shortly, everyone stopped and waited, though some very reluctantly.

Then a voice cried out in wonder. A child was gliding across the water toward them. His face was disfigured by crying. His shoulder was bleeding where it had scraped something. When he got closer, they could see the gray doraado supporting him. Behind him others began to appear.

Each refugee was hauled aboard and welcomed with tears and hugs. Sometimes they were recognized, sometimes not, but all were greeted with equal warmth.

When the second wave rocked Marjilee, some recognized its potential and watched breathless as it continued on. Those who were en route to the ships were at first obscured by its bulk and then appeared on top of it and slid down the other side toward the ships. Each silhouette was cheered as it crested the wave. But once the roller hit the reef, a new roaring began. There were no more silhouettes, and no more cheering.

Sand saw it coming and held her breath. When the roaring

began, she began searching for him. "M'ridan!" Through contact with him she felt a blow on his ribs and the echo of a terrible sharp pain and a crushing pressure that faded immediately. She waited in agony. "M'ridan!" No answer.

She stood, balancing on the gunwales of the little tanth, and then vaulted into the water and struck out for where the island used to be. For a long time she swam and the emerging treetops grew no nearer. And then she could see that she was gradually—oh, how gradually!—drawing closer. At intervals she felt for him, despite the fact that she needed her strength for swimming.

Then she felt a faint flicker. "M'ridan! Hold on! Guide me!" She focused on his touch and concentrated on holding it.

Toward the shore, the water was choked with debris and the undertow was terribly strong. She bruised her foot on a submerged tree trunk, but barely noticed. She saw several bodies supported by the wreckage, but they were beyond needing her help. When her feet at last touched bottom, she gasped with relief.

She scrambled ashore. Feeling him still, she visualized his thought patterns as a thread and put her own mind's fingers around it to follow it. She recognized nothing on shore. Before her was the wreckage of a raeth holding, but whose was beyond her knowing.

"Sand!" She felt her name in a surge of energy and then—nothing. Continuing in a straight line, she followed the direction she felt him to be in. The trees were full of debris caught and strung between them. Some of it belonged on land, some of it in the sea, but it was all tumbled together here, obstructing her way and her vision.

And just when she had begun to despair of finding him, she saw something gray and smooth half hidden by the branches of a fallen tree.

It was he. She recognized him by the old mating scars on his back, though there were many new cuts and scrapes now that she'd never seen before.

She looked wildly around herself, cursing. She turned and made her way back to the broken raeth house as quickly as possible. Circling it, she found a way in. Crawling gingerly over the rubble, she ducked through a small space where two collapsed walls supported each other drunkenly. Finally she found a bedroom. The sodden blankets from the sleeping pallet were plastered to the floor like seaweed left on the beach by the tide.

Sand peeled one off, rolling it as small as she could. She retraced her route in, rolling and pushing the blanket before her. When she got outside, she scrambled to her feet and stood there shakily for a moment before going on. Behind her she heard a crash as something in the house gave way and another wall collapsed.

Running, leaping, picking her way through the debris, she reached him again and threw herself down beside M'ridan. She called his name, stroked his side tentatively, and her salt tears bathed his scraped hide. In the joy and terror of hope, she saw his blowhole open and heard the air whistle through it.

She unrolled the blanket beside him. Digging her heels into the sodden ground, she braced herself and, with a mighty heave, rolled him onto it.

Picking up two corners, she tried to pull the blanket. She couldn't budge it. Her mind was blank. Frustration, rage, and despair fragmented her. She sent her distress outward like a beacon, and felt Lucius instantly in her mind. "I'm here. Use your talent, Sand. Your unique talent. Visualize! If I can lend you my strength, I will." Her mind was completely blank for a moment. Then she imagined his mindtouch as a brimming lactus reed. She lifted him to her lips and began to drink. His strength burned in her like lactus brandy. She drank and drank and—

"Enough!" He warded her off with a gasp.

She gathered the corners of the blanket again, braced herself, and pulled. It began to slide, and she stumbled forward, dragging it behind her. As long as she kept it moving, the going wasn't too hard. But there was so much debris on the grounds of the raeth holding that she spent too much time going around some things and moving others. By the time she reached the strand, she kept on only by the sheerest will.

At last she pulled him into the water. She held him in her arms, praying he was still alive. His blowhole whistled open and shut. She sat down on the sandy bottom and bent her knees. She cradled him in the valley between her knees and her chest, letting the sea bathe his skin, but keeping his blowhole above the surface.

She sent her thoughts into his mind like a fish sent through a dark, alien sea. Far ahead of her in these unknown, internal waters glimmered a light, like the pale electric glow of an angler fish. She surged after it. The strangeness of the surroundings they swam through pressed at her, but she forged on. Finally she caught up to it and swam beside it. Try as she might, she could see it only as a bodiless, pale glow, passing through dark water.

She focused on the pale light and poured strength into it, adding the torch of her strength to the candle of his. Her physical ears registered the sound of his blowhole whistling open and shut.

When she felt herself getting dizzy, she stopped stoking the light. It burned a little brighter, she thought. "M'ridan."

"Mudball." A whisper only in her mind. "I want you to know how dearly I have loved you." She waited, but he said no more.

Renellus and Berran found her hours later. When they had met Lucius on the shore by what was left of the temple, he told them that Sand lived. "At least, she did a few hours ago. But she was desperate and weak." He staggered and they asked no more of him than in what direction they should seek her.

"At the water's edge," he called after them.

Her body was racked with chills in the night water, but she refused to leave the doraado. Renellus said gently, "You know they never survive when they beach themselves, Sand. Why don't you let him go?"

She shouted at him, furious. "He didn't beach himself! He was beached trying to help some stupid raeth—" She began to sob.

Berran waded into the water and lifted him from her arms. "I'll hold him while you warm up."

She released him reluctantly. "You have to keep his blowhole above the water," she showed him.

"I will, I will. Go get warmed up."

They spent the rest of the night taking turns in the water and by the fire.

Sand took the watch near dawn, forcing herself into the icy water. She held him and laid her soft cheek against his even softer skin. She spoke to him at intervals, but there was no answer. She drowsed. When the first edge of the sun showed over the rim of the world, she started fully awake. Horrified, she realized she hadn't noticed his blowhole opening for a long time. How long? she wondered, panic-stricken.

She laid her ear against his side, but all she could hear was the surf of her own pulse in her ears. She tried to send a cry into his mind, but she couldn't find it. She put her lips to the crescent shape on the top of his head and blew, but the blowholes of the doraado are designed to keep seawater out at high pressure and she couldn't force air in.

"M'ridan!" she screamed aloud. Sobbing wildly, she held him and rocked his body back and forth.

When the long gray bodies began brushing up against her, they did it so gently at first that she hardly noticed. Then they touched her mind, and she relaxed and let her sorrow join with the grief of the pod, who were mourning the many, not this one.

One young female touched her mind and told her to give him to them.

"Is he dead?" she sobbed.

"Give him to us," she gently insisted.

At last Sand relaxed her hold on him and they took him from her. The only comfort she had was that they carried him under his flippers, holding his blowhole up in the air. She stood in the shallows and wept.

Renellus and Berran left her with her grief for a long time. But eventually they persuaded her back to the fire. She shambled up onto the shore, weeping bitterly, shivering uncontrollably.

She stripped off her wet clothes and rolled herself in the damp, sandy blanket. Before she fell asleep she licked her lips and tasted him on them.

Chapter Twenty-three

A survivors' camp was set up in the center of what had been the fish market. Destroyed buildings were pillaged for whatever salvageable materials could be used to build temporary shelters. Everyone was grateful for the work; everyone needed to do something. There were so few survivors, compared to the original population of Strandia, that those who had survived, whether they were raeth or Midislanders, now had a common bond. Everyone wanted to be physically close in the following weeks, to hear other human voices just a little distance away in the dark.

Sand knew she should feel grateful. The survivors included so many people she cared for: Jinny, Daulo, Berran, Kemahl, Renellus, her family, many of the weavers. But with M'ridan's loss, she felt too numb for joy or pity or relief. She didn't think there was any more room in her heart for pain until the next day when she looked at Jinny and said suddenly, "I haven't seen Monarri."

Jinny hugged Kemahl close to her as she'd been doing

unconsciously all day. "I'm sorry, Sand. She was on shore when the wave hit."

Sand couldn't believe her. "She'd been living on the boat for weeks!"

"But she kept going home to look after her grandfather. When she heard about the earth shaking, she went back to force him to come to the boats."

Sand felt black despair overwhelming her.

Gradually she learned the names of those who had died: Tamin, Alesk; and many, many raeth families. She determined that she would rejoice over those who were left, rather than mourning those she had lost. But of course the sadness wasn't so easily defeated.

The biggest loss in her life continued to be M'ridan. She had found him again after her sickness such a short time ago, and now he was gone forever. No more gentle touch in her mind—no more uncomplicated, unconditional, joyous loving. It was a loss beyond healing.

Berran and Renellus tried to set a pace that didn't allow her to mope. Between building and doctoring they tried to keep her so distracted that she didn't have time for pain.

But still there were many hours that she lay staring into the dark when she should have been asleep, and there was no distraction for her then. She began to wonder if she wasn't secretly becoming eldrin. She couldn't stop thinking about M'ridan. She couldn't stop crying. And sometimes she woke up certain that she'd just been joined with him in her dreams, and then she had to adjust to his loss all over again. But worst were the times during the day when she was absorbed in some task and she was suddenly certain she'd felt his mind touch faintly. "Mudball."

She'd freeze, drop what she was doing, and send her consciousness out like a seeking arrow. But there was never anything there, though she'd stand motionless and searching for half an hour at a time.

The two men learned very quickly not to disturb her at such times. Berran tried to get her attention one day as she was quivering with the intensity of her inner listening. "Sand. Sand. Sand!" He reached out a hand and shook her. Her eyes flew open and she looked at him with such fury and rage that he withered in the heat of her glance. She cursed him, something that left them both gaping with its violence.

Hours later she returned to him and apologized. "I thought I heard M'ridan. I thought I was getting close to finding him."

Berran and Renellus were developing a mutual trust and respect based on many things, including the grueling pace they each set for themselves and then surpassed. But what united them most of all, and divided them at the same time, was their growing feeling and concern for the raeth daughter.

After several weeks, people's need to be together to celebrate their survival began to relax. They began planning a new way to live on the island. So few raeth were left that anyone who wanted to could now have a piece of the beach for their own. Masons spent several days traveling the perimeter of the island and knocking down the old beach markers. Even the raeth that were left didn't object. In the face of all that had happened, class privilege just didn't seem to have any meaning. They were enjoying the connection they felt with the other islanders.

That was the way people began to refer to themselves. As islanders, not raeth or Midislanders. And Sand began to feel very excited about the possibilities of this. With the labels starting to fade, so did the limits. No one was proscribed from doing anything. Whether you were a raeth woman or a fisher, you could live where you wanted and do anything you had the courage to attempt.

Sand began to feel lonelier than she ever had in her life. Because she'd been the one who'd brought the saving ships to the island, people began to assume that she knew more than she did. Even that she had supernatural powers and knowledge. They sought her out for advice, for help, for approval. They looked to her for guidance. But nobody looked to her for friendship.

Jinny was wrapped up in her family and the rebuilding of the weavers' house. Berran and Renellus were both too careful of her feelings and of not poaching on the other's territory, now that they had grown to like and respect each other. Her family and she still had too many unsaid things between them. And if the truth be known, even her family felt there was something fey and unnatural about Sand.

Finally she couldn't stand the loneliness in the heart of the community. One day she made her way to Monarri's house. Pausing outside, she prayed silently that she wouldn't find anything too grisly within. And yet, when she went inside, the very innocuousness of what she did find left her feeling unsatisfied. Two sodden sleeping pallets, the blanket that Monarri had bought her grandfather with the money from the bottle fish so long ago. A few other odds and ends, dry now but smelling moldy.

She couldn't shake the eerie feeling she'd had lately: that all the people she'd known that had disappeared in the wave would somehow come back.

She squared her shoulders and set herself to clearing out the house. A small room at the back had collapsed, and the porch had actually separated from the building, but the central room was still solid. She scraped seaweed and sand from where it had collected in the corners of the rooms. She washed and dried the blankets that remained.

271

Sand worked there alone all day, and when evening came she returned to the camp to pick up her blanket and announce her intention of moving. No one tried to dissuade her. In fact, people seemed relieved. They had all found living with someone who so obviously had the Mother's favor a bit of a strain. It was like living with a priestess in their midst.

Only Berran and Renellus seemed concerned. But when she agreed that she would return to Midisle every day to work, they reluctantly acquiesced.

Eventually the sailors began making noises about leaving. They'd already stayed much longer than they'd originally intended to, and they knew that those on the continent would be worried about them. Lucius and Andronius were going to stay. So were several of the men with no families at home who'd been comforting the new Strandian widows. Sand was appalled at how fast people seemed to adjust to grief and loss and then move on to building a new life, without out apparently thinking about the past. Her loss of M'ridan was like a weight on her heart every hour, every day.

The night before the ships left, she had Jinny, Daulo, and Berran out to the cottage for a farewell dinner for Renellus. They all went down to the beach together and the four guests splashed into the water and held the net while Sand made a light catch for them. They each picked out their fish and a thank-you treat for the doraado and then let the rest scoot off back to the ocean. Daulo had unearthed a bottle of lactus brandy—"Literally unearthed it," he told them. "I buried it years ago to ripen and the wave didn't touch it"— and they drank to old friendships and new friendships and the passing of many things.

When the three islanders left, Renellus stayed on for a few minutes. Sand steeled herself against what she sensed was coming.

"Sand, will you come back to the continent with us?"

She looked at him compassionately. "You know I won't."

"If you're not sure whether or not there's a place for you there—"

"It's not that."

"I want to tell you that you're an enormous help to me and I care for you deeply. I'd be happy to take you home as my wife."

There was a silence. She gave him a long, hard hug. "Thank you. But I want to stay here. There I would be a help to you, but here I'm really needed."

"I need you, too."

She gestured to the island with her hand and smiled sadly as she echoed M'ridan's words to her. "This is *real* need. Everything is changing. There's room here to be myself. I want to find out everything I can be. I can't even imagine what that is right now. But I want it all. On the mainland I would just be a part of you, the doctor's wife, the doctor's helper. I don't want to be anybody's anything. I want to be Sand of Strandia." She blushed at the sound of it. "That's all. Can you understand?"

He hugged her back and said, "Yes, and the better side of me wants you to be all yourself. It's only the selfish side that wants you to be mine."

She reached up and turned the hand that rested on her shoulder palm in. She kissed the center of his palm and then curled his fingers around it to hold the kiss. "You have no selfish part. Only a lonely part. We all have that."

❖   ❖   ❖

The next afternoon as she was working in the weavers' house reconstructing a smashed spinning wheel and thinking of Renellus heading home, she heard Berran's step behind her.

"Sand?"

273

He beamed with joy. His step held so much spring that he literally bounced around her. "We're going to be so happy!" he announced.

"I'm glad." She couldn't help smiling in return—his joy was infectious. "What brought this on?"

"I saw him go—leaving on the ships. And you weren't with him! I was so afraid you were going to leave and didn't know how to tell me. I'm hardly able to keep my boots on the island. I'm glad the tools in my apron are so heavy— they keep me anchored to the earth!"

"I thought you liked him!"

"He's a fine man. But to see him go and know you were staying!" He threw his hands wide, measuring the joy he felt. "I've already looked at some of the beach that's available. I think I've found the perfect spot for us, but of course you'll have the final say. You'll have the final say in everything. I'm going to use everything my father ever taught me about working with wood—"

"Berran."

"—and I'm going to build the most beautiful house that Strandia's ever seen—"

"Berran!"

"—with lots of rooms for children—"

"Berran!"

He stopped and looked into her eyes.

And though it saddened her, she was relieved to see the joy fading out of his face like an ember cooling to gray ash.

"Sand?"

"Berran, you've made all the wrong plans."

"But when I saw Renellus leave . . ."

"You thought . . . ?"

"I knew you'd chosen me."

She looked at him.

"Well, you didn't choose him!"

She let the silence lengthen.

He sat down as if his weight had suddenly grown too great for his legs to support.

"Berran, you once opened my eyes for me by telling me that Midisle women were free to choose whom they would lie down with. Are they also free to choose not to lie with anyone?"

"Of course."

"That is my choice."

"So the answer's no?"

"The answer is no."

He leaned forward and took the pieces of the smashed wheel from her. There were several minutes of silence as he fitted them together abstractedly. Finally, still looking down at his hands, he asked, "Are you saying no because you miss the doraado?"

She closed her eyes. "I suppose it's partly that. I miss him enormously. And yet sometimes I think I can hear him. Sometimes I'm sure he's just far, far away and he'll be back. But also, it's just not right. I don't want to be anyone's wife."

He shook his head. Ignoring the last part of her statement, he argued with her: "Sand, the doraado was hurt. He was beached. They almost never survive being beached. It's been months since they took him away."

"But the others held him up so he could breathe! Surely they wouldn't have bothered to do that if he was dead."

"Who knows why the doraado do what they do? You've got to stop hoping for the impossible."

"Why?"

The silence between them lengthened. Finally he shrugged. Handing the wooden spokes back to her, he said, "Good question. Why indeed? I'm going to keep hoping for the impossible, too."

＊　　　＊　　　＊

Sand found that it got harder and harder to have any time to herself except in the few moments before she fell asleep. People automatically delegated authority to her, with her position as a favorite of the Mother and her experience with both sides of island society. They looked to her for everything from medical advice to decisions on land claims on the newly available beaches.

She returned to her old habit of pre-dawn swims to have some time alone to think. These were the times when she missed M'ridan the most, especially when she'd awakened from her recurring dream with his voice still in her mind and his briny scent all around her. But paradoxically, they were also the times that she felt most comforted.

Occasionally one of the providers would surface and roll sideways to examine her. She would greet him courteously while her heart spasmed with regret. She would halfheartedly exchange a few thoughts with them before they lost interest and swam away.

One day a full-grown male surfaced near her. His gray skin was crisscrossed with white scars. He whistled. She put her hand under the surface and waggled her fingers slowly. "May the sea be plentiful for you."

He slapped his tail at her and submerged, to reappear a moment later with a small trawna clamped delicately between his jaws. He swam up close and gave it to her.

She thanked him gravely, denied being hungry, and offered it back to him.

It disappeared in one snap.

Politely he asked her name.

Her heart contracted, and she took a deep breath before replying. "Sand."

"Too unspecific," he told her. "I think I will call you . . .

276

Mudball!" At that moment he flung himself into the air and breached, cascading her with water.

Crying, choking, she flailed out blindly toward him and he flowed against her. She cupped one hand under his chin and stroked it, while tracing his scars with the fingertips of her other hand.

"Where have you been?"

"Far, far away. My pod took me to a place where the water is shallow and the seaweed is so thick it's like lying on a mattress, and it held me above the water to breathe. My body was crushed, Sand. I almost died."

"Sometimes I thought I heard you."

"Sometimes I dreamed of you in my sleep. But I was always too weak to reach you."

Finally, when she was able to think more clearly, she said, "Your mind touch feels different. You seem different."

He agreed. "Life seems less full of jokes than it was before. So many of my pod are gone—their bodies rot among the trees of your island. Too many of your pod rot on the ocean floor. But I rejoice more than I can say that you are not one of them."

"And you! Oh, M'ridan, I've been so sad. Sometimes I was sure you were dead."

He regarded her sideways. "Not a bad joke, seeing as I swim here beside you. Already you raise my spirits, mudball!"

They floated together as color returned to the earth, rejoined, rejoicing, and making plans for their new world.